Good Karma, Bad Karma

Shannon L. Coates

Fictional Novel

Copyright © 2024 by Shannon Coates

All rights reserved. No part of this publication may be stored in a retrieval system, reproduced, or transmitted in any form, except for the inclusion of brief quotations in a review, without prior permission in writing.

Dedication

This book is dedicated to my incredible husband, Raimon – thank you for always inspiring and pushing me to reach my fullest potential. To my mom and dad, whose unwavering belief in me has shown that any dream is possible. And to my wonderful children, whose love and encouragement fuel my journey every day. I am deeply grateful to God for blessing me with an incredible gift and for guiding me to discover it.

Table of Contents

1. The Ending and Beginning 01

2. Rejection While Longing for Acceptance 06

3. Creating a Story Rather Than Living Your Reality 11

4. Your Past Travels to Your Present 22

5. Wisdom From the Matriarch 25

6. A New Day, A New Beginning 38

7. Everybody Needs Somebody 61

8. Game Over 66

9. Exploration of Foreign Territory 76

10. What Goes Around Comes Around 82

11. Babies and Circumstances Change Everything 92

12. Same Man, New Life 110

13. Success Does Not Always Breed Happiness 154

14. The Honeymoon Has Ended 170

Chapter 1

The Ending and Beginning

Oh my GOD. What has happened to me? I can't help but feel helpless. I feel a tightening in my chest and an aching in my heart. I feel like the inside of my body is going to erupt because of my endless bawling and utters of grief. My heart is pounding because of the anger, fear, and sadness I feel because of this current chapter in my life. The shoulder-length, beautiful, silky dark brown hair that I once took pride in is now thrown into a reckless ponytail with loose strands scattered across my head. My once flawless and radiant mocha-colored complexion is now rough and dry because of the tears that keep rolling down my thin yet round-shaped face. The brown-colored almond-shaped eyes that once intrigued even my worst enemies have become empty holes in my face that bare my soul. In only a matter of weeks, my 5-foot 6-inch, and 150-pound frame has been depleted into a 120-pound empty shelter that only provides refuge and protection for the love that I have for my children. The burning in my heart and in my soul can be attributed to the man that I have lost. I killed the unity of his family, his sense of security, and ultimately his pride. This was never my intention. Honestly, I never knew who I really was, so I destroyed the love of my life. Since I have been dead inside for so many years, I have been unable to truly breathe life into anything in my life, including my own relationship.

Before you can understand my present situation, I need to tell you about my past and about how everything started with the love of my life. I met my love, my soulmate, and my heart during a terrible November winter storm in Buffalo, New York. The day began normally; I went to work as usual. During this time, I had just graduated from college and was working as a nurse. As the end of my shift began to approach, I realized that thc weather had become relentless. Everything had become engulfed in heavy white snow. It took me nearly an hour to clean the mounds of snow that concealed my small white two-door vehicle. It took me even longer to get to the highway that had taken me home so many times before, within minutes.

After being stuck in traffic for two hours and not moving an inch, I realized that I may not make it home. Eventually, I decided to utilize the shoulder of the road to get off at the nearest exit. Once I reached the exit, I realized that the entire city had become a ghost town. Cars, trucks, SUVs, and even buses had been left abandoned in the middle of the streets. Despite the desolation my eyes encountered, I still had faith that my little white, two-door car would have the toughness and durability to overcome all odds and make headway through the treacherous environment that Mother Nature had created. It was not long before fear overcame me; darkness had fallen, and thunderstorms soon followed. My vehicle could no longer maneuver its way out of the thick white snow, and I was stuck. Then, my eyes fell upon a man who seemed to have emerged out of a snow cloud. As he approached me, he became taller and taller. His 6-foot, 4-inch build hovered over me as his chocolate skin and bright white teeth gave me a sense of relief. His presence made me feel safe because he had such a warm and welcoming spirit. Then I heard a deep voice say, "Hey, I'm Alonzo. I see you're stuck."

"Hey, I'm Karma. I've been out here forever. I need some help." I had no idea that this man would someday become the love of my life.

After Alonzo had made several attempts to push my vehicle out of the snow as I pressed on and off the gas, hardly any progress was made. "I guess we better get somewhere warm because neither of us is getting anywhere with a car tonight," Alonzo said.

"I'm far from home. Do you know of any hotels nearby?" I asked.

"No, but I'm headed towards my aunt's house to bunker down for the night. You're welcome to come with me until the weather lets up."

I accepted the invitation but not without reservations, and I had already planned my escape if Alonzo was a predator seeking out helpless women during the storm. That night, Alonzo and I walked, climbed, and stumbled on our way to his aunt's house.

Our hour-long journey to Alonzo's aunt's house did not seem to be an hour because Alonzo and I talked, laughed, and got to know each other. During our walk, Alonzo explained to me that his Aunt Betty was like a mother to him. Alonzo had tried to drive to his aunt's house before meeting me; he wanted to make sure that she was alright. Alonzo's car had gotten stuck in the snow that night as well. I admired the concern and compassion that Alonzo had for his aunt. I asked Alonzo if his aunt would be okay with allowing a perfect stranger into her home. Alonzo replied, "Look, tonight you'll be my friend, and whoever is a friend of mine is a friend of hers." Honestly, I found Alonzo's straightforward attitude and take-charge demeanor sexy.

Alonzo and I approached a mid-sized white home with a brown trim, which stood two stories high. It was obvious that the house was surrounded by a white wooden fence; however, the snow had submerged the fence, leaving only the sharp triangular-shaped tips for view. Alonzo walked up to the house in relief. "Finally, we're here," Alonzo said. I instantly became nervous because I did not know his aunt; I didn't even know Alonzo. I did not know how long I would be stranded here, and I didn't even have a change of clothes. We practically walked over the fence as Alonzo held my hand to prevent me from stumbling. The snow had accumulated a couple of feet, and it was laborious to navigate through. As we got closer to the door, I could see a figure pushing the curtains aside a frosty snow-coated window. Before we could even get to the door, it opened with a short, heavy-set, grey-haired woman standing beside it. Her eyes were filled with excitement and obvious concern. "Aunt Betty, I am so glad to see you. You good?" Alonzo said.

She smiled and replied in a Southern accent, "I'm fine boy; you should not be out in this type of weather." Aunt Betty looked at me and said, "He's always worried about me; I told him that I'm grown and that I can take care of myself."

Alonzo interjected as Aunt Betty was speaking and said, "Aunt Betty, this is a good friend of mine, Karma."

"Hey, honey, it's nice to meet you. You so pretty, I see why Alonzo is friends with you."

Alonzo showed me around the house and made me feel safe and welcomed. Soon, the scent of fried chicken and warm, flaky homemade biscuits began to saturate the house. Aunt Betty called Alonzo and me to the kitchen table. I was so focused on the delicious meal that sat before me because I barely ate that day; I was incredibly hungry. I fixed my plate and began eating immediately. When I looked up, I saw Alonzo and Aunt Betty with their heads bowed down, silently saying their grace before eating. I felt a little embarrassed that I had started eating like a savage before even thinking of saying my grace. I just continued eating because it was too late to say my prayer; I had taken huge bites out of my perfectly fried chicken. It was silent at the dinner table. When I lifted my head up from being only inches away from my plate as I ate with contentment, I witnessed Aunt Betty looking at Alonzo and I. Aunt Betty and I made eye contact. "Is everything good?" Aunt Betty asked.

"Oh yes, I have not had a meal like this in ages," I replied.

Growing up, my mother wasn't the best cook, my siblings and I ate a lot of microwavable meals and canned foods. My mother was too busy working to cook good meals, which took time.

After dinner, Aunt Betty brought out some blankets and told me that I could sleep in a guest room and Alonzo could sleep in the pull-out bed concealed in a couch with a red and orange floral design. Alonzo and I decided that we were not tired yet and would stay up a little longer to watch television.

"Yall better behave!" Aunt Betty playfully said as she walked towards her bedroom.

Alonzo and I sat side by side, drinking hot chocolate as we were still thawing out from being in the frigid elements. We really had a chance to get to know each other that night. We talked for hours. I know it sounds crazy, but I really felt like I was falling for Alonzo. As cheesy as it may sound, it was close to love at first sight. Every word he spoke had me wrapped in the sound of his deep yet peaceful voice. I thought that Alonzo was so attractive; I could see his chiseled chest through his ordinary cotton long-sleeved black shirt. His upper arm muscles were like mountains that bulged from within his shirt. The guys that I had been with before were little boys compared to this amazing sculpture that I had come to know as Alonzo.

As Alonzo and I talked, I made sure to sneak in, "So, how would your girlfriend feel about me being here with you and spending the night at your Aunt Betty's house?"

"Well, it's a good thing I don't have a girlfriend because if I did, I'm sure she wouldn't like it at all."

"So, do you want a girlfriend?" I immediately felt stupid and was kicking myself for asking such a direct and desperate-sounding question.

"I haven't thought about that in a while. I just graduated from law school, and I have been pretty focused on my career. I must say, you are gorgeous, and although I don't know you well, I wouldn't mind having a girlfriend like yourself."

Before I knew it, my emotions took over, and I grabbed Alonzo's face and began to kiss him. Just as I kissed Alonzo, he pushed me away. I was so embarrassed. Alonzo then turned away and said, "I think it's about time for you to go to bed; the guest room is to your right." I slowly got up and tried to collect my pride as I silently proceeded to the guest room. I did not get much sleep that night because I was so embarrassed. I had never been so aggressive with a man. Usually, the man always makes the first move. This was simply bad judgement on my part. I thought that I should have been smarter.

The next morning, I awakened and quickly glanced out the window, feeling a wave of relief washing over me as I saw the sun melting the snow. The plow trucks had cleared most of the streets, which meant that I would be able to go home.

The sound of gospel music and the aroma of breakfast being made eventually captured my attention. I began to walk towards the kitchen. Aunt Betty had just finished making sausage, grits, cheese eggs, and toast for breakfast. Aunt Betty greeted me by saying, "Hey baby, I see you decided to get up. Alonzo left with a neighbor to go pick up his truck. Did you want something to eat?"

"Yes, it smells so good in here."

Right after I finished my breakfast, Alonzo entered the front door and yelled for me to get my coat on. I hugged and thanked Aunt Betty for her generosity and put my coat and boots on.

Once I got into the black SUV that belonged to Alonzo, I felt nervous and flustered. I apologized for my reckless behavior as Alonzo and I drove down the streets. Initially, Alonzo was silent as I explained that my behavior was totally out of the ordinary and that I was really a nice girl. Eventually, Alonzo looked at me and said, "It's cool, let's stay in touch." Alonzo and I exchanged phone numbers and social media, although Alonzo warned me that he rarely used social media.

When Alonzo drove me to my car, and shoveled my car out of the snow, I admired his manliness. I always admired a man who knew how to take care of the women in his presence. Before I knew it, I was on my way home, and I was wondering if Alonzo was just going to fade into a memory from my past.

Chapter 2

Rejection While Longing for Acceptance

There is a reason why I am the way that I am. Furthermore, there is a reason why I became so aggressive with my emotions when I was at Aunt Betty's house with Alonzo. I have always felt the need to be liked, and if you did not like me, I would make you like me. Now that I am an adult, I know deep inside that you cannot make anyone do anything. But you couldn't tell me that in my youth. Even when a person displayed disinterest in me by either making rude comments or just plain ignoring me, I would adjust my personality, my style, and even my demeanor to appease these individuals. I started this destructive habit at around the age of six and kept it going for many years of my life. I eventually realized that I could not make everyone happy. Also, I realized that I had no identity because I was constantly bending to become the person that others wanted me to be. My need to become a person that others would accept made me realize my need to be wanted. I don't want to be alone. I have always needed a boyfriend and/or friends to fulfill me. I have an array of acquaintances that serve the purpose of making me feel validated.

I have been rejected all my life. My siblings rejected me. The main reason why my siblings rejected me was because I was the youngest and I had a different father from my other siblings. My skin complexion is darker than that of my siblings. My older brother Matthew is fair-skinned, like my sister Celine. Even my mother is fair-skinned. Growing up I stood out like a sore thumb. I did not look like I belonged in my family.

My siblings blamed me for breaking up their family unit. Matthew and Celine's father, Michael Collins, was physically and verbally abusive to my mother. My mother, Donna left Mr. Collins when Matthew was ten and Celine was seven years of age. When my mother left Mr. Collins, she was pregnant with me. Apparently, she had started a relationship with my father, Eric Jamison, before she could leave Mr. Collins.

My father, Eric, was also married when he and my mother started their affair. Eric's wife, Linda, contacted my mother when she learned that my mother was pregnant with me. Linda urged my mother to end her pregnancy, claiming that since she was also expecting, Eric would never be a part of my life. My mother told me stories about how Eric even threatened to kill her if she did not abort me. My mother told me that Eric's wife had lost her baby a week before I was born. This is why I was named Karma. My full name is Karma Destiny Robinson, and I have my mother's maiden name. My mother said that Eric and his wife focused on my death so much that death came upon their doorstep instead, and that was their karma. I always hated this story. I wanted my father to get his karma by seeing me become a huge, successful movie star. I dreamed of having fame and fortune and for Eric to make attempts to reach me, but I would ignore him as he did me throughout my life.

Growing up, my mother, Donna, was vengeful. If someone did her wrong, she would get them back someway somehow. She even took me with her to visit what she called a Witch Doctor once because she wanted a curse placed on our landlord, who was mean and unempathetic when she was having a hard time paying rent. I have seen her cheat on boyfriends if they cheated on her. It always seemed as if my mother was focused on making sure that she paid people back for any wrongdoing done to her.

My mother and I were close when I was growing up. My mother knew that my siblings did not like me, so it was almost like she was trying to protect me. Being around my mother so often resulted in us being close, and this caused the strain between my siblings and me to worsen. My siblings pretty much ignored me most of the time. It didn't help that their father would pick them up from our house and totally ignore my existence. There were times when my sibling's father Mr. Collins would bring them back home with candy, clothes, toys, and fun stories to tell me about going to amusement parks and grandparents' houses. This would hurt my heart. I would physically feel stinging in my soul as my eyes would swell up with tears. I longed to have that type of love and sense of belonging. I wanted someone to love me enough to buy me things and take me places.

When I was old enough to go to the store alone, I would buy candy for the kids on my street with any money that I could get my hands on. I was trying to create my own love and safe haven amongst friends. The candy persuaded the kids to play with me. Sometimes, the kids on my street would be mean to me after they finished eating the candy that I purchased for them. I would pray for a friend who was so cool that we would play with each other while the other kids watched in envy. My childhood was very lonely.

Once I reached my teens, I began to blossom, and people began to look at me differently. By this time, I stopped buying friendships with money. I had matured a lot, both mentally and physically; however, my longing for acceptance was evident. The main reason why my peers were interested in becoming friends with me was because I was best friends with the most popular girl in school, Grace. Grace was very popular because she was pretty, smart, and she was involved in every activity within our high school. I looked up to Grace. I wanted to be Grace's friend because I knew that being around her would attract more friends, and I could finally have that sense of belonging that I had been yearning for.

Besides being my friend and role model, Grace was a guy magnet. There was one guy named Darnel who was enamored by Grace. Darnel would carry Grace's books to class and wait with her at the bus stop. He would even bring her lunch some days. Grace did not like Darnel at all, but I did. Darnel had a horrible reputation amongst the girls at school. He was known for hopping from girl to girl. I thought that Darnel was amazing and that those other girls just weren't a good fit for Darnel. Darnel embodied star appeal: he was charismatic, athletic, and so handsome. Darnel had a beautiful chocolate brown complexion, wavy black hair, he was tall and had beautiful brown eyes. He literally looked like he stepped right out of a movie. I was constantly trying to get Darnel's attention.

Eventually, Darnel realized that I liked him, and he asked me out. Grace said that she was cool with us dating, but she warned me to be careful when dealing with Darnel. Like a fool, I started dating Darnel, and after about two weeks, I lost my virginity to him. I recall the sex being horrible because neither of us knew what we were really doing. Darnel would tell me that it would get better, but it never really did. After several sexual encounters with Darnel, our relationship ended because he decided he liked another girl. I was crushed. I tried to make it seem like I was not bothered by Darnel's betrayal when I was around Grace, but she knew that I was heartbroken. I was determined to move on. Girls in my neighborhood would say that the best way to get over a guy is to get under another guy.

Meeting new guys was not hard because Grace and I had a party to go to every weekend, whether it was a high school party or a college party. We were popular girls. I was popular by association at this point. I remember one high school basement party where I was looking amazing. My hair was curled in spirals that reached down to the middle of my back; this was all my real hair. My tight red shirt fit around my perfectly round-shaped breast, and my blue jeans looked as if they were painted on. Not to mention the brand new sneakers I purchased that very day. Grace and I were the hottest girls at the party. We partied hard. Towards the end of the party, I needed to go to the bathroom, and I asked Grace to help me find it. We opened a brown wooden door that creaked as we walked up the stairs from the dark basement. We walked into the kitchen, where the walls were decorated with red and brown wallpaper with pictures of plates, drinking glasses, and spoons. The tile on the kitchen floor was in a white and black checker design, and it was worn with pieces of tile missing. It looked like someone's grandmother's house that had never been remodeled. Grace and I continued to walk through the kitchen until we found ourselves in the family room. To our surprise, we found a separate party. There was a group of people gathered in a family room looking at a large screen television, this television was at least 70 inches. The television nearly engulfed the entire room. Grace and I were bold, so we walked into the room to see what was going on. I looked at the screen of the television and saw me and Darnel naked and having sex. It was almost impossible for me to wrap my mind around what was occurring. I quickly realized that Darnel had been secretly making videos of us having sex without my consent. I was flabbergasted, embarrassed, ashamed, and infuriated. Then, I looked into a corner and spotted Darnel. Instantly, I ran toward him and punched him in the face. His friends pulled me off of him. I screamed out, "I can't believe that you would do this to me. You recorded us having sex." Then I blurted out, "Shrimp dick!!!!"

The guys in the room burst into laughter. One guy decided to mock me and said in a baby-singing voice, "Schrimp diiick."

Then another guy walked up to me and said, "Chill, it's not like it's the first time we've seen the video."

I was sick to my stomach, and then it was like I instantly went into autopilot; I just started running out of the house in tears, and after that, everything was a blur. My need to feel accepted allowed me to start a relationship with someone that I knew wanted me for sex. Darnel wasn't ashamed to have entertained his friends at my expense because I had not placed enough value on myself.

Chapter 3

Creating a Story Rather Than Living Your Reality

After Darnel, I jumped from one volatile relationship to the next. During the time that I met Alonzo, I had just gotten out of a relationship. I still longed for companionship, although my experiences with men were not pleasant. Each of my relationships consisted of men cheating, lying, and breaking my heart. I was hoping that Alonzo would be different; furthermore, I was hoping that I had not ruined my chances with Alonzo when I practically threw myself at him only for him to totally dodge my advances. Also, I was slightly intimidated by Alonzo because he seemed so mature and so sure of himself. During this time, I was doing a lot of soul-searching. I didn't know who I truly was and had no idea what I wanted to do. I was only a nurse because my mother wanted me to be a nurse. I always wanted to be a Hollywood actress but was not sure how this would happen while living in Buffalo.

It took two whole weeks after the snowstorm for Alonzo to call me. I remember it like it was yesterday. I was sitting on my couch in my small yet cozy apartment, watching television. I was browsing through social media to see if Alonzo had posted anything; he didn't. Then my phone rang. I saw that it was Alonzo. I was trying to compose myself because I was accustomed to guys texting me when communicating with me. I cleared my throat and said "Hello," in the softest, sweetest voice.

The deep and distinguished voice of Alonzo said, "Hey, Karma." I swear the sound of his voice made my uterus contract.

"Hey Alonzo, how are you?"

"Fine, I have been thinking about you and wanted to know if I could take you out. I want to take you to a comedy show this Saturday. I remember how much you like late-night comedy shows and everything."

I was impressed that Alonzo took note as we watched the late-night shows at Aunt Betty's house during the snowstorm. I told Alonzo that I would love to go out with him. After hashing out the details of where to pick me up and what time, Alonzo and I engaged in a little friendly conversation. I was so excited and looking forward to being in Alonzo's presence again.

Preparing for my date with Alonzo was difficult for me. I was very meticulous in finding the perfect outfit, accessories, and creating a sexy hairstyle. I decided to go with a short silver dress that hugged my curves and accentuated my legs. The tiny straps from my dress laid across each of my shoulders, which helped my strapless push-up bra make my breasts sit high and proud. I wore my dark brown hair with a part in the middle, and my loose curls cascaded down the middle of my back. I oiled myself with body oil; I made sure my arms and legs were glistening. I sprayed on my favorite perfume, which had a fruity floral scent with hints of jasmine. This fragrance made me feel sensual. I wore my 6-inch rhinestone closed-toe heels. I put on a faux fur coat, ignoring the fact that I would still be cold because Buffalo was still in the depths of winter; however, most of the snow had cleared up. I could not wait for Alonzo to see me; he was going to have the opportunity to see me at my best and forget about the distressed snowstorm version of me.

Once I was completely ready for my date with Alonzo, I grabbed my silver rectangular-shaped clutch purse and tucked it under my arm while looking out my living room window. When I saw Alonzo's black SUV pull up, I quickly closed my curtain and sat on my couch. I did not want Alonzo to know that I was anxiously awaiting his arrival. It was not long before I heard footsteps outside my apartment door, and the doorbell rang. I slowly walked to the door and opened it. Alonzo was looking so incredibly fine. His smooth, dark skin was freshly shaven and glowing. His haircut was low, and his lineup was perfect. Alonzo was wearing a black suit that looked as if it were made just for him. The crisp white shirt underneath his suit jacket was opened at the top and displayed a hint of chest definition. Both the collars of Alonzo's shirt and suit jacket gripped one another without any sign of shifting. After I finished admiring Alonzo's beauty, I stepped outside and closed my door. I looked into Alonzo's gentle eyes and said, "Nice to see you; you look great."

"Likewise," Alonzo replied in his sexy and deep voice.

Once Alonzo and I arrived at the comedy club, we were greeted by a long line that consisted of an assortment of people. The people in line were black, white, Asian, Hispanic, young and old. Alonzo gave a hand signal to one of the doormen, and instantly, Alonzo held me by the small of my back and guided me toward the comedy club entrance. The people who were waiting in line all looked at us in envy. I felt like a queen. Alonzo and I sat at a table in front of the stage. The bartender came to our table and asked if we wanted any drinks, I asked for an apple martini, and Alonzo asked for a pop. This prompted me to ask Alonzo if he drank. He told me that he did not drink because he grew up around alcoholism, but he did not want me to feel uncomfortable about drinking in front of him. Of course, his issues with alcohol made me uncomfortable, and I was unable to finish my drink. I drank pop with Alonzo for the rest of the night.

The comedy show consisted of about four comedians. During one of the comedian's standup routines, Alonzo suddenly had a coughing fit. I tried pushing Alonzo's pop towards him so that he could drink it and hopefully stop coughing before catching the attention of the comedian on stage. But it was too late; the comedian's attention went straight towards Alonzo. The comedian looked at Alonzo and said, "Bro over here got COVID; he's trying to get us all sick." Then the comedian looked directly at me and said, "Wait, dude over here with Broke Yonce." Then the comic looked at Alonzo and said, "Who you supposed to be because you sure as hell ain't HOV, you COV. Covid ass nigga. If y'all have a daughter, her name gone be Boooo Ivy." We both laughed it off a little bit, but it was so embarrassing. The whack-ass comedian talked about my entire outfit; I don't even remember everything that he said. But I was trying my best to keep my cool and anxiously waited for the comedian to just move on to some other jokes.

After the comedy show, Alonzo took me out to a nice Italian restaurant called Romano's. I had heard of this place but never went because it was so expensive. This place had dimmed lit chandeliers' that were probably shipped from Italy and red candles placed at each circular table. Romano's was an elegant and romantic restaurant. During our dinner, Alonzo and I had the opportunity to get to know about each other's plans for the future. Alonzo articulated his audacious goals of becoming a high-powered entertainment attorney. This was perfect for me because although I was a nurse, I wanted to get into the entertainment industry as an actress. I loved how Alonzo listened to me and encouraged me while I discussed my dreams. Everyone that I talked to about my dreams of becoming an actress pretty much told me to let that dream go. Alonzo told me about how he had just passed the Bar Exam and finally found a job with a law firm. I was extremely impressed and could see myself being with a person like him.

Alonzo was a perfect gentleman throughout the night. I never wanted the date to end. During the ride home, Alonzo asked me what I would like to do for our next date. I told him that I loved going to the movies. I was excited to hear Alonzo making plans for our next date. When Alonzo walked me to my door, I promised myself that I would not make myself look foolish like I did during the snowstorm when I threw myself at him; Alonzo had to make the first move. Once Alonzo and I were at my apartment door, he told me that he had a great time. He grabbed the small of my back, pulled me toward him, and kissed me so gently on my lips. His lips were soft and smooth, and his tongue slowly caressed mine as we kissed. After about a few seconds, Alonzo softly separated my hips from his by slowly pushing me away. After our kiss, I told Alonzo that I was looking forward to seeing him again as I pulled out my key to open my door. Once I walked into my apartment, I turned to Alonzo and said, “Be careful going home.” We both said bye, and Alonzo walked to his vehicle. That man was on my mind all night. I had the scent of his cologne all over me. I almost dreaded taking a shower the next morning because I did not want his scent to leave me.

After the first date, I try not to anticipate the man’s text or phone calls. I hate the disappointment of rejection. I must admit that in the back of my mind, I was thinking about Alonzo and why he had not reached out to me. When Alonzo finally did call, a week after our first date, he told me that he had a death in his family and was consumed with making funeral arrangements, etc. When I asked Alonzo who passed away, he told me that his father passed away suddenly. I asked Alonzo if he would mind me going to the funeral to offer him support during his time of grief. Initially, there was a little hesitation on Alonzo’s part; he did not seem very comfortable about giving me the funeral details. I told Alonzo that I did not want to overstep my boundaries, but he then insisted that I come to the funeral. He said that he needed support.

Heavy rain saturated the city of Buffalo during the morning of the funeral. The sun hid behind the heavy grey clouds, making the day gloomy. I began to have reservations about attending the funeral because I was kind of nervous. I wondered if I had forced Alonzo to give me the funeral information, I wondered if I was pushing myself on him, I wondered how he would respond to me being at the funeral. Eventually, I put on my foundation and nude-colored lip gloss, slipped into a black dress along with a long sleeve black blazer and black heels. I put my hair into a ponytail, threw on my black button-up trench coat that went to my knees and tied at the waist. Before I knew it, I was on my way to the funeral.

Once I arrived at the church, I saw so many people standing outside, consoling one another. There was a mound of stairs between the ground and the entrance door of the church. People were standing at the bottom of the stairs, middle of the stairs, and at the very top of the stairs next to the door that led into the sanctuary. I was very nervous because I did not know any of these people, and I was nervous about seeing Alonzo as well. As I began walking up the stairs, I was greeted by Alonzo's Aunt Betty, who provided me with shelter during the blizzard. She noticed me before I noticed her, and she was so welcoming. As soon as Aunt Betty saw me, she said, "Hey baby, thank you for coming."

"It's so nice to see you, I just wanted to give the family my condolences and support during this time, and I know that it can be hard to lose someone," I replied.

"Yes, but this is a joyous occasion because Willis has gone home to be with the Lord."

Aunt Betty went on to greet others who were on their way into the church to pay their respects. The line to the casket seemed to be long and was moving slowly. I did not mind the wait because I had no plans on looking at the body in the casket anyway. Once I got to the front of the line and in front of the casket, I quickly turned toward the first pews of the church to offer my condolences to the family. I just shook everyone's hand until I got to Alonzo, and I gave him a hug and a sympathy card. Alonzo whispered in my ear, "Thank you so much for coming," and kissed me on the cheek.

"I am here if you need anything," I replied. I continued to shake hands, making my way to the end of the front church pew when I shook hands with Darnel Young. The Darnel Young from high school who recorded us having sex without my knowledge. My heart dropped once I saw his face. But I kept my cool and pretended not to be phased as I continued to shake hands. I walked towards the back of the church to a woman and asked her where I could find an obituary.

"Actually, there was an issue with the obituaries, and they just arrived; you will be receiving one of the first obituaries," the woman said.

I thanked the woman and bolted out of the church. I ran to my car, opened the obituary, and went straight to the last paragraph. There

I read: Willis Washington leaves to cherish his loving memory, wife Tina Washington, three children Alonzo Rodgers, Darnel Washington, and Persia Washington. I could not believe it; Alonzo and Darnel are brothers. I was in disbelief.

After Alonzo's father's funeral, Alonzo and I began to spend more and more time together. During this time, I never brought up Darnel. Surprisingly, Alonzo never spoke much about his family, and I never asked. I was just hoping that Alonzo did not figure out that I had been with his brother Darnel. I was terrified of being exposed. Alonzo was always so sweet to me, and he would invite me to his family gatherings; I always declined. My fear of running into Darnel and Alonzo finding out about my previous relationship with Darnel horrified me. During this time in my life, I was trying to redefine who I was. I did not want to be known as the girl that a man could never turn into a wife. For the first time in my life, I was with a man who was more interested in my mind and spirit than he was in my body.

It would be a month and a half before Alonzo, and I made love. We did not plan it, but I sure as hell anticipated it. It was a night that I will never forget. Alonzo came to my apartment after working 12 hours at his law firm. He was so tense, and I could tell that he had a very stressful day. His tie was loosened, his shirt unbuttoned at the top, and there was only a hint of his cologne left for me to savor. Alonzo was not trying to be sexy; however, being sexy came naturally to Alonzo. He was sitting on my couch watching television with his legs open. I told Alonzo to go to my bedroom to lie on his stomach so that I could give him a back rub. Alonzo walked to my room, plopped on my bed, and turned to his stomach. One thing that I knew for sure was that I could give a sensual back rub. I pulled out one of my body oils and rubbed it in my hands so that it would not be cold once I applied it to Alonzo's back. I started rubbing his shoulders first in a circular motion. Then I worked my way down his back and rubbed him gently yet firmly. This exercise of me rubbing Alonzo down made me yearn for him sexually. I knew that Alonzo could sense my intense sexual energy at that moment. Suddenly, Alonzo began turning around, and I lifted my body so that he could turn around and face me. Once Alonzo turned completely over, he sat up straight and wrapped my legs around his waist. Alonzo began kissing me passionately. He started kissing my breast, and then he slowly caressed his tongue around my nipples. He laid me down flat on my back and slowly yet gently worked his tongue down to my belly button. Alonzo continued to kiss me lower and lower until kissing between my legs as if his only mission in life was to make me cry out moans of ecstasy; Alonzo devoured me and accomplished his mission. I was moaning and making sounds that I never heard myself make. Before I knew it, Alonzo was inside of me and stroking with force while being gentle at the same time. Alonzo is a take-control type of guy, and he strives to be the best at everything he does, including making love. After it was all over, I could not stop shaking from the orgasmic experience. No one had ever made me feel this way. I literally experienced aftershocks of uncontrollable shaking after we finished making love. I soon realized that I had just made love for the first time. Alonzo taught me that having sex is completely different from making love.

After Alonzo and I made love, we became official. I was his woman, and he was my man. We could not get enough of one another. However, Alonzo continued to invite me to his family gatherings, and I continued to decline. I always pretended to have an important engagement when Alonzo invited me to anything that involved his family. One day, Alonzo expressed to me that it was very important for me to come to his family reunion. His family reunion was being held at a park down the street from my apartment. He told me that I had two months to prepare and that he would not take no for an answer. I was hoping that a distant aunt or uncle would die during his family reunion date so that I could have yet another excuse not to make his family gathering. This is how much anxiety and worry the thought of running into Darnel caused me. I had to come up with something, and I had two months to figure it out.

Accepting my past so that I could welcome my future had become a priority for me. I could not spend the rest of my life hiding from the mistakes that I had made in the past. I had decided to define myself and not allow others to decide who I was. It had become time for me to come clean with Alonzo. If Alonzo decided to characterize or judge me for my past actions, I would just have to deal with it and move forward. I waited a week before Alonzo's family reunion to speak to him about his brother Darnel and me sleeping together. Alonzo and I were lying in bed one night when I revealed to him that there was a reason why I did not want to be seen at any of his family gatherings. When I began to speak, my voice was shaking. I looked into Alonzo's eyes and said, "I have to tell you something about your brother Darnel."

"If it's what I think it is, you don't have to say anything else."

I went from being nervous to being inquisitive. "What are you talking about?"

"I really don't want to talk about it," Alonzo said. Alonzo was silent for a few seconds before proceeding to say, "You used to date my brother, and he made a video of you both having sex, right?"

"You knew?" I asked.

"I realized it shortly after we met during the snowstorm when you started talking about the high school that you went to, and your name definitely sparked my memory because there aren't many Karma's runnin around. Plus, I recognized you from the tape and from a house party where you went crazy on Darnel."

Alonzo's nonchalant recollection of the events surrounding his brother made me feel crushed, deceived and betrayed. Alonzo continued to say, "Your history with Darnel was the main reason why I wasn't trying to take it too far at Aunt Betty's house that night during the snowstorm. It was difficult for me to be with someone that my brother has already been with. But I'm over that now."

In a shaking voice, I replied, "Why didn't you say anything when we first met?"

"We was chillin and I was enjoying our conversation. I wasn't going to ruin that by mentioning my brother. I know that Darnel can be an asshole and I figured that mentioning him would probably trigger you."

I looked Alonzo in the eyes and said, "Why haven't you said anything for all of this time?"

"It's just not important enough to bring up. I guess I have the same question for you. Why didn't you mention anything?"

I instantly began to relive the house party, and my emotions took over, and I just yelled out, "Fuck you, Alonzo. What is this, a game to you?"

Alonzo looked at me in confusion and said, "You knew that Darnel was my brother; why didn't you tell me that you slept with him until now? I guess we both are at fault."

Alonzo had made a pungent point that penetrated my soul. "When did you find out that me and Darnel were brothers?" Alonzo asked.

"At your father's funeral."

I calmed down and felt further embarrassment because I thought I was keeping a secret, and Alonzo knew about me and Darnel all along.

I asked Alonzo if Darnel knew that we were currently in a relationship. Alonzo told me that he and Darnel spoke about me the day that Alonzo drove me back to my car after leaving Aunt Betty's house in the snowstorm. He said that Darnel told him that he was young and dumb for taping us having sex and that I was really a good person. Alonzo told me that Darnel told him not to judge me by the video and to take me out if he was interested in me. It took Alonzo a while to call me because he was debating on whether he wanted to pursue a relationship with someone who had a previous relationship with his brother. But Alonzo explained to me that he could not stop thinking about me and decided to ask me out on a date.

Alonzo knew that I was very upset with him for not telling me that he knew about my previous relationship with his brother. My anger prompted Alonzo to demonstrate some transparency when it came to his history. Alonzo revealed to me that he and Darnel were close, although they were not raised in the same home. It was interesting to find out some details about Alonzo's history because Alonzo did not spend a lot of time talking about the details of his life. Alonzo told me that he and Darnel have different mothers and the same father. After Alonzo held me in his arms and told me that he would never deliberately hurt me, I realized that he truly loved me, and external factors did not consume him. He was a real man.

The day of Alonzo's family reunion picnic could not have been more perfect. The sky was blue, the sun was shining, and the temperature was just right. When Alonzo and I were on our way to the family reunion, he explained to me that I would be meeting his deceased father's side of the family. Many of the people who were at his father's funeral would be at the family reunion. When we pulled up to the park, Darnel was the first person we saw. Alonzo parked right next to Darnel, who was standing outside of his car. When I got out of Alonzo's car, Darnel said, "Hey Karma, long time, no see," and proceeded to hug me. I hugged Darnel back to be cordial. Alonzo and Darnel then slapped each other up and embraced. Then Darnel introduced an extremely handsome man who was around 6 feet tall and had long black locks that hung down his back. Darnel told Alonzo and me that the handsome gentleman's name was Tim, his fiancé. Alonzo slapped up Tim and said, "It's nice to finally meet you; Darnel talks about you all of the time."

At this point, I felt even more deceived; Alonzo and I had just had an entire conversation about Darnel, and Alonzo neglected to tell me that Darnel was not only engaged but engaged to a man. I didn't know whether Alonzo had an issue with communicating or if he was intentionally withholding information from me. Either way, I was beginning to feel that Alonzo did not value me enough to be completely open and honest with me.

While attending Alonzo's family reunion, I was able to determine that Alonzo came from a very close-knit family. Everyone was getting along so well. Aunt Betty seemed to be the matriarch of the family. She was always surrounded by people, and everyone made sure that she had everything that she needed. All I heard was, "Aunt Betty, do you want anything else to eat?" "Aunt Betty, do you have enough shade?" She was truly loved. I had the opportunity to see Alonzo's sister, Persia. I met Persia when I was dating Darnel. When we were reacquainted, it was a little uncomfortable. However, it was not long before Persia began introducing me to the whole family. During this time, Alonzo was playing football with the kids at the park. After a couple of hours, festivities began to wrap up, and Alonzo was ready to go home. We prepared food to take home with us and said our goodbyes.

Conversation and laughter filled the car as Alonzo, and I chatted during our ride back to my apartment after the family reunion. Once we were in my apartment, Alonzo hopped on my couch and turned on the television. He turned to the sports channel to get his daily sports update. I sat next to him and said, "Why are you not transparent with me?"

Alonzo turned to me and smiled while saying, "Just like a woman, what now?"

"Nothin, but why didn't you tell me that Darnel was gay and engaged to a dude after we had a whole conversation about him recently."

"Look, I don't understand how Darnel's sexual preference and relationship status has anything to do with you."

Alonzo's harshness and dismissal of my concerns regarding his transparency pierced through my hurt feelings like a million sharp needles. I explained to Alonzo that, as his woman, he should feel comfortable enough to tell me about things relevant to conversations. I told Alonzo that when we talked about my previous relationship with Darnel, he had to think about the fact that Darnel was gay and engaged. Alonzo continued to tell me that he did not understand my point and that Darnel's business was none of my business.

Then Alonzo finally said, "Karma, from now on, I will work on being more transparent; what do you want to know?"

"I am interested to know when Darnel came out as being gay?"

Alonzo reluctantly provided me with some background. Alonzo explained that he pretty much always knew that Darnel was gay, but Darnel did not come out as gay because he feared disappointing their father. Alonzo said that Darnel had told the entire family that he was gay about two years ago. Alonzo stated that Darnel disguised being gay by always having a lot of girlfriends. Alonzo told me that in high school, a boy somehow figured out that Darnel was gay, and in a desperate attempt to prove or deceive everyone into thinking that he was straight, he filmed us having sex and would play it often. The video dispelled the potential of anyone believing the boy who figured out that Darnel was gay. I asked Alonzo if he had anything to do with recommending that Darnel record us having sex. Alonzo said in a deep stern voice, "Hell no! I thought that shit was dumb as hell." Everything that Alonzo told me that night was a lot to take in. I had an entirely new perspective of Darnel after my conversation with Alonzo. Although I was still upset that Darnel recorded me having sex with him, I felt some empathy towards him.

Chapter 4

Your Past Travels to Your Present

Love is very complex. Although I always knew that Alonzo loved me, it took him a very long time to tell me so. Alonzo did all the things to show me he loved me. He was one of the most reliable people in my life. If I needed anything, Alonzo was there to ensure that my needs were met. He would bring me lunch, make sure I ate dinner, give me flowers, show me affection, and he would do all the things a woman dreams of from her man. I did not understand why Alonzo could not say the words, I love you. I did not understand what occurred in his past that would prevent him from being able to tell me he loved me.

Early in my relationship with Alonzo, he would become visibly agitated when I would ask about his past. However, as time went on, Alonzo began to open up to me about his past, although he seemed most comfortable discussing his future. We were together for over a year before he discussed his mother and his feelings towards her. Alonzo had told me that his mother and father never married, and this was why he thought he did not carry his father's last name, which was Washington.

Alonzo told me that his mother had been an alcoholic for years. Her addiction to alcohol began when Alonzo's father left her for Darnel and Persia's mother, Tina. Alonzo was around one year old when his father left. Alonzo's mother, Sybil Rodgers, was very abusive to Alonzo and resented him because he reminded her of Alonzo's father, Willis. Alonzo told me that when he did something that Sybil disapproved of, she would say, "You are just like your daddy." Being just like his daddy was a negative, although Alonzo's father was a good guy. According to Alonzo, Willis always tried to remain a part of his life. Unfortunately, Willis's new wife, Tina, was not very accepting of Alonzo. Tina would completely act as if Alonzo did not exist when he would visit his father. The situation had become so uncomfortable that Willis decided to take Alonzo to Aunt Betty's house when he wanted to spend time with him.

Aunt Betty was Willis's oldest sister, and she had never had children of her own.

When Alonzo was about six years old, he went to Aunt Betty's house after school to visit his father. Alonzo said that he was outside playing after heavy rain had fallen. While playing in the wet yard, Alonzo said that he slipped and fell. He said that his clothes were completely muddy after the fall. Alonzo told me that as Aunt Betty was helping him take off his muddy clothes, he started whining and crying about his back hurting. Aunt Betty put Alonzo in the shower. When Alonzo got out of the shower, Aunt Betty was there to give him a fresh T-shirt to wear while she was cleaning his clothes. Alonzo said that after Aunt Betty entered the bathroom, he heard a loud gasp, and Aunt Betty nearly fell to the closed toilet seat. Alonzo said that if it weren't for the toilet seat, Aunt Betty would have surely fallen to the floor. Aunt Betty sat on the toilet and quickly turned Alonzo around so that she could fully examine his back, which was covered in red whip marks from where his mother had beat him with an extension cord. Alonzo said that he could hear Aunt Betty trying to conceal her whimpering as her eyes fell upon his back. The whips were from the top of his back to his bottom. When Alonzo told me the story, I imagined the red, sore, and swollen whip marks on his little six-year-old body. Alonzo said that tears streamed down Aunt Betty's face as she called Willis into the bathroom to look at Alonzo's back. Alonzo said that Aunt Betty told Willis, "You are not taking this baby back to Sybil."

"Well, he can't come home with me," Willis said.

Alonzo said that when his father told Aunt Betty that he could not come home with him, it felt as though his father's words were a torch that burned a hole in his soul. The hole in his soul was filled with feelings of resentment towards his father that he carried for the rest of his life. Alonzo said that he felt loved by Aunt Betty while feeling neglected by his father. He said that the pain from his father's words hurt more than the scars from his mother's vicious extension cord beating. Alonzo was never sure about what exactly transpired between Aunt Betty and his mother, Sybil, but Alonzo lived with Aunt Betty from that day forward. Aunt Betty legally adopted Alonzo.

Initially, Sybil would visit Alonzo from time to time. But there was one visit that Alonzo would never forget. Sybil came to Aunt Betty's house and told Alonzo that she would be leaving to move to Las Vegas. After Sybil moved to Las Vegas, she rarely communicated with Alonzo.

Aunt Betty would hear from Sybil sporadically, but Alonzo had not spoken to his mother in years. I believe that Alonzo's mother has a lot to do with Alonzo's issues with saying "I love you."

Love is a dynamic force that alters one's life. Many of my own issues stem from love or a lack of love. The absence of love from my father, Eric, caused me to yearn for the love of a man. I only saw my father a handful of times in my life. My father's cousin Debra was friends with my mother, and Debra would take me to the park, come to my birthday parties, and take me around my father's side of the family. Debra mostly took me to see her aunt and uncle, who were my grandparents, on my father's side. Debra kept me far away from my father and his wife.

One time, when I was about eight years old, Debra took me to my paternal grandparents' house. My grandparents were so good to me. They acted as if they adored me. On this one particular day, my father showed up with his wife Linda and their daughter Jennifer, who was about two years old at the time. Everyone was shocked when the doorbell rang, and everyone was even more shocked when they saw my father and his family enter the house. Clearly, my father stopped by without communicating with my grandparents. I remember my father losing it and yelling at Debra and his parents. I don't remember everything that my dad said, but I do recall feeling bad about my existence. I knew that my presence was met with hatred. This was a crushing moment in my life. I wished that my dad could love me like my siblings' father loved them.

Chapter 5

Wisdom From the Matriarch

Aunt Betty was an important part of Alonzo's life, and it was not long before she became an important part of mine. Although I never heard Aunt Betty tell Alonzo she loved him, she showed it every day, and she showed me so much love as well. I would ask Aunt Betty for advice, and she would give me honest answers. Her honesty was kind, loving, and empathetic, not cruel, hurtful, and lacking sympathy.

Aunt Betty and I became close when I volunteered to take her grocery shopping once a week when Alonzo had become consumed with work. Aunt Betty did not drive. Eventually, I just scheduled time out of my week to take her shopping while receiving her words of wisdom. I remember asking Aunt Betty why Alonzo had not asked me to marry him after being together for almost two years; she replied, "Why do you think Alonzo has not asked you to marry him?"

"Honestly, I don't know; I guess that is why I am asking you," I replied.

"That's an Alonzo question, baby. The best way to get an answer to a question is to ask the source. If Alonzo decides that he does not want to get married, you will need to make decisions that are best for you. You need to find out if you both are on the same page because if you're not, you both are wasting your time. But I am sure you both will figure it out."

I respected Aunt Betty's honesty even if it stung me to my core. I did not want to fathom Alonzo not wanting to marry me.

I remember one night when Alonzo returned home from work; I cooked him his favorite meal, shrimp alfredo, and garlic bread. The smell of sauteed Shrimp mixed with green peppers, garlic, onion, and a creamy alfredo sauce filled the house. We sat at the kitchen table and ate, he talked about his day, and I talked about mine. When there was a moment of silence, I went in for the kill.

"Alonzo, Aunty Betty, and I had a very interesting conversation."

"Oh really," he said with an inquisitive expression on his face with his eyebrows raised, as he continued to focus on his food and look towards his plate. He took another fork full of his shrimp alfredo, took a few chews, swallowed, and said, "Tell me about this conversation that you and Aunt Betty had," with a smile on his face.

I did not know if he and Aunt Betty had already talked or what, but it seemed as if Alonzo had been given a heads-up on what I was about to talk to him about.

I continued, "Me and Aunt Betty talked about you and I getting married."

Alonzo looked at me with his sexy dark brown eyes and said, "So, you want to be my wife?" Then Alonzo said in a joking way, "Do you think that you can handle being my wife?"

I got up from my chair, walked over to Alonzo and sat on his lap. As I sat on Alonzo's lap, I wrapped my arms around his neck and said, "I have proved that I can handle you night after night," as I kissed the side of his face and neck.

"Don't worry, I have plans for us. Be patient," he said.

Life can change in an instant. I will never forget the day that I received the devastating news. Alonzo called me on my way home from work to tell me that Aunt Betty was being rushed to the hospital. She had suffered a heart attack while visiting a friend's house. Alonzo's voice was consumed with grief. I could feel his pain through the phone. Alonzo's voice began to crack when he said, "I need you; I need you to get to the hospital."

When I arrived at the hospital, I walked to the Emergency Room's Nurse's Desk and immediately felt someone grab my hand from behind. It was Alonzo. Alonzo looked into my eyes and said, "Aunt Betty may be taking her last breath soon." Alonzo proceeded to grab my hand tight and intertwined his fingers between mine. We went into Aunt Betty's room, where she was hooked up to various machines. Each agonizing breath that Aunt Betty took seemed to be a struggle. It was as if Aunt Betty was gasping for every morsel of air that she could capture through her body. Then suddenly, Aunt Betty looked right into Alonzo's eyes and took a deep, strenuous breath. Aunt Betty closed her eyes, and she was gone; Alonzo fell to his knees and began to bawl uncontrollably. I wrapped my arms around Alonzo and began to sob alongside him. Although there were a few family members in the room, at that moment, it seemed to be only me and Alonzo. Aunt Betty's death was devastating to me because I had lost a second mother, a friend, and a part of Alonzo.

It's strange how tragedy can sometimes cause people to make sudden decisions. Perhaps spontaneous actions are used as a distraction from the pain a tragedy has caused. One day, Alonzo took me to Niagara Falls, Canada, for a day of shopping and sightseeing. He wanted to stay the night in Niagara Falls. When we arrived at the hotel, the bed was covered in red roses in the shape of a heart. There was champagne, cookies, chocolates, and more. As my hands were over my mouth because of the shock of it all, I turned to thank Alonzo, who was on one knee with a ring in his hand. In his hands, there was a 2-carat princess-cut diamond ring with a platinum band. Alonzo stared me in the eyes and said, "Will you marry me?" I said yes about ten times as Alonzo put the ring on my finger. At that moment, I felt like my dreams were coming true. I did not want a wedding or our future marriage to act as a temporary bandage for the pain that Alonzo was feeling inside. I even told him that I did not want to marry him if it would only mask the sadness, he felt over Aunt Betty's death. Alonzo assured me he loved me, and that marriage was always part of his plans for us. We planned to marry the following summer.

Just like a giddy little girl, I could hardly compose myself when it came to my wedding. When I thought about it, talked about it, or indulged in the planning process for it, I was overwhelmed with excitement and pure happiness. I had a sense of confidence when it came to my wedding. When I spoke to others about my wedding plans, boy, did I make it seem larger than life. When I went to visit caterers, bakeries, and florists, I meticulously looked over each detail and demanded the personal touches that I thought would add elegance to the wedding and reception.

I was so confident in my wedding planning yet not so confident in my relationship with Alonzo. His involvement in the planning process was minimal. After Aunt Betty passed away, Alonzo and I moved into a house together. When Alonzo was not working, he would come home and play video games. When I would complain to Alonzo about us spending quality time together, he would always talk about how he needed to spend endless hours in the office to secure our future and make money. Alonzo would say that he needed to play the video games in order to relax. Meanwhile, I was tired of feeling alone.

During the time that I was planning for me and Alonzo's wedding, I was reunited with my high school best friend Grace. Grace had moved to Atlanta, Georgia to attend college, and she had worked there for a few years. Grace rarely came back to Buffalo to visit, so I was surprised that she had come back to Buffalo to live. Grace had returned to Buffalo to live temporarily because her mother had passed away, and she wanted to get her affairs in order. Grace was the only child, so she had to decide whether she would sell her mother's house and other assets.

Being reacquainted with Grace was wonderful. It was just what we both needed. Grace was in a lonely and grieving space, and so was I. Grace and I literally started where we left off. We would go out to dinner, shop, and hang out with each other. Grace and I even started going to church together.

During the months that I was planning for my wedding, Grace and I grew very close. Grace started assisting me in planning my wedding. This worked out great since Alonzo was not very involved in the process, and I had become overwhelmed.

I had started to neglect myself because I was working extra hours at the hospital to cover some of the wedding expenses. Then, one day, working hard and not taking good care of myself finally caught up with me. I was at work and began feeling extremely tired and jittery. My manager took my blood pressure, which was normal, but she still insisted that I go home. I called Alonzo because I did not want to drive home feeling the way that I was feeling; Alonzo told me to hang in there for a while and that he would be on his way. While waiting for Alonzo, I called Grace to tell her what was going on, and Grace told me to tell Alonzo that she would pick me up. When I told Alonzo, he seemed relieved. When Grace arrived, she started telling me how she was feeling weak as well because she had started her menstrual cycle. Grace then said, "That's probably why you are feeling depleted, between being on your period, working all those hours, and planning for your lavish wedding." My heart instantly began to pound at turbo speed. Grace and I had been hanging around each other so much that we would start our menstrual cycles at around the same time each month. By the way, it is scientifically proven that women who spend a lot of time together somehow end up having their periods at the same time.

"How long have you been on your period?" I nervously asked Grace.

"I'm on day four, it should be ending soon. What about you?"

"Take me to a pharmacy to get a pregnancy test now."

When Grace and I arrived at my place after leaving the pharmacy, I immediately grabbed the pregnancy test and ran to the bathroom. I read the instructions carefully to ensure that I did not make any mistakes while taking it. I peed on the pregnancy test stick, and as soon as I lifted the test to see it, the word pregnant started showing up on the test. I was so upset with myself, with Alonzo, and our carelessness. I went from feeling upset, dumb, scared, anxious, to excited and optimistic. I figured that I could still pull off the perfect wedding while being pregnant. By the time the wedding would come around, I would be about four months pregnant.

I did not tell Alonzo that I was pregnant right away. It took me about a week before I told him because I was so nervous. I did not know how he would take the news. In all my life, I had seldom witnessed a couple excited about a pregnancy. Where I am from, I saw women get pregnant by men that they were not actually in a relationship with, teenagers getting pregnant, or women getting pregnant with men who were not ready to be fathers, etc.

The night that I told Alonzo that I was pregnant, we were both exhausted from finally cleaning out Aunt Betty's house; Alonzo was getting ready to put the house up for sale. That day, Alonzo had insisted on keeping the red and orange floral design sofa that I remembered so vividly from the night of the snowstorm when I met him. I hated that sofa with a passion, but Alonzo insisted that he keep it because he purchased it for Aunt Betty, and she told him that it was the best gift that anyone had ever given her. She loved that couch. I agreed to keep the couch because Alonzo was already going through enough emotionally, and I did not want to add more to his plate. Our living room was crammed with furniture. There was my beautiful chocolate brown leather sofa nestled next to that ugly red and orange floral sofa. Alonzo was sitting on the sofa that belonged to Aunt Betty, and I was sitting on my chocolate brown leather sofa. We were both watching television. I turned to Alonzo and said, "I have something that I have been meaning to tell you." I felt so stupid wording it this way, but these were the only words that I could devise.

"Okay baby, what's up?"

I said nervously, "I'm pregnant."

Alonzo immediately sat up, looked at me with wide eyes, and froze for a second. "What did you just say?" he asked.

Again, I uttered, "I'm pregnant."

Alonzo got up, walked over to me, grabbed me by my hands, pulled me from the sofa, and began to hold and kiss me. When Alonzo's lips parted from mine, he had the biggest smile and started rubbing my belly and saying, "We're having a baby, wow I can't believe this." I felt so happy, and I was even happier that I could be in a relationship where my fiancé was excited about us bringing a new life into the world.

Being pregnant and planning a wedding is very strenuous. I had to buy a new dress and sell the original one. Not to mention that I had become very irritable and agitated by everything. Further, Alonzo was becoming increasingly agitated with the expenses associated with the wedding. Alonzo was working all the time and when he was not working, he was playing more and more video games. Grace told me that I should be happy that he was not in the streets playing with women and just playing video games. But I was beginning to feel that Alonzo was becoming more and more distant.

Tough times seemed to be a consistent theme in my life. I worked countless hours so that I could contribute more to my wedding financially. At this point, I was about three months pregnant and a month away from my wedding. Of course, my car broke down during this time. The repairs required to fix my car added up to more than it was worth. I decided to just get rid of the car. I had been through college, snowstorms, and hell with that little white two-door car. The car had served me well, and it was time for us to part ways. Instead of getting a new car, Alonzo insisted that I just get rides from him, my mother, or Grace to and from work until after the wedding. I was okay with this deal because I was determined to have the wedding of my dreams, and I could not afford to make such a large purchase.

Working at the hospital as a nurse had become annoying and exhausting. I just started to feel that I was not living my purpose. Also, the patients were starting to get the best of me. I had one patient in particular who had been admitted for hypertension. I was assigned as his nurse for a day or two. This patient's name was Stephen, and he was very flirtatious. Now, I have had flirtatious patients in the past; I never took them seriously. However, this man was extremely strange, and he made me feel very uncomfortable. He was very inappropriate, constantly making comments about wanting to take me home with him.

He even told me that God brought me into his life for a reason. I could tell that Stephen did not realize that I was very pregnant and very uninterested in him.

Stephen was a fifty-two-year-old, tall, and thin Caucasian man with bright blue eyes that really stood out. He was bald with an oval-shaped head. His teeth were yellow, which was a shame because he had perfect teeth otherwise.

The day that Stephen was discharged from the hospital, he came back to my unit stating that he had left a gold necklace. My charge nurse was asking around about Stephen's gold necklace. When Stephen saw me, he said, "You going home with me, baby?" I just ignored him. Further, I was just happy to be clocking out soon.

That night, when I finished my shift at the hospital, I was waiting outside for Alonzo to pick me up, and he was nowhere to be found. After about ten minutes, I called Alonzo, and he told me that he was running behind and asked me to be patient. I was infuriated. I was waiting outside for Alonzo after working a 12-hour shift. I was pregnant and tired, and the hospital where I worked was not in the best neighborhood. After about an hour of waiting on Alonzo, I was on fire. I called and texted my mother and Grace, but no one was getting back to me. I was growing more and more impatient. Plus, Alonzo had stopped answering his phone. I was tight on money because of the wedding, so I decided to take the cheapest route and get on a bus. A million things were going through my mind. I felt totally neglected and abandoned by Alonzo. I thought to myself, "How could a man leave his pregnant fiancé out in the streets waiting on him and not answer his phone."

After walking a block or two in the dark, in an unsafe neighborhood, my eyes welled up with tears. It was like my heart was beating deep and fast. The fury in my soul caused my face to become physically hot; both of my fists were clutched tight as I walked. I felt tingling throughout my body because of the embarrassment, sadness, anger, and emotional pain that I was feeling all at once. I was feeling embarrassed because I feared that one of my co-workers would see me catching the bus. Everyone that I worked with knew that I was working a profusion of overtime. If any of my co-workers saw me at the bus stop, they would assume that I was really mismanaging my money. Past traumas of those closest to me not being available when I needed them the most brought about my array of emotions.

As I was getting closer to the bus stop, I felt headlights behind me. I felt compelled to turn around. When I turned around, I saw the patient from the hospital, Stephen, driving a green sedan with his passenger window down. Soon, I was looking at Stephen in his blue eyes. I started to walk faster. Stephen pulled his car up a couple of feet in front of me. At that moment, I began to feel an excruciating pain in my stomach. My stomach began to hurt so badly; it was like no pain I had ever experienced. I just sat on the ground. Then I heard Stephen's car door slamming. Before I knew it, Stephen was standing over me saying, "Are you okay? Are you alright?" I could barely speak. Then he said, "Come, get in the car with me."

I mustered up enough energy to scream, "Noooooo."

"Alright, alright. Do you need me to call an ambulance?" Stephen asked.

The pain was so intense that I could only shake my head up and down to gesture yes.

Soon, I heard sirens, and then I was put on a stretcher. Within minutes, I arrived at the same hospital where I had just finished a shift. My mother returned my call on my way to the hospital, but Alonzo did not return my call. My mother was close by and was able to meet me at the hospital.

When Alonzo arrived in my hospital room, I could not even look at him; I was so angry. My mother told Alonzo that I had a miscarriage, and he walked out of the room and into the hallway. When Alonzo returned to my room, his eyes were red, and I could tell he had been crying. My mother excused herself. Alonzo then began to explain. He said that when I initially called him, he was preparing to leave the office. However, his boss requested that he complete one last task. Alonzo said that once he was done, he rushed out of the office and accidentally left his phone behind. He said that he did not notice that he left his phone until he was driving to the hospital to pick me up. Alonzo explained that after waiting outside of the hospital for a while, he eventually went into the hospital to see if I was in the lobby, and I was not there. He said that he went back outside looking for me. Then he drove around the neighborhood looking for me for about thirty minutes before returning to the hospital. Alonzo said that he went to my unit looking for me. He was told that I had left well over an hour ago. Alonzo said that he was on his way out, and one of my co-workers ran up to him. She said that she had heard that I had been brought to the hospital via ambulance. Alonzo said that this is how he found out I had been admitted to the hospital. I looked him in the eye and said, "Are you even ready to have a wife and a family? You couldn't even be here for me, and all I needed was a ride home. What if we had the baby? Would you be there for us when we need you?" I then just turned away from Alonzo because, for me, this moment was not about him or me; it was about the baby that we lost. At this time, I partially blamed him for losing the baby. I felt as though the circumstances that Alonzo had created brought about the loss of my child, and I did not know if I could ever forgive Alonzo.

After the miscarriage, things really changed between Alonzo and me. I felt that he was dealing with grief, and I was not qualified to help him through it. Additionally, I think that we were both dealing with depression at this point. We both were drifting further and further apart. Eventually, the inevitable had to happen. I called off the wedding. Initially, I called off the wedding because, after losing my unborn child, I felt that I had no reason to celebrate. My relationship with Alonzo was not worth celebrating at this time; I felt that Alonzo had failed me as my fiancé. Further, Alonzo had not fully grieved his Aunt Betty; he buried his feelings in his work and video games. The love that we had was not enough to hold us together. Although I loved Alonzo, I had dreams for myself, and I could feel myself drifting away in my own sorrows, and I needed to save me.

A time will come when you realize the obvious; you realize it's over. Alonzo and I were in the process of looking for a home to purchase. Aunt Betty left Alonzo everything she had, although she didn't have much. Alonzo sold Aunt Betty's house and had plans on using this money to make a down payment for a new home. However, after the miscarriage, everything came to a screeching halt. The lease on the home that we were renting was almost up. Alonzo was talking about getting an extension on the lease. Alonzo was talking as if the wedding plans and house-buying plans were just on hold. Unfortunately, in my mind, our relationship was over. Alonzo was not showing me any attention. I was getting more attention from the men at the grocery store than I was from Alonzo. Alonzo was excelling at work and spending money on all the things that he wanted while I was just at home wallowing away in my sorrows. Alonzo did buy me flowers, jewelry, and he even purchased me a new car; however, I was not happy. I just could not understand how Alonzo was able to just move on with life after everything that had happened. Especially since deep down inside, I blamed my miscarriage on Alonzo. I resented him.

Grace was a great source of support during this difficult time in my life. One day, Grace and I were out at a restaurant eating dinner. Grace revealed to me that she had just found out that her mother had left her a substantial amount of money after her death. She was ready to start over. I sat at the restaurant table with my head hanging low, and I said, "I sure do wish that I could start over."

"What do you mean?" Grace asked.

"Girl, I'm ready to leave Alonzo's ass. I'm just trying to figure out how."

"I'm moving to Los Angeles in a few weeks; if you want to move with me, you are welcome to do so. I think this may be a good move for you," Grace said.

For the first time in a long time, I felt a glimmer of hope. I immediately began to think of the possibilities. I knew that I was beautiful and talented, and I had always wanted to be a Hollywood actress. I thought to myself, maybe everything happened for a reason. Maybe it wasn't meant for me to have a baby with Alonzo. My lease was almost up, Alonzo and I were having a hard time, and Grace came to me with this proposal at the perfect time. I looked at Grace and said, "I am so ready to go; it's time for me to enjoy life."

I only had three weeks to plan my move to Los Angeles. I was really uneasy about the thought of telling Alonzo that not only was it over between us, but I would be moving across the country. I started feeling empathy towards him because he had dealt with a lot recently. But then, I would quickly think of my miscarriage and the part he played in it. A part of me felt that Alonzo deserved to be neglected and deserted because this is how he made me feel.

I informed Alonzo that I would be moving to Los Angeles two weeks before the move. Alonzo came home from work with some Chinese takeout. He set the food on the table. Before Alonzo got too comfortable, I said, "Alonzo, we need to talk." Alonzo's facial expression immediately turned to agitation.

"Baby, can I at least fix my plate first?" Alonzo asked.

"You can do whatever you want to do, but I need to tell you something."

Alonzo sat at the kitchen table, looked at me, and said, "What?"

"Alonzo, things have not been right between us since the miscarriage; there is a clear divide between us."

"I know, we both have gone through a lot. We just need to get on the same page."

"There is no need to get on the same page because I have torn the pages out of the book; I'm leaving you and moving to Los Angeles."

The energy in the room became cold and dark, and I knew that it was because of me. Alonzo looked confused, shocked, hurt, and disappointed. Alonzo said with great passion with a slightly elevated voice, "You have been making me pay for the miscarriage ever since it happened. I have tried to make amends. There is nothing that you can do to me that would punish me more than I already punish myself. The torment that I endure in my mind is inescapable. Sometimes, I feel like a prisoner in my own grief, and I don't know when my sentence will end. Sometimes, I wonder if I will have to serve a life sentence. So, to try to find some solace and forgiveness, I have been trying to make things right with you without avail. I hold you to comfort you, but you don't return my embrace. I bring you flowers, and you don't stop to smell them. I try to talk to you, but you're quiet. I apologized more times than I can count, and you dismissed me. I even buy you things, and you won't even open the bags. I am in a situation where I feel as though you don't want to be happy, you don't want to make things better, you don't want to forgive me or yourself."

At this point, the tension was so thick you could cut it with a knife, pick up the slices, and serve a thousand people. The tension in the room was accompanied by an atmosphere of a somber feeling. I then said, "Alonzo, all you do is work and I am left to always pick up the pieces of our lives. I had to be the one to notify everyone that there would be no wedding this summer, I take care of the house while you're working, plus, I have to go through my own grieving process."

"Karma, do you realize that I work so hard because one day I want to make sure that you don't have to work at all? I really have been doing all of this working for you and our future kids. Do you understand how much I love you and how much I sacrifice for you?"

At this point, I was beginning to second-guess my decision. Alonzo never poured out his heart to me in this way. Alonzo rarely said, "I love you". For the first time, I felt as though I understood Alonzo's perspective more than I ever had in the past. However, my mind and heart were set on moving to Los Angeles. There was no turning back now. Alonzo asked, "What's in Los Angeles?"

"My new life is in Los Angeles," I replied.

The next two weeks of living with Alonzo were awkward. I made it a point to sleep on the couch every night. Alonzo was coming home later and later. I think that Alonzo was trying to avoid coming home because things had gotten so weird. The day that I moved out, surprisingly, Alonzo was only in the office for a few hours before returning home. When Alonzo did come home, he was greeted by a U-Haul truck, Grace, and movers. All of the boxes that I had packed were finally leaving the house. Alonzo grabbed me by the hand when he got into the house, walked me into our bedroom, and shut the door.

"I know you are not leaving," Alonzo said.

"Alonzo, we already had this discussion."

Alonzo grabbed me, kissed my lips, and said, "You know you love me, and you know we belong together. There is nothing in Los Angeles for you. What can I do to make you stay?"

"There is nothing else that can be done, Alonzo, it's over."

Alonzo kissed me again; my face began to get wet from Alonzo's tears. I pushed Alonzo away so that I could see his face; I wanted to confirm that Alonzo was really crying because I was leaving. However, when I pushed Alonzo away, he quickly rubbed his hands over his face in an effort to conceal his tears. Then Alonzo looked at me and said, "Do me a favor; please tell me if you are leaving because you want to punish me or because you really want to go to Los Angeles."

"I really want to go to Los Angeles."

Honestly, I was not 100% certain about my answer. Now that I look back, I think initially I wanted Alonzo to suffer. Alonzo showing so much emotion made me feel conflicted, but it was too late. I wanted to escape my pain, and LA seemed like the antidote.

"I really hope you find happiness because I would love to be reacquainted with happiness again myself," Alonzo said.

I held Alonzo and said, "I love you more than you will ever know; you are a good man. In fact, you are the best man that I have ever known. But Alonzo, you and I both know that we are not happy. It's time to sever this bond that was once a bond of love and now is a bond of anguish." Before long, I found myself getting into the U-Haul truck as Alonzo entered the house, lowering his head as he closed the door behind him.

As I was leaving Buffalo and moving to Los Angeles, I said very few goodbyes; I have heard people say, "Where's the good in goodbye?" I had a totally new understanding of this question as I was chartering new territory and leaving my old life behind. Grace and I went to my mother's house before we left town. My mother was surprisingly supportive. All she wanted was for me to become a nurse and to have a steady income, yet here I was chasing a wild dream of becoming an actress. My mother made sure that I departed with her words of wisdom. Before leaving, my mother said, "Baby, your life is all that you have; although it can be durable, it can be fragile at the same time. Be careful about how you choose to live. Make decisions that will illuminate your life, not decisions that will darken your paths. And when I say darken your paths, I am referring to inviting dark energies into your life that will remove whatever clarity you have. Remember, turbulent times will come; do your best to ensure that those days aren't self-inflicted." That was a lot for me to absorb, but I tried to take in the wise words that my mother so eloquently expressed.

Chapter 6

A New Day, A New Beginning

It took about four days for Grace and me to drive from Buffalo to Los Angeles. When we arrived, my heart began to pound, and my eyes were wide open. I had never visited Los Angeles before and could not believe that this would be my new home. I did not know what to expect because, honestly, I did not have a legit concrete plan of how I would reach my goals of stardom. I knew that Grace would take care of me until I was able to get my feet on the ground. However, I became overwhelmed with anxiety after coming to terms with the fact that I had made a life-altering decision by moving to Los Angeles. I quickly realized that I did not leave my internal issues in Buffalo. Further, my anxiety had me thinking a million things at once. I thought to myself, "What if I am unable to find work? What if Grace gets sick of me, and I'm forced to move back to Buffalo? What if something happens to Grace, and I am left penniless?" I was consumed with thoughts and emotions. Reality had hit me like a ton of bricks. Now, it was up to me to make the move a success or a failure.

Grace had leased a small 2-bedroom apartment in Los Angeles that we were going to have to make work. This was not a luxury apartment. The appliances were white and outdated with rust, the wall-to-wall carpet was a light brown color but was worn, and the walls were an off-white color. The smell of the apartment consisted of a musty melody of cigarette smoke, possible mildew, and soil. This is the best way that I can describe the apartment's scent. The cost of living was unbelievably high, and we had to adjust accordingly until we were able to afford something nicer.

When I arrived in Los Angeles I refused to renew my nursing license. I wanted to force myself to focus solely on acting. Plus, working as a nurse would not allow me the flexibility to pursue my acting career, so I took on bartending, which was fun. Grace found a job as a software engineer shortly after we moved. During the day, I was either taking acting classes or going to casting calls, and at night, I was bartending and partying. If my mother knew what I was doing at that time, she would have lost it. But I wanted to have fun for once in my life. I had no interest in being stuck with a man or being stuck in a career; I just wanted to be free.

In Los Angeles, there were lots of opportunities to meet wealthy men. Grace seemed to be out on a date at least three times a week with guys that had money. As always, she was a guy magnet. Men just loved her. Grace would sometimes come back home with shopping bags full of things. I don't know what her trick was. As for me, I was not looking for anything serious. I was cool with a guy taking me out or taking me shopping, but I was in no way, shape, or form interested in a relationship. If there was a guy who could just take me to the movies, I would have been happy.

Grace would tell me that I needed to learn the art of flirting. She would try to give me some pointers here and there on how to flirt. Unfortunately, twirling my hair, staring at a guy, or bending down to pick up shit that I dropped on purpose was hard for me to apply in a real-world setting.

It wasn't long before Grace mentioned that she had met a guy named Dane, who owned a prominent record label. Dane was famous. We had seen him on television since our teens, talking about his role in different artists' careers and even his imprint on pop culture. Dane was about 5 feet 10 inches tall with a bald and shining head. He was thin and had the smoothest-looking black skin that gleamed. Grace met Dane at an industry event that another guy took her to. Grace said that she and Dane had been making eye contact all night long. She said that as soon as the guy that she was with walked away, she walked right over to Dane, and the next thing she knew, they were leaving the event together. Grace said that she and Dane had sex that night. She said that Dane was hung like a horse. After she met Dane, Grace told me that she didn't even want to be with anyone else because she said she did not think that she could find another man to satisfy her sexually like Dane did.

Dane introduced Grace to a life she had never experienced before. Dane would send drivers to our raggedy ass apartment to pick her up. He would send her red roses at least four times a week. Sometimes, he would even take her on impromptu trips out of the country in his private jet. Grace suddenly stopped working altogether, but the bills were getting paid. She was home less and less. When Grace did come home, we would talk about all the celebrities she met. Grace had even started putting Dane on her social media platforms, and he was doing the same. I started to quickly realize that I needed to become more stable financially because Grace seemed to really be getting serious with Dane.

Finding friends in Los Angeles was not hard for me. At the restaurant where I worked, I got to know a lot of people. There was a girl that I was intrigued by; her name was Aiko. She was a fellow waitress and bartender at the restaurant. She was black and Japanese but was born and raised in New York City. I loved her New York accent. Aiko had been living in Los Angeles for two years. She was stunning and fun to be around. She moved to Los Angeles in hopes of becoming a Hollywood actress like so many others. Aiko knew a lot of people and seemed to hang around with a lot of celebrities. She always had the best clothes, the best jewelry, and the best handbags. I mean, she would wear thousands of dollars' worth of clothing every time we went out. I often wondered what she was doing to afford her luxury lifestyle. I knew that waitressing and bartending alone could never generate the money required to live the life that Aiko was living. I just did not understand how she could afford all these things. Whatever she was doing, I certainly wanted to get in on it. I once asked Aiko if she was getting her beautiful things from men. Aiko said no with fierce conviction. She was deeply offended by my question. I was unbothered and still curious about Aiko's streams of income.

One night, Aiko and I were leaving work. It was raining, and I was waiting for a Taxi because the car that Alonzo had purchased for me before I left Buffalo was burglarized the night before, and my windows were busted. Aiko said, "Girl, I will take you home tonight; I know you have had a tough couple of days." I happily accepted. As Aiko was taking me home, we both decided that we were not ready for the night to end; we decided to go to a club. When we arrived at the club, we drank, we talked, we danced, and we laughed. We were having such a great time, and then I saw Grace's boyfriend, Dane, walk into the club and enter the VIP section. This instantly caught my attention because I then began looking for Grace. I figured that Dane and Grace would be able to get VIP treatment for Aiko and me. I started walking towards the VIP section and figured that Grace would be within close proximity. However, instead of seeing Grace, a man walked up to Dane as he was sitting in the VIP section. The man was extremely feminine in the way that he walked and his mannerisms as he was speaking to Dane. He and Dane spoke for a while and were very close to one another during their conversation; perhaps it was because of the loud music playing in the club. I decided to abort my mission to greet Dane in the VIP section. I went back to dancing on the dance floor. After a few minutes of dancing, I looked back toward the VIP section where Dane had been sitting; Dane was gone and so was the man. I felt like I had witnessed something that I was not supposed to see.

Aiko and I began spending more and more time together. We began to become good friends. We hung out often because we had a lot in common. Neither of us did any drugs, although we could drink with the best of them. We loved the same TV shows, and we both had dreams of becoming mega movie stars. One day, when we were hanging out and doing girl stuff, once again, I was itching to ask her how she made extra money. We had already shared our history, likes, and dislikes with one another, but I could not get Aiko to tell me what else she did for money.

One day Aiko and I went to one of our favorite restaurants called Surtain's. It was a family-owned restaurant, but it was so elegant. The restaurant had black and silver décor. The black linen napkins were wrapped in silver jewel cuff napkin rings. The crystal wine glasses that sat on the table were almost mesmerizing; it was hard to keep your eyes off them. Even if you looked your hardest, you could not find a fingerprint, smudge, or flaw on any glass. The lights were dimmed in the restaurant, and all you could smell were delectable scents of freshly cooked foods and marinades. There was a miniature silver and crystal-dimmed chandelier that hung over our table. The ambiance alone gave me the courage to speak my mind with Aiko. How could anyone, including Aiko, get mad at a place like this? I said to Aiko, "Girl, I need to know how and where you get your money from. We essentially do the same thing, and I cannot afford half of the things that you have."

"Well, girl, I am not sure if you are ready for the big leagues; what I do is not for the faint at heart, and it's not a game."

This really sparked my curiosity. "I have seen and done a lot of things in my life; I'm a big girl, Aiko. Just tell me what you do?"

Aiko sighed and placed her right hand over the top of her forehead in frustration. Then, with a look of contemplation, she sat quietly for a few seconds as she looked at me. Then Aiko said, "Karma, I am doing homework at our job. My job requires a lot of local travel; I go on business trips."

"What the hell are you talking about?" I asked.

"I will explain more when we leave here, let's just enjoy our dinner for now."

I tried to play it cool during dinner, but the anticipation was overwhelming. I figured that if Aiko was willing to speak about what she did, she might be able to get me in. I would not have to worry about relying on Grace or trying to find a roommate before she inevitably left. I was sure that this job would suit me just fine, even if I had to do it temporarily. I just needed to get the name and number of the contact person, and I would be able to move forward from there. I refused to go back to nursing.

When Aiko and I left the restaurant, she dropped me off at home and said that she had an emergency and just left. I was pissed; I felt that Aiko had just played me for a fool. Some people feel better knowing that they are doing better than you, and I was beginning to feel that Aiko was one of those people. To my surprise, when I walked through the door, Grace was home. I was so excited because Grace and I hadn't seen each other often since she had started dating Dane. Plus, I wanted to catch up with her so that she could give me the tea about the celebrities that she was now mingling with. That night, Grace seemed super excited. She ran to me and just grabbed me and began hugging me as she was jumping up and down, and my natural reaction was to jump up and down as well. Then Grace stopped jumping and pulled away from me. I looked at Grace and said, "What is going on?"

"I am engaged to get married; Dane proposed to me," she yelled with excitement in her voice. Then Grace started screaming.

By this time, Grace and I had only been in Los Angeles for six months, and she had been dating Dane for only about three of those months.

"Grace, you don't even know him." Instantly, I regretted saying this. But I had no idea that I would be so angry that Grace was getting married. I could not conceal my emotions. I then said, "This may not be a good idea at all; what do you know about him? Have you met his family? Hell, do you know if he has kids?" I looked at Grace's ring finger, which had no ring, and I said to her, "Where is the damn ring?"

Grace's joy instantly turned into rage. Grace said in a condescending tone, "Sweetie, once you stop relying on me, pay all of your own bills, purchase your own car, oh yeah, and find your own man, then you can question my decisions."

"Let's not forget, I have been engaged before," I said.

"Yeah, to the brother of the guy who you gave your virginity to and broadcasted you having sex with him to an entire city. I doubt if Alonzo was ever going to really marry you. Oh, and speaking of Alonzo, you may want to call him to congratulate him because he is expecting a baby."

Grace grabbed her designer handbag and walked out the door. I was speechless. I just laid my back against the wall that I was standing near and slid down as I held my face and began to cry uncontrollably. I cried continuously for about an hour. Almost everything that Grace said about me was true; however, I was just praying that what she said about Alonzo was a lie. My heart could not handle that. It's not like I did not expect Alonzo to move on, but I did not expect him to move on so quickly. This came as a total shock to me. Grace's harsh words towards me made me realize that it was time for me to make some changes in my life. I had to stand on my own two feet. I vowed to myself that I would never again place myself in a situation where a person could look down upon me and crush my spirit because I relied on them.

Once I dried my tears, I mustered up enough courage to stroll through Alonzo's social media pages. I knew that Alonzo hardly ever posted on social media. While strolling through social media, I found a post where a really basic looking girl posted that she and Alonzo were expecting. Alonzo was tagged in the photo, but he was not in the actual photo. The photo was posted that day. The girl had thin, stringy shoulder-length hair that you could see through as if she had extensive hair damage from hair relaxers. She had a part down the middle of her hair, and some of her thin hair was tucked behind her ears. She appeared to be tall and thin; she was shaped like a pencil. She was holding her small and bulging stomach. Maybe I am hating a little bit, but of course, I am going to be critical of the woman who is with the man that I love. I wanted to reach out to Alonzo, but I could not find any words to say to him. I was disappointed in Alonzo for running off and getting someone pregnant so fast, but I really did not have a right to be upset. I could not help how I felt. Grace revealing this awful news about Alonzo, coupled with her harsh words, hurt me to my heart.

Weeks went by without me seeing and speaking to Grace. The power ended up getting shut off at one point in the apartment because I was having a hard time paying the bills alone. I thought about taking Grace to court for not paying her portion of the bills. I even thought about going back to nursing, but I was determined to find another way to survive financially. I had to borrow money from Aiko; I really had to put my pride to the side in order to do that. I asked Aiko if she needed a roommate, and her response to me was, "I don't do roommates." Which ultimately felt like a "Hell no" to me.

I really wanted to know what Aiko was doing on the side to earn money, but she was just so damn secretive about it. I was between a rock and a hard place; I needed some extra money. I was betting on my persistence paying off in the world of acting. None of my acting auditions were working out. I had to find a way to make it in LA; going back to Buffalo was not an option. I was going to ask Aiko what she did one last time, and if she did not let me know, I was going to have to reconsider our friendship. Friends look out for each other, and if she was unwilling to help me out in my situation, that would confirm that she was not a real friend. Aiko was aware of my financial struggles and all I needed was some extra income. I was wondering if Aiko was thinking that if I started doing what she was doing for extra money, perhaps I would make more money than her. Was Aiko's fear of me doing better than her preventing her from letting me in on how she made extra money? Did Aiko enjoy being around me because my circumstances made her feel better about herself? I really hated the idea of being anyone's charity case, and I really hated the idea of Aiko hanging around me because I was down and out, and my misfortune made her feel superior.

Navigating challenging or uncomfortable situations is not much fun, especially when you are strategically setting up a friend. I had arranged a time for Aiko to come to my apartment for a fun girl's night. I had plenty of alcohol and food. Besides having fun, I really wanted to speak to her about how she viewed our friendship. By this time, Aiko and I were as close as Grace, and I once were. Aiko was under the impression that we would just be doing fun girl stuff. I had other plans in mind.

I was looking forward to seeing Aiko. When I heard the knock at my door, I opened the door with a smile on my face. Aiko stood there with a smile as she held her brown and gold monogram canvas Louis Vuitton travel bag on her shoulder. She was wearing a black jacket, and her long, black, straight hair laid across the middle of her back while the part in the middle of her head allowed her hair to fall against her face and cascade past her chest. She was always so pretty and so well put together. Her nails were short but painted red. She was wearing patent pointed-toe red-sole Christian Louboutin shoes. Each inch of Aiko's 5-foot 3-inch, 100-pound frame seemed to be cared for. She wore false eyelashes and foundation that made her skin flawless. Her hair had a shine, and her body was toned. She even smelled amazing. I could not even afford perfume for myself. At that very moment, I realized that I was a little jealous of Aiko. I could feel the tension in my chest, and my eyes damn near began to water. I quickly got it together, but I desired to have it all just like Aiko. Sadly, I was unable to afford a fraction of the things that Aiko possessed. The designer bags, designer shoes, and all the high-fashion clothes and accessories were far out of my reach. I knew that I deserved to have those beautiful things, but for some reason, Aiko was not willing to help me obtain what she had.

Aiko and I started off the night in our pajamas, making homemade pizza. We used Alfredo sauce instead of tomato sauce to try something different. We topped the pizza with mozzarella cheese, red onions, bell peppers, spinach, mushrooms, and black olives. We talked, we laughed, and we drank lots of Moscato. Moscato was my favorite wine; I did not care that it was a dessert wine; I would drink it whenever I felt like it. As Aiko and I sat on the cold brown leather couch that I had brought from Buffalo, we were stuffed. Then I went in for the kill and said to Aiko, "Why are you secretive about your side gig?" Aiko then rolled her eyes. I said, "Don't do that, Aiko; I am serious; we hang out all of the time; you know how hard I am struggling. Why won't you just let me in on what you do so that I can at least figure out whether or not it's right for me or if I am even qualified." Aiko just looked at me without saying anything. Then I said, "Sometimes I feel as though our friendship is predicated on me making you feel superior to me due to my current circumstances."

A befuddled look fell upon Aiko's face, and she asked, "What is that supposed to mean?"

"I feel that our friendship works because I make you feel elite while you persist in looking down on me. You could easily help me out by giving me information about your side job, but instead, I think you like to see me struggle." I immediately started to feel relieved for expressing my thoughts and remorseful because I did not want to lose my friendship with Aiko.

After my rant, Aiko sat up straight on the couch, looked me directly in the eye, and said, "Really, is this what you think?"

"Well yeah," I said.

"First and foremost, if you are trying to imply that I am interested in hindering your progress because I enjoy seeing you struggle, you are sadly mistaken. I have been nothing but a great friend to you. I help you out because we are friends, and I have the means to assist you when you need it. Furthermore, you owe me money that I have not asked you to repay. I certainly do not enjoy giving my money to you if that's what you believe. I am a damn good friend to you; it's unfortunate that you can't be a good friend to me. And lastly, stop going through life expecting people to help you or rescue you. No one owes you shit. The difference between me and you is that I don't expect shit from anybody. I get what I want. If there is no way, damn it, I make a way."

When Aiko was speaking, I could feel the emotion in her voice. Her eyes became filled with tears, and she was trying to restrain them from falling down her face. Her voice cracked as she spoke with passion, disappointment, and agitation. I really felt foul for the things that I had said to Aiko. I should never have doubted our friendship. I then said to Aiko, "I'm so sorry, and maybe you are right. There is no denying that I have some things that I need to work on within myself. I feel like I'm in a ditch trying to climb my way out, and I'm waiting for someone to throw me a rope, a ladder, or something. I know that I have to become determined to dig my feet and fingers into the dirt and climb my way out of this." Then I jokingly said, "I just hate getting dirty." Aiko and I just burst out into laughter.

"Yes, climbing your way out will make you stronger; someone throwing you a ladder will not be as gratifying as knowing that you got yourself out of the situation regardless of how dirty you have to get," Aiko explained.

Aiko hugged me, and I just broke down in tears. Aiko just held me as I cried; she began to cry as well. "I'm sorry," Aiko said. Eventually, Aiko and I were released from our embrace, and I got up to grab some tissues to wipe our tears.

When I returned from the bathroom with the tissues, Aiko was still sitting on the couch and had started scrolling through her phone. Aiko then looked up at me as I was preparing to sit on the couch and said, "Let's talk about what I do on the side. But before I utter a word, I need you to promise never to tell anyone."

"Of course not." Then I sat down next to Aiko.

Aiko faced me and grabbed me by the shoulders, and said, "If you tell anyone what I am going to tell you, it has the potential to forever ruin my life. What I do is not a game, and I take it seriously."

My curiosity was at an all-time high. Aiko continued to say, "You know how we go to nice restaurants and clubs often?"

"Yeah," I replied.

"We are not only there to have a good time; I'm there doing research."

Then, I became perplexed. Aiko continued, "What I do is research celebrities and their habits. I go to celebrities' and wealthy people's social media pages, find out where they live, and rob them. Sometimes, others pay me for information, and they rob celebrities and rich people. When I know the wealthy person or celebrity is out of the country or not at home, I take what I like to call a business trip to their house and take things of value. Now personally, I only take small yet very expensive things like jewelry. I take things that I know they may not miss right away. When I take things, I don't make it obvious. I don't trash houses or take everything in the jewelry box. I want the person to think that perhaps they misplaced their valuable item or that someone who works for them took something. Now, as for the people who pay me for information, I don't know, nor do I care about what they do with the information. I just want my money."

This disturbing yet captivating second life that Aiko was living had me yearning for more details.

"How do you get into the celebrities' houses?"

"There are many ways. I enter the home as a guest and roam the house until I find the primary bedroom and take things. I have literally taken keys from under carpets, plant vases, amongst other things, and walked right into houses. When I know that a celebrity or rich person is out of the country, it's like striking gold. It feels like stealing candy from a baby."

I tried to maintain calmness to avoid showing my true internal feelings, which were feelings of Immense excitement. I did not want Aiko to think that I was unable to handle the information that she had entrusted me with.

"When you go to people's homes, are you alone?" I asked.

"I have been doing this alone because people talk too much. I have learned that people don't get caught because of their own miscalculations; people get caught because someone ran their mouth. This is why it's so important for you to never speak of this."

Aiko continued to explain to me that she is friends with celebrity fashion stylists, hair stylists, agents, and more. Aiko said that between casual conversations with people who are hired by the rich and famous and social media posts, she finds out how long her victims will be away, exactly where they are going, who they are going with, and if anyone will be left behind in the home. Aiko said that her strategy is to make sure that she is long gone before the authorities are called. Aiko's main goal was to prevent the authorities from being contacted at all. This is why Aiko said that she strives to keep each home that she enters intact with no traces of a burglary. Aiko proceeded to provide me with an example of when we were together, and she was doing her research. Aiko was friends with a guy named Terry Tea, who was friends with a lot of celebrities because he was a fashion stylist to many of them. Aiko was trying to get me to remember him, but nothing was ringing a bell. She explained that he was a really good-looking, brown-skinned man whose keen fashion sense should have sparked my memory, but nothing reawakened my memory bank. Aiko stressed that Terry Tea has no idea what she does; however, he always tells her which celebrities are going to be where. He would even tell her if a celebrity had family in town. I had witnessed Aiko have these types of conversations firsthand with an array of people and never thought twice about it. Aiko stated that she would use Terry Tea's information to calculate her next move and determine where she would take her next business trip. These business trips involved nothing more than Aiko going to the person's home and stealing some of their valuable belongings. She continued to say that she even had friends who were paparazzi. Aiko said that she would talk to her paparazzi friends because she sometimes acts as a paparazzi, and they will tell her exactly where celebrities live and where they will be. Aiko said, "I just want to let you know that the more that you and I hung out, the more I began to adore you as a friend, but I must admit, having you around helped me with my research because it would look strange if I were to go out to dinner alone. You know our favorite restaurant, Surtain's? That's also a famous comedian's favorite restaurant as well. I was trying to get to know his habits because I really wanted this diamond necklace that I have seen him in during interviews. I was just learning his habits so that I can eventually go in for the kill. And by the way, I was able to get the necklace."

As Aiko continued to talk, I looked at the wine bottle that I barely touched, but Aiko had drunk so much, that there was only a sip left. I guess I can thank the Moscato for allowing Aiko to divulge so much information that night.

The night that Aiko told me what she was doing to earn extra money was the night that would redirect my entire life. Aiko told me that she would allow me to go on one business trip with her. This was all that I wanted. I wanted to feel the exhilaration that Aiko felt when partaking in such a dangerous adventure. Aiko explained to me the six important rules of being what she described as a heistist. Aiko explained that she created the term heistist to describe a professional female thief. She explained that the rules of being a heistist were as follows: #1 keep your mouth shut; never tell people what you are doing, even the people who are unknowingly and inadvertently involved in the heist itself. #2 Know your designers and know when pieces are made specifically for the celebrity. You sell those pieces, and you never wear those pieces. #3 Remain on heightened alert and never let your guard down. #4 Always have a contingency plan, just in case the person comes home during the heist. If you are caught in the house, work your way out of the situation. You better act like a maid or something. #5 Remain well connected; if you can't befriend the celebrity personally, become friends with their friends. When their friends are bragging and sending you text messages saying that they are in another country with the celebrity, you go on a business trip, i.e. steal from the celebrity's house. #6 Maintain relationships with business owners, waitresses, stylists, paparazzi, etc. When you go to hang out with business owners such as jewelers, they will tell you who came to their business and what they bought. These business owners are completely clueless that they are telling you what is available for you to steal. Waitresses may talk to football players or celebrities and then call me and say, "Hey, this particular football player will be at this particular club. Do you want to come?" Now I know that the football player is not going to be home, and I can take a business trip." It seemed like celebrities were Aiko's easiest targets.

After learning more about being a heistist, I can't even lie; I wanted to tell Grace all about it. She had been my best friend, and we told each other almost everything. Although I was educated and very intelligent, I was excited about going on one business trip with Aiko. The thought of being a heistist was very exciting, but the thought of being caught was extremely frightening. I felt lonely not having someone like

Grace in my life. I was far too stubborn to reach out to Grace, and I knew that she was far too stubborn to reach out to me. My current best friend and the only person that I trusted had the most dishonest profession. This best friend was Aiko.

The things that Grace said to me during our argument were really disheartening to me. I had to come to the realization that we were no longer connected. One day, while I was gone, Grace came to the apartment and moved all her things out. I did not even bother to reach out to her after that. I was still upset about how she vengefully broke the news to me that Alonzo was expecting a baby. I did, however, low-key stalk her social media pages. I had seen that she married Dane on some island somewhere, and there were no guests at the wedding from what I could see in the pictures. I was really hurt seeing Grace getting married without me there. My imagination had never allowed me to envision either of us getting married without the other there to support. The reality was that we were now navigating life without each other, and this was painful for me.

All of Grace and Dane's wedding pictures reminded me of what things could have been like for Alonzo and me. There were plenty of nights that I sat by the phone contemplating whether or not to call Alonzo. It was like torture. I really did miss Alonzo and our sometimes-deep conversations and all the fun we had with each other. I sometimes fantasized about Alonzo coming to LA to fight for me, but I knew that I had pushed him away and that he never deserved to be handled that way. The more time I spent alone, the more time I had to think things through, and there were points when I felt that I made a mistake by leaving Alonzo and not completely being there for him when I should have.

One day, I decided to give Alonzo a call. It took every fiber inside of me to pick up the phone and make that call. I began pacing back and forth in my apartment as I was calling him. When the phone started ringing, I started thinking about hanging up, but I already knew that my name would show up on his phone and that he would know who was calling him. My heart was pounding; then the phone stopped ringing. There was silence on the other end for a couple of seconds. I heard Alonzo's voice saying, "Hello."

The only words that I could get my mind, body, and soul to generate was, "Hey." I continued to hear silence.

"Listen, I am on my way out the door; let me call you back a little later."

"Okay, bye," I said. I felt so stupid. I should have never in a million years called Alonzo. What the hell was I thinking? I felt so foolish, embarrassed, and desperate. I did not want to leave an impression on Alonzo that I wanted him in any way, although deep down inside, I did. Alonzo, not dropping everything at that moment to speak with me made me understand that I was in an entirely different place in his life. He demonstrated to me that I was no longer a priority. Although I didn't expect to be a priority in his life, the way he displayed his dismissal of me was totally unexpected. I had to gather my feelings and snap out of this immense mournfulness that I was feeling. This was the moment that I recognized the finality of Alonzo's relationship with me. Furthermore, I began to realize that I had never mourned the end of our relationship. This was a very difficult day for me.

Aiko and I did a lot of research before she took me on my first heist. On one specific research assignment, Aiko and I went to dinner with her friend Terry Tea. I was looking forward to seeing Terry Tea because Aiko insisted that I knew him and assured me that once I saw him, it would spark my memory. Aiko and I arrived at dinner first, and she was prepping me for our evening with Terry Tea. As Aiko and I were sitting, a tall, thin well dressed, very feminine, brown skinned man walked up to us. He was gorgeous. Terry Tea had jet-black hair, and he wore eye makeup, foundation, and lip gloss. His smooth, clean-shaven face had no blemishes at all. I could not put a finger on it; but I knew this man from somewhere. Then Terry Tea started to talk; he said, "Well, hello Bitches," in a sweet and excited tone. Terry Tea's smile brightened up the dinner table. Both me and Aiko laughed and greeted Terry Tea; his energy was infectious. We began talking to him and asking him about how everything was going. It was not long before Aiko started talking about her rendezvous and wild sex adventures. I was drawn in, and I think that half of the stuff that was coming out of Aiko's mouth was bullshit. Aiko was talking about threesomes with women and being given oral sex by a news broadcaster. However, I quickly learned Aiko's strategy. She was just baiting Terry Tea so that he could tell her about what he had been up to. After Aiko finished telling Terry Tea a slew of what I believed to be fabricated sex stories, Terry Tea was so anxious to top them. Terry Tea said, "Well, you know my boo thang and I have been spending a lot of time together. I started off as his stylist and now he is my man. I am not sure if I told you about this guy, but he is gorgeous and rich. I am really starting to catch feelings for him. But he is not out and accepting of his sexuality." Aiko and I just sat there looking at Terry Tea; he had our undivided attention. Terry Tea continued, "In fact, he says he is not gay, but how is he not gay when I am on my knees damn near every night pleasing him until he blasts off. Let me tell you, I detonate that missile every night."

Just as I was connecting the dots about where I knew Terry Tea from, he remarked, "Sugar Cane Dane loves me but hasn't come to terms with it yet, much like he hasn't recognized that he is gay." I was stunned, Terry Tea had been sexually involved with Grace's new husband Dane and Terry Tea was the guy that I saw Dane within the VIP section of the club.

"Is Sugar Cane Dane in a relationship with a woman?" I asked.

"Yeah, some raggedy bitch named Grace. She can't dress worth a damn, but she is fucking gorgeous. I call her Grace the Face because there is no denying her beauty. But baby, girlfriend can't do the same things for Dane that I can do."

Aiko and I responded to Terry Tea's comment by laughing. Terry Tea continued, "My Sugar Cane has always been honest with me, he was honest that he had a woman. I see her on his social media; you can tell that she thinks she is the shit. But if she was all that she thinks she is, my Sugar Cane Dane would not be with me damn near every night." Terry Tea even talked about how he has been within Grace's presence while styling Dane. Terry Tea said that he has even styled Grace a few times. I learned that Dane had been giving Terry Tea money as well. All this information was a lot for me to comprehend. It took everything in my soul not to say that I knew Grace. The man that my former best friend married is having an affair with a man. I was focused on the salaciousness of what Terry Tea was saying, meanwhile, Aiko was asking questions like, "Is this the famous Dane? The one who has his own record label." Where does he stay?" As Aiko was asking Terry Tea a plethora of questions, I was trying to digest all the information that I received, and I was trying to figure out how I was going to tell Aiko that Dane cannot be her next target because I knew him and his wife. Then, there was a part of me who felt that Grace was getting what she deserved. Grace had gotten to the point where she thought that she was above me, and that gave her the authority to tell me about Alonzo expecting a baby with evil intent. The difference between me and her was that Alonzo and I were not together; however, Grace had a whole husband who was in another relationship. Terry Tea continued to drink and talk about how Dane loved him and how they shared their hopes and dreams with one another. Then Aiko said, "Yeah, I bet that bitch that Dane is with is only with him for the money; they probably don't even have a connection. I bet they go on vacations all the time; she is just using that man's money." Aiko was steadily fishing for details about when Dane and Grace would not be home. Then Aiko said, "So when is the next time you will be seeing Dane?"

"Although they had their wedding on an island, Dane and that bitch are on their honeymoon in Paris as we speak," Terry Tea said.

"Well, when they come back, you should tell Dane how you feel," Aiko said.

"Girl, that is exactly what I will do." Then Terry Tea took both of his hands and cascaded them from the top of his head down to his hips as he said, "Dane can't resist all of this. I just may be able to get him to see the light, honey."

I just did not feel right, and I was trying to convince myself that I was not wrong and that Grace was getting what she deserved.

After me and Aiko's dinner with Terry Tea, I felt compelled to let Aiko know that I knew Dane and his wife. As soon as Aiko and I got in her car from the restaurant, I began to explain that I knew Dane and that his new wife was my former best friend, Grace. Aiko just sat in silence. Then Aiko said, "Either you are in, or you are not. This is why I did not want anyone else involved. You can't take what we do personally. Karma, are you in or not?"

I looked Aiko in the eyes and said, "I am in, but I don't want to put your operation in jeopardy by going into Dane and Grace's home. I have known Grace for years. If anyone described me to Grace, she would know exactly who I am."

Then, in a tone that I have never heard Aiko use, she said, "I'm serious; this is life or death. Do you understand what I am trying to say to you?"

I was afraid at this point and said, "Aiko, you know that I would never do anything to jeopardize this."

"Okay, are you ready to go on a business trip?" Aiko asked.

"Right now?" I replied.

"Yes."

"Damn, I guess so"

This caught me entirely off guard. Looking back, I think that this was Aiko's way of making me complicit, just in case I got a change of heart and decided to turn her in or tell Grace and Dane of her plans.

During the car ride to the person that Aiko and I were essentially getting ready to rob, I was nervous. My heart was going to jump out of my chest. I was just praying that we were not on our way to Grace and Dane's house. Aiko was calm and was briefing me on what we were going to do once we got there. Aiko showed me the home's floor plan; apparently, Aiko had studied the home.

"Look, we are going to Sophia Silva's house," Aiko said.

"Do you mean the movie star?"

"That's exactly who I am talking about," Aiko said in an agitated tone. Aiko took a deep breath and said, "We are going to first, knock on the front door and ring the doorbell. If no one answers, as I suspect, we will try just turning the doorknob to open the door. If the door is locked, we have to look to see if she keeps a spare key outside of the house."

I was looking at Aiko like, "Are you serious?" I could not believe that it would be that easy to enter someone's house. I was from the hood where we kept the doors and windows locked, and we for damn sure never kept a spare key outside of the house. Aiko then reached into the back seat of her Mercedes SUV and handed me a hat. "Put this on," Aiko said. Aiko opened her glove compartment, pulled out two pairs of sunglasses, and handed me a pair. "Put these on too," Aiko commanded.

I literally watched Aiko turn into a different person as she looked at me and said, "When we enter the house, be sure to keep your head down the entire time. The rich will sometimes invest in a surveillance system. You do not want to be seen on camera. When we ring the doorbell, say that we are looking for Jason Jones."

"Are you talking about Jason Jones, the professional football player?"

"Yes, he lives next door. Now, if someone comes home and actually catches us before we are able to get out, pretend to be drunk and tell them to get out of your house. Pretend that you are drunk and that you walked into the wrong house. Then get the hell out of there."

I must admit, I thought that this operation that Aiko was running was much more complicated.

Before I knew it, we were parked. The sky was dark, and so was the atmosphere. When we exited Aiko's vehicle, the thrash of the wind on my face seemed to be a sign that this wasn't the wisest choice. I had my hat down low and my shades on. Aiko said, "Hold my hand, and let's start swinging our hands back and forth. We need to look like two harmless little girls."

In my mind, I was thinking, "Bitch, what?" But I just went with the flow. Aiko explained that we didn't want to appear dangerous or suspicious. At this very moment, all 28 trillion cells in my body were telling me not to follow through with this. I felt that it was too late to turn back. I was completely in.

Aiko and I began to walk up the circular driveway with our heads down. We got to the entrance; there was a huge cherry wood double door. Each door had a golden handle. At this time, Aiko put on some plastic gloves and gave me a pair to put on, too. We first knocked on the door, and then we rang the doorbell. After ringing the doorbell about five times, Aiko grabbed the door handle to open the door. To my surprise, the door opened right up. No alarm, no dog, no nothing. Aiko told me that there may be cameras, but our goal was to get in and out. We were both focusing our gaze downward as Aiko proceeded with caution. Aiko kept saying, "Remember to look down."

When we walked in, the lights were on, and the first thing that I saw was the double staircase and the white marble floors. The handrails were golden. My eyes were hurting from trying to see everything while my head was down. Aiko immediately started going up the stairs, and I followed. Aiko walked right into the primary bedroom. She went straight to the closet; she opened a huge duffle bag that she had concealed in her shirt and started putting things into the bag. She only took about two pairs of shoes and some pretty outfits. Then Aiko went to the dresser, and her eyes were fixed on a jewelry box. She was sifting through the jewelry carefully and methodically as she selected the pieces to take. I was assuming she took the pieces that she thought were the most expensive. Suddenly, my phone began to ring. I tried to silence it when I noticed that it was Alonzo. My heart skipped a beat. Aiko looked at me and said, "Put your phone away; in fact, turn your phone off." Then Aiko walked to a handbag that was sitting on a leather Chaise in the bedroom. Aiko went through the bag and pulled out a stack of 100-dollar bills. Aiko grabbed her bag full of stolen items, and we ran out of the door with our heads down. Literally, it looked as though no one had even been in the house. We did not leave a mess. It may be a while before the beautiful actress Sophia Silva even notices that some of her belongings were missing. Aiko stressed that she takes very few things, but they are very expensive. When Aiko and I left the house, we held hands again and began to swing our arms back and forth. Off to the car we went. I felt such a rush. I felt a high that I had never felt before.

Being a heistist was exhilarating. Initially, Aiko said that I could only go on one business trip with her. I actually ended up going on several. I felt like I was invincible after a while. I was a professional in my mind. Furthermore, I had gotten so good at being a heistist that I was feeling financially sound for the first time in a long time. Things were looking up for me. However, in the back of my mind, I knew that when you are going through life speeding, at some point, you will either run out of gas, be forced to slow down by a speed bump, or crash. None of these outcomes were desirable to me. My intentions were to continue the business trips until I felt comfortable and could get myself together financially. But this lifestyle was a rush. I wanted to stop, but I just could never accumulate enough money to stop. Nothing was ever enough. And every time I felt a little guilt about what I was doing, I would just think, "These people are millionaires and will not miss the items that were stolen."

Aiko had a contact person that she would not allow me to meet, who purchased the items that we would steal during our business trips. I did not ask many questions because I honestly did not want to be that involved. I wanted the perks, but I did not want any additional responsibilities or to have to keep any more secrets. Aiko did not talk about her contact. The only thing that Aiko would do is give me the money a day or two after the heist and make mention of the contact person. She would simply say, "Hey, this is from the contact." I didn't even know the person's name.

There were several business trips where I took items and did not tell Aiko about them because I did not want her to sell them to her contact. There was this one time when we went to a rapper's house; his name was Lil Pharaoh. He walked around with one of the most amazing chains that I had ever seen. We went to Lil Pharaoh's house, and I went to the jewelry box. To my surprise, the chain that I had seen him wear in interviews was right there. I was in shock. I slipped the chain into my loose-fitting pants without Aiko knowing about it. One thing about Aiko, she had a rule about us not keeping stolen items in our possession. Of course, there were some exceptions to this rule, such as popular handbags or shoes that were our sizes. For the most part, she sold nearly everything to the contact. She did not want us to do anything that would lead the thefts back to us.

Once, Aiko and I dressed up like maids and went to a singer named Michelle Thompson's house. We knew that she recently broke off her engagement to a famous basketball player. Michelle Thompson's engagement ring had made headlines; it was a huge 8-carat emerald-cut pink diamond ring worth almost 1 million dollars. When we arrived at her house, I went to the jewelry box, saw the engagement ring right away, and pocketed it. Aiko approached me and asked, "Did you find it? Did you find the ring?"

"No girl, she probably gave it back to him." There were just certain things that I kept as keepsakes and that ring was one of them.

I began working Los Angeles like you would not believe. My contact list had become so impressive. I had made friends with so many people who were friends with celebrities. Furthermore, I even made friends with some celebrities. After about three months of being a heistist, I had acquired some nice things. Not to mention the fact that I had a personal trainer. I had built the perfect body for myself, wore the latest fashions, and went to a celebrity hairstylist weekly. Plus, I bought myself a used Mercedes. It was only about two years old, but it was beautiful. I was "That girl" as an adult, and I loved it. I felt that I could be considered an equal to Aiko. I felt that I had one up on Grace because a man was not providing me with everything that I had. I continued to bartend so that I could meet people and have a legal gig. My life had changed for the better.

I had a lot of friends that I kept close because I really had an ulterior motive. I wanted to gain relationships and access to places where I could eventually plot my next heist. My main friends were now Aiko and Terry Tea. Terry Tea always gave us the gossip about Grace and Dane. The more that I heard about what was going on with Terry Tea and Dane, the more I felt like telling Grace. I honestly wanted her to know so that she could get off of her high horse. I also wanted to tell Grace because I wanted her to hurt like I was hurting when she told me about Alonzo. I did not think that I could ever forgive her for that. However, I had to be careful about what I told Grace because Terry Tea did not know that I personally knew Dane, and Dane did not know that I knew Terry Tea. Revealing that Terry Tea was having a sexual relationship with Dane to Grace could ruin Aiko's relationship with Terry Tea; he would never trust us again. Terry Tea was well-connected and gave a whole lot of pertinent information that allowed Aiko and me to have successful heists. I did not despise Grace enough to interfere with my money.

One night, at around 8 p.m., I received a phone call. I looked at my phone and saw that it was Grace. I was just lying in bed, wide awake, because I could not sleep. Initially, I hesitated to answer the phone. But I must admit, I was really interested to know why Grace was calling me. I answered the phone by saying, "Hello."

"Hey Karma, do you have time to talk?"

Instantly, my inquisitiveness replaced my feelings of anger towards Grace. "Yes," I replied.

"I apologize for being so nasty towards you. I understand that you were trying to tell me how you felt about me getting married. You are entitled to your opinion, and I should never have reacted the way that I did. I should not have told you about Alonzo having a baby in the way in which I did. I just wanted to hurt your feelings because you hurt mine."

I was filled with emotion. As I tried to hold back my emotions, I said, "Grace, I am so happy that you said that; it really made me feel a lot better." Tears were flowing down my face. I really missed my friendship with Grace. Before our falling out, Grace and I were so close and us not speaking ate at me a little each day.

"Girl, since you are up, can I come by your apartment tonight and we can have a girl's night?" Grace asked.

I was not really in the mood, but I knew that something had to be wrong for Grace to make this request. As teenagers, every time something was going on with Grace, she would spontaneously call me and ask me to spend the night at my house and have a girls' night. It was her way of saying that she really needed someone to talk to.

When Grace came to the apartment, she smiled at me with her beautiful wide smile. We embraced each other at the door with a hug. Grace was teary-eyed when we departed from our embrace. We both simultaneously began apologizing to one another. Grace sat down and told me how difficult it was in Los Angeles because she does not have any real friends and that Dane is all that she knows in Los Angeles besides me. At one point during our conversation, Grace made mention of how beautiful I was, and she began to ask what I had been up to. I told her that I was bartending and picking up some small acting roles here and there, which was true. I had got some parts as an extra. I had even booked a gig in a commercial. I noticed Grace looking around the apartment. I think she noticed that I had refurnished the apartment and made it a serene atmosphere compared to the serial killer ambiance it had when we first moved in. Grace said, "I see you made some changes."

"Yeah, I had to add my own touch to the place."

"Impressive."

Grace started explaining to me that she felt bad about leaving me to fend for myself in the new city that she invited me to. She said that she wished that she could have handled things differently. Then Grace pulled a check out of her purse and said, "This should cover my portion of the lease for the rest of the year and my half of the utilities."

With great pleasure, I looked at Grace and said, "It's okay; I took care of it." Then Grace looked confused. I proceeded to say, "I have it covered; I already paid the lease for the rest of the year," which wasn't completely true. Money was streaming in from my business trips with Aiko, so paying the lease was not an issue.

Grace looked so confused and asked, "Oh, so do you have a new man?"

I quickly said, "No, I don't need a man to pay my bills." I couldn't resist the opportunity to throw a little shade in Grace's direction.

Grace put the check back on the table and said, "Girl, just keep the check."

"You can keep the check there, but I am not cashing it." I did not want Grace to feel like I needed her money at all. In the past, Grace had maliciously brought up the fact that she was assisting me financially, and I pledged never to place myself in that predicament again.

Dane was on my mind the entire time that Grace was at my apartment. She and I had a couple of glasses of wine and were talking. I finally mustered up the courage to ask Grace, "How is Dane doing?" Grace paused for a moment as if she was debating whether to be honest or to give me a generic answer.

"He is doing well," Grace said. Grace looked down for a moment, and then, in a regretful tone, she said, "I think something is going on with him."

"What do you mean?"

As Grace sat on the sofa, she looked at me and said, "I hired a private investigator, and I found out that he rents a hotel room in

Beverly Hills. He goes there at least three times a week. He is having an affair."

I was completely immersed in her story, wondering how much information she would divulge. Hoping that she would talk about Dane having an affair with Terry Tea. Grace proceeded to say that she had not confronted Dane about his affair. I instantly asked Grace, "Why haven't you confronted Dane yet?"

Grace said in a sorrowful tone, "I don't even know how."

I knew I had to be cautious in my approach with Grace, especially since we were just getting to a better place, and she was going through a traumatic situation.

"Girl, it's okay; just be honest with Dane and let him know that you are aware of his affair with this man," I said. I could not believe what I had just said. I quickly scrambled and said, "I mean, woman, girl, this wine is starting to get to me."

Grace looked at me with a peculiar look. Grace started to grab her things and said, "Yeah, girl, well, I am going to head out. It was so good talking to you; I have to get home."

I walked Grace to the door and said, "I really enjoyed seeing you. Please let me know if you need anything from me. Remember, I am literally a phone call away."

Grace and I hugged, and we said our goodbyes. I felt like such a dumbass. I could not believe that I practically told Grace that I knew that Dane was having an affair with a man. I was hoping that Grace believed that it was just the wine and that I did not know something that she did not want me to know.

Chapter 7

Everybody Needs Somebody

After ending my relationship with Alonzo, I vowed to take my time getting into another relationship. However, one man caught my eye. He was a sherriff, go figure. His name was Deshaun. I met him at the restaurant where I bartended and sometimes waitressed. One night, I was working, looking good, and wearing a low-cut shirt that showed my cleavage, the usual for a night at the restaurant. Then, a towering figure entered the restaurant with broad shoulders and a bright smile. He walked straight to the bar. Oh, my goodness, he smelled so good. He had a beautiful caramel complexion. He had big strong hands and huge feet. He was just beautiful to look at. His presence made my heart melt. He was kind, considerate, and charming. He had beautiful, luscious lips, a bald head, and a shiny jet-black well-groomed beard. I was extremely physically attracted to him, and I knew that he felt the same about me.

The first thing that Deshaun ever said to me was, "If mind-blowing beauty was a person, it would be you." His pickup line was just what I needed that day. Deshaun and I would talk every time he came into the restaurant, and I enjoyed it. I rarely gave my phone number to customers, but Deshaun was different.

For our first date, Deshaun invited me to his skyrise condo in Los Angeles. Deshaun told me that he wanted to serve me since I always served him at the restaurant. When I knocked on his door, I had no expectations for the night. I thought that having no expectations would protect me from disappointment.

That night, I made sure I looked good. I was wearing my hair back in a ponytail, and my long hair flowed from the top of my head down past my shoulders. I was oiled up, and my makeup was perfect. I was wearing nude-colored lip gloss and my favorite fragrance. My sexy high heels were extremely expensive; I picked them up during a heist. I had a small gold and brown clutch Chanel purse that I had tucked under my arm. I was wearing a brown silk dress with a plunging neckline and no bra. The sexy black thong that I wore was the perfect pairing for my sexy dress because a panty line would ruin this ensemble. I looked like I walked right out of a movie.

When Deshaun opened the door, he looked very pleased. He greeted me with a warm embrace and a beautiful smile. He was wearing a black button-up shirt. The first three or four buttons were not fastened, which allowed his shirt to open and reveal the definition on his chest. He was wearing black dress pants and black leather dress shoes. He smelled so good.

As I walked into the skyrise condo, I noticed how chic and modern it was. Yet, the condo was very cold; it needed a woman's touch. The aroma coming from the kitchen was heavenly. There was a table in the dining area. The table was a golden brass, which was accompanied by brass chairs with black leather seat covers. There were candles lit in the middle of the table. Deshaun pulled out a seat for me, and I sat down. Then Deshaun walked into the kitchen, brought two plates out, and placed one in front of me and the other in front of him as he sat down. The plates were occupied with filet mignon, grilled asparagus, lemon garlic shrimp skewers, and a baked potato topped with chives, bacon, butter, and sour cream. To top it off, Deshaun pulled out the wine; we had Cabernet Sauvignon. I was excitedly surprised and asked, "Deshaun, did you cook all of this?"

"Of course. Baby, I was raised by culinary geniuses. This was light work"

"Okay, I see you," I said as I giggled.

During our dinner, I learned a lot about Deshaun. He told me about how he grew up in Detroit, Michigan, and how he moved to Los Angeles to go to college and never looked back. We talked about the things that we loved, and we talked about life. He said that he did not have any children and that he was not in a relationship. Deshaun said that he was looking for something serious. Although Deshaun talked about himself, he seemed much more interested in me, which was refreshing. I didn't mind telling him about my history in Buffalo and how soul-searching and big dreams landed me in Los Angeles.

After we finished dinner, he looked at me and said, "Baby, I know you didn't think that was it. Hold on, I have something else for you." Deshaun walked towards the kitchen and came back with two more plates. He had mocha molten cakes with freshly cut strawberries that laid across the plate.

"Oh, my goodness, this looks delicious," I said.

Deshaun walked away again and came back with a dozen red roses. I felt so special. I was totally infatuated with Deshaun, and I could not believe how charming and romantic he was. I just looked at him and said, "This is the sweetest thing ever, thank you." Deshaun and I continued talking as we ate our dessert.

At one point during dessert, I noticed Deshaun having an extremely difficult time taking his eyes off me. Finally, Deshaun said, "How are you so fine? You are really so beautiful, and I am not trying to gas you up. I want you." I began blushing and smiling. Deshaun then walked over to me as I sat in my chair. He grabbed both of my hands to assist me in standing out of my chair. Deshaun softly wrapped his arms around my waist and began kissing me. Kissing his warm and soft lips made me feel deeply desired. He picked me up, and I just naturally wrapped my legs around his waist as we kissed passionately. He grabbed my plate of dessert with one hand and held me with the other. He took me into the kitchen and placed me on his black granite island. This was done so effortlessly; Deshaun was so strong, and he handled me with such care. Then he pulled my brown dress straps off of my shoulders, and my dress practically fell down to my waist. Deshaun put the chocolate molten on my nipples and passionately licked it off. Deshaun proceeded to lay me completely flat on my back and slid off my thong. Then he opened my legs, rubbed the molten chocolate between my legs, and proceeded to eat the chocolate while pleasing me. Deshaun was gently moving his tongue back and forth in long and intense strides. Before I knew it, I had erupted into pure bliss. Deshaun then carried me into his bedroom and continued to kiss all over me. He was so damn sexy. Deshaun bent me over the bed and gently entered me. He began thrusting in a rhythmic motion. He pulled my ponytail and smacked my ass. Then he slowly exited my body, turned me around, and laid me flat on the bed. My legs were in the air, facing the ceiling as he held my ankles. Deshaun penetrated me again and continued to stroke, sending me into a transcendent euphoria. Deshaun had huge windows in his bedroom that overlooked the city of Los Angeles. Eventually, Deshaun picked me up and carried me a few feet before placing my naked body on the window and continued his rhythmic motion as I held on to his neck with both hands. When we finished, we both collapsed to the floor. I don't know if it was because I had not had sex in nearly a year or if Deshaun was that good. But by far, this was the best sex I had ever had in my life. I could not believe what I had done, but I was glad that I did it.

After having sex with Deshaun, I got up and went to the bathroom. I looked into the mirror and saw a disheveled, yet beautiful and free version of myself. My ponytail holder was so loose that it only took two fingers for me to glide it out of my hair. I felt like I had a glow. I was proud of myself for doing what pleased me. Everyone around me was having sex, and I was getting tired of hearing about everyone's wild nights while my nights were monotonous. This was a night that made me feel liberated. It was nothing like I had ever experienced before.

My life was moving at turbo speed. I was always doing something. I did not have a plan, and I was living in the fast lane. I was getting really small acting roles here and there, but it was getting more and more difficult for me to dedicate the time that I needed to my acting career. I knew that I had to get it together. I had been doing well with my business trips with Aiko, and my new relationship with Deshaun filled a huge void in my life. I fell for Deshaun, and I fell hard. Within a month or two, I was head over hills in love with Deshaun, and all I could do was hope that he felt the same. Deshaun once told me that he did not like saying that he was "in" love. Deshaun said he did not like to be "in" anything because when you are "in" something, it feels hindering. Deshaun preferred to say that he felt love for me, and I felt love for him, too.

Deshaun spent a lot of time working as a sheriff, which was fine with me. He spent every second of his free time with me. When we saw each other, it was passionate. We both needed a vacation and would talk about going somewhere romantic. Deshaun said that he enjoyed going to Italy a few years back and said that he would love to go there again. I came up with the perfect plan by suggesting Deshaun take a week off work for a trip to Vegas. Little did he know, I was secretly planning to surprise him with a trip to Italy. Once Deshaun said that he was able to get time off of work, I started making plans and asking questions about his passport being up to date, etc. One night, as Deshaun was asleep, I went into his wallet to get his license. I needed his license because I wanted to make sure that I spelled his last name correctly and needed to see if he used his middle initial in his identifications. Something peculiar happened as I was booking our flight. I noticed that the address on his license was not the same as the address that he lived in. I quickly took a picture of Deshaun's driver's license so that I could capture the address. Then I woke Deshaun up; I asked him about his address being different from the address on his license. Deshaun said that he had moved and had not had the time to change his address. He said that he moved into the skyrise right before meeting me. Deshaun sat up straight in the bed and saw his wallet next to me with his license in my hand. He proceeded to say, "Why are you in my wallet? Why are you looking through my things?"

"I was trying to surprise you with a trip to Italy and was booking our flight," I said.

Deshaun kissed me and said that this is why he had a love for me because I was so sweet and thoughtful. Deshaun told me not to buy his ticket and that he would purchase his own ticket. I told Deshaun that this was a gift from me to him, but he insisted that I not purchase the ticket. He said that he would purchase his in the morning. I went ahead and purchased my ticket, but insisted that he purchase his ticket along with mine so that we could be seated together. Deshaun said that he would purchase his ticket in the morning, and when he got paid, he would upgrade both of our tickets to first class. I stopped going back and forth about the damn plane tickets after this. A multitude of thoughts were going through my mind at once. I was wondering if I had overstepped my boundaries by going through Deshaun's wallet. Was I moving too fast by trying to surprise Deshaun with such an expensive trip? Was the life that I was living, causing me to be paranoid and always think the worst of people? Something was not right in my spirit. I just was trying to decipher the internal uncertainty that I was feeling.

Chapter 8

Game Over

I had talked to Aiko about wanting to end our heist or business trips together. I was in a relationship with Deshaun, who was a sheriff. I was becoming more and more afraid that my time was running out. Aiko told me that she wanted me to come with her on one more business trip before I decided to call it quits. Aiko wanted me to go on a more sophisticated business trip than usual. Aiko said that there was a football player that had just been drafted. The football player was a guy named Samuel Roth. She said that she knew a guy who designed and created custom-made jewelry. The guy was going to meet with Samuel, who was going to purchase a $100,000 custom-made necklace in cash. The plan was to go to Samuel's house the night before he was scheduled to meet up with the guy with the necklace. Since the scheduled pickup for the necklace was early in the morning, Aiko figured that Samuel would have the cash the night before in his home. Samuel had a birthday celebration scheduled at a club the night before the jewelry pickup, so he would not be home for hours. Our goal was to find the cash and get out of the house.

The night that we were going to take a business trip to Samuel's house, I was more nervous than normal. Our disguise was a little more complex than usual. We both purchased blond lace front wigs and had them glued to our heads. We both still wore hats. We both dressed in short trench coats, heels, and lingerie underneath the coats. Our contingency plan would be to act as if we were women sent to the home to entertain Samuel for his birthday, if anyone was still home or if anyone returned home during the heist.

Aiko and I waited outside Samuel's house. Before we knew it, Samuel and a group of guys who appeared to already be inebriated came stumbling out of the home laughing. They all seemed to be carefree as they loaded into vehicles. As Aiko and I looked onto Samuel's driveway from Aiko's car, we watched each large black SUV pull off one by one. After all of the vehicles were gone, Aiko and I exited her vehicle. We went towards an unlocked back door. I felt that someone must have left this door unlocked for Aiko because Aiko walked to the door as if she was 100% certain that it would open with the turn of a knob. Aiko and I entered the house. The house was already well-lit and as always, we went straight upstairs to the primary room of the house. The primary room was so cheesy. The bed was covered in leopard-designed sheets. The colors were safari colors, which included rich browns, yellows, and some reds. If this bedroom was any indication of what kind of man Samuel was, he was corny. Lying alongside the bed was a duffle bag. I looked at Aiko and said, "There is no way that this is the money." Aiko walked over to the duffle bag and opened it up; it was loaded with $100 bills wrapped, just like in the movies. Aiko closed the duffle bag, and then we both heard a noise. Aiko put the duffle bag down, and she slid under the bed before I could even react. Then, in the blink of an eye, I was staring in the face of Samuel.

Samuel was a fierce offensive guard for a professional football team. He was Caucasian with blond hair and blue eyes. He was about 6 foot 5 inches tall and 330 pounds. He had a blond beard and shoulder-length hair. He was very intimidating. Aiko and I always did our research before going on a business trip. When researching Samuel, I learned that he almost was not drafted because of his temper. In college, he was arrested for beating a man at a club after the guy made some derogatory remarks towards Samuel's female friend. Samuel did come from humble beginnings. He came from a two-parent household. His mother suffered from bipolar disorder and his father suffered from substance abuse. Samuel suffered verbal and physical abuse from both his mother and father. Therefore, Aiko and I knew that if we were caught in Samuel's house, it could be dangerous. This is why our contingency plan was so imperative. Most importantly, our contingency plan had to be believable.

When I found myself looking Samuel in the face, my survival instincts kicked in. Samuel looked at me confused. I walked over to the foot of his bed. I allowed my trench coat to drop to the floor and threw off my hat. Samuel looked at me and said, "Wow, Happy Birthday to me! Did David send you?"

"Let me just put it like this, I am a gift," I replied.

Samuel gazed at me in ultimate bliss. Then he looked over at the duffle bag and said, "Wait right there, don't you move."

I was hoping that he would not see Aiko as he bent over to grab the duffle bag. When Samuel seized the duffle bag, he damn near jogged to his closet with it. I heard something open, and then I heard something close; it sounded like a safe. I knew right then that Samuel was locking his money up. Samuel came back into the room and said, "So, where were we?" Samuel walked to the left side of the bed where I was standing and started kissing me. He took off his shirt, and then he took off his pants and threw them to the side of the bed, where I saw Aiko slide under. I told Samuel to lie on the bed. As Samuel laid on the bed, I saw Samuel's pants being pulled under the bed. At that moment, I thought to myself, I can't believe that as I am about to give the most intimate part of myself to this man to save both me and Aiko, the only thing that Aiko can think about doing is picking Samuel's pockets. I felt so cheap. I felt that my actions were depreciating my value and that I had become someone who would do anything for money. When you are willing to get dirty for money, the only type of money that you will get is dirty money. Nothing I had been doing was upstanding or ethical. Everything I was doing came at a price, and now the price had become too expensive for my moral bank account to cover; my moral bank had overdrawn. I sat on top of Samuel's genitals with my legs bent along each side of his waist. I looked at his face, and tears began to fall. Samuel looked at me and said, "What's wrong? Did I do something?" I was anticipating this huge, monstrous man to lose control and harm me. Instead, Samuel looked at me with a sense of concern and urgency and said, "How can I make you stop crying; do you need some water? Please don't cry, please don't cry." Then Samuel became frantic and said, "You're not going to lie on me and say that I raped you or anything, are you?"

"No, no, no, it's not you," I said.

Samuel sighed in relief and said, "Let's talk. Is there anything that I can do to make you feel better? I am not sure what you are going through, but you look lost; you don't even seem like you should be here. Whatever you are going through, it will get better; I have been lost before; you need to ask God to help you find your way."

Before I knew it, Samuel was quoting the bible and said, "Psalm 34:17-18 says, "The Lord hears his people when they call to him for help. He rescues them from all their troubles. The Lord is close to the brokenhearted; he rescues those whose spirits are crushed."

I felt a sense of calm overtake my body. I nearly forgot what I was supposed to do at Samuel's house. In the midst of me attempting to do the most ungodly thing, I received the most holy message. I got up off the bed, picked up my trench coat from the floor, and said to Samuel, "Your words mean more to me than you'll ever know; I am sorry for wasting your time."

Samuel then got up from the bed and softly grabbed my hand. "I can tell that you are not the type of girl to do this. You just need to follow your path to true happiness. This is not what makes you happy," Samuel said.

It was as if God was talking to me through Samuel. Samuel had no idea that I was there to steal from him and really had no intentions of having sex with him. Yet, he said that I was not the type of girl to do this. He was right; I was not innately a thief, and I surely was not someone to have sex with, just anyone. I broke down crying yet again. Samuel just held me and caressed my back as I cried. Once I was finished crying, I looked at Samuel and said, "Thank you so much for being so kind and understanding."

"I understand; if I was sent to have sex with me, I would break down and cry too," Samuel said. We both laughed, and Samuel walked me out of the house. I thought about Aiko at this time, but I was so disappointed in her for not looking out for me. I really did not care about Aiko's well-being at this point.

I walked for a long time in the dark that night, just collecting my thoughts and reflecting on things. I called Deshaun a couple of times, but he did not return my calls. I called a shared ride service to pick me up and take me home after walking for about an hour. When I got home, I reviewed the missed calls that I was ignoring from Aiko, and there were 10 of them. I did not care; I was not in a rush to speak with her. What I did know was that I needed purpose in my life. I didn't know where I was going, and nothing I did truly had meaning. I was just surviving and obtaining things, but I was not living a fulfilling life.

I sat in my house doing a lot of self-reflection after my last business trip with Aiko at Samuel's house. I did what Samuel told me to do; I prayed for God to help me. I wanted to talk to someone, but the only entity that I could turn to was God. I had gotten myself in a situation that was not only illegal but immoral, and confiding in someone could lead me behind bars or severely judged. God was all that I had.

I yearned for the company of Deshaun, but he was always working. A few days after my last heist/business trip with Aiko to Samuel's house, Deshaun arrived at my apartment unexpectedly with two dozen roses and some food. During our conversations, I just told Deshaun that I was trying to figure out some things in my life and that I was confused about what direction I wanted my life to go. I was debating if I should just go back to nursing or if I should continue pursuing my acting career. Deshaun was very understanding; he dried my tears, kissed my lips, and reassured me that I had our trip to Italy to look forward to. I was excited to know that he was just as excited about the trip to Italy as I was. Nonetheless, I felt somewhat let down since Deshaun didn't upgrade our tickets to first class as he had promised. I didn't dwell on this too much because Deshaun was such an amazing man. I could not imagine my life with anyone else at this point.

I was avoiding Aiko like the plague. Every time Aiko called, and I answered, I would just rush her off the phone by telling her that I was really busy or that I was out and about. I had not put myself in a situation to see her face-to-face. I quit my job as a bartender where we both worked, and I stopped going to places where I knew she frequented. One day, Aiko just came to my house uninvited. I heard a knock at my door. I opened the door, and there stood Aiko. I did not say a word; I simply opened the door wide and walked to the couch.

"Girl, what is up with you? How could you just leave me at Samuel's house and then ignore me for days," Aiko said in a frustrated tone.

"You abandoned me. I was there about to sacrifice my body to that man to save us both, and all you could do was pick his pockets."

"What do you think we were there for? We were there to take money, and we already knew that we had lost out on the chance to get the $100,000. We needed to get what we could."

"But at my expense? I mean, you could have pretended that you were there to entertain him too, or you could have distracted him in some way. I just felt like you did not care about me and that all you cared about was what you could get."

"Action is the key to life; I had to take action to get what I was there for. I wasn't going to leave there empty-handed. I knew that yo ass was not built for this. I would have done the same thing you did; the only difference is I would have done it proudly. There would have been no tears. I would have gotten the job done and done well."

"Well, I guess we are not the same."

"I guess not."

"Look girl, I am leaving for a trip in a few days, and I have to start packing and getting myself together. Thanks for stopping by Aiko."

"Alright girl, I really hope that we can get back to at least being good friends; we don't have to do business together. And Karma, if you ever kept any items that could be traced back to us during our heists, please either give them to me now or get rid of them immediately. We don't ever want shit to catch up to us."

I hugged Aiko as she stood by the door and said, "I don't have anything, and we will talk more when I get back."

I had no guilt about lying to Aiko about keeping some things that could definitely be traced back to specific celebrities. I figured that she had kept some things for herself as well. As Aiko left my apartment, I knew deep down inside that there would be no conversation when I got back from Italy. In fact, the hug that I gave her was more of a farewell hug than it was a see you soon hug.

The day before my trip to Italy, Deshaun called me during his lunch break, and we talked about how excited we were to take this trip and how it was long overdue. He told me that he had so much love for me and that he was happy that I was his woman.

It was my wish that me and Deshaun's trip to Italy would bring us closer together. It was hard for me to get to know Deshaun better because he did not have any siblings, and both of his parents were deceased; therefore, I could not get a feel for what his traditions were or see how he loved others. I did meet Deshaun's cousin Richard briefly at his skyrise but that was it. I was determined to show Deshaun true love, and I was convinced that I could show Deshaun how to truly love a woman instead of just having love for her.

The day that our flight was going to leave, I was all packed, but I had not heard from Deshaun. I called Deshaun, texted Deshaun, and there was no response. I would just calm myself down and say to myself, "The ringer on his phone is probably off." As time got close to our departure time, I became increasingly concerned. I was hoping that nothing horrible happened to him. I knew the risks that Deshaun faced daily by being a sheriff. I knew something had happened to Deshaun. I called Deshaun's job at the Los Angeles Holding Center. The person who answered the phone said that they did not know Sheriff Deshaun. I just assumed that a new employee must be answering the phone and that they didn't know Deshaun. I called a couple more times and spoke to different people, but no one had heard of Deshaun. I was devastated and frustrated. I did not want to come to terms with the possibility that Deshaun had been lying to me.

I rushed to Deshaun's skyrise and started pounding on the door. A half-dressed man that I had never seen before answered the door. I looked at him and said, "Where is Deshaun, and who are you?"

"Deshaun ain't here," the guy said.

I pushed past the guy and started looking around the skyrise. I went to the bedroom, and there was a naked female in Deshaun's bed. I yelled at the girl and said, "Who the fuck are you?" Then, I looked under the bed for Deshaun. I proceeded to walk around the skyrise yelling Deshaun's name and looking in every closet and every room. The unknown man kept saying to me, "Who the fuck are you?"

Finally, I yelled back, "I'm Deshaun's woman!"

The gentleman pulled me outside of the door of the skyrise and said, "When I see Deshaun, I will tell him you stopped by."

"Why are you in his house? Me and Deshaun are supposed to be traveling to Italy today," I yelled.

The man completely closed the door to the skyrise and stood outside the door as he was shaking his head with his left hand across his forehead, gripping his temples. In a frank tone, the man said, "This is not Deshaun's skyrise; well, actually, it's kind of his. Listen, me and two other friends rent this skyrise and we use it to entertain our bitches. Sorry, you are one of Deshaun's bitc...I mean, female friends. I suggest you move on and take that flight to Italy alone."

Then that man proceeded to slam the door in my face. I felt like I had just been sucker punched in the face and then in the stomach. The wind was blown out of me.

I thought back to when I looked at the license that was in Deshaun's wallet. I was smart enough to take a picture of the license because I wanted to keep the address just in case I needed it. I got into my car and traveled to the address on the driver's license. The address was in Glendale, California, which is a suburb of Los Angeles. As I was driving to the address, I passed multimillion-dollar homes. I was so angry, and my anxiety was at an all-time high. I did not know what I would do when I arrived at the address, but I was determined to get to the bottom of what was going on. There was no way that I was going to allow Deshaun to get away with playing me like a fool. He was going to know that I am not a toy; therefore, I am not to be played with. My anger only intensified each time that I looked at my phone, and there were no calls from Deshaun. When I finally arrived at the address, there was no turning back.

I sat in the car for a while to collect myself once I was at Deshaun's real house. The neighborhood was absolutely beautiful. It was a very affluent neighborhood. I pulled out my cell phone and took pictures of the house. Then, I saw a car pull out of the driveway. This was Deshaun's silver Mercedes Benz. I began to follow the vehicle for about 5 miles. The car pulled up to a grocery store. Then I saw an older lady getting out of the car with a head full of grey hair. I was so confused. Deshaun was only thirty-seven years old; this lady looked at least seventy. I thought this must be a mistake. When I looked at the license on the Mercedes Benz, I saw that it had the same fraternity license plate frame as that on Deshaun's car. This was, without a doubt, Deshaun's vehicle. I waited for about 20 minutes for the elderly woman to exit the grocery store. The elderly lady got back into Deshaun's car and drove back to the beautiful home where Deshaun apparently lived. Eventually, the lady walked into the house and closed the door behind her. Either this older lady was Deshaun's mother, or she was his cougar.

After taking a few deep breaths, I walked to the door of the house, and as I was walking, I sent one of the pictures that I had taken of the house to Deshaun and texted, "Bitch, do I have your attention now?" I waited a few minutes, but Deshaun did not respond. I proceeded to walk around the house and noticed that this massive house had windows all around it. I thought to myself, "Perfect, I can at least take a peek inside." I then peeked into a window along the side of the house and saw a kitchen. I saw Deshaun sitting with a little girl on his lap at the kitchen table. The little girl looked like she was about seven or eight years old. I saw two small little boys who seemed to be two and four years old. There was no one else in the kitchen. Suddenly, I saw Deshaun look down at his phone, and his eyes widened, and he had an "Oh shit" look on his face. I figured that he must have just seen my text along with the picture that I had taken of his house. He quickly moved the little girl from his lap and began to hurry towards where the front door was. I then began running towards the front door as well. By the time that I made it to the front door, my phone was ringing, and it was Deshaun. When Deshaun opened the front door, he gasped and quickly closed the door behind him. Deshaun angrily said in a low yet stern voice, "What the fuck are you doing here?"

"Why did you do this to me? Why would you lie to me," I said in tears.

"I did not lie to you."

"Then please explain your definition of a lie," I yelled.

Deshaun was trying to walk me away from the house as I was yelling and crying.

"Why are you walking me away? I'm sure you have a wife. What, you don't want your wife to know what you've been up to?" I screamed.

Eventually, the older lady who had been driving Deshaun's car came outside.

"Is everything okay?" the older lady asked as she looked at me and Deshaun.

"Yeah, Mom, go back inside," Deshaun said to the older lady.

"Mom, I thought your mother was dead; you're a fucking liar," I yelled.

Before Deshaun or the older woman could respond, one of the most beautiful women I have ever seen in my life walked outside. She looked like she could be Miss Universe. She had the most beautiful flawless chocolate skin and was about 5 feet, 8 inches tall. She was in perfect shape; she had curves and beautiful long legs. She was toned; she had definition in her arms and shoulders, not like a bodybuilder, but like someone who gets up every day at 5 a.m. to work out. I was so stunned by her beauty that I was speechless. The beautiful woman looked at Deshaun and said, "Honey, what is going on?"

"Beautiful, it's nothing; I will be inside in a moment," Deshaun said.

I was like, damn, she is so gorgeous that her name is Beautiful. The woman continued to stand there, and finally, Deshaun said, "Babe, please go back inside."

Then I snapped out of whatever trans I was in and yelled out, "No babe, you are right on time; I think you should stay," I said.

"If you don't get the fuck away from my house, I'm calling the police," Deshaun yelled.

"Wait, I thought you were the police. I found out today that you lied about being a sheriff. Go ahead, call the police and tell them that you have been having an affair and lying to me for months."

Deshaun proceeded to get increasingly agitated and said, "Mom, babe, don't listen to her; she is crazy as hell and lying. She is stalking me and obsessed with me."

"Tell Mom and babe how we were supposed to go to Italy today, and the reason why I am here is because you stood me up."

The beautiful woman who was clearly Deshaun's wife looked at Deshaun with her eyes filled with tears and said, "Italy, that's where we went for our honeymoon. Is this true, Deshaun? Are you having an affair?"

"No, go in the house, babe," Deshaun begged.

Deshaun's wife ran into the house bawling, and Deshaun ran after her. The older woman, whom I now know as Deshaun's mother, swung her hand to wave me away and said, "Go on now, you have caused enough trouble for today."

"You are the reason why he is like this; I can tell that you don't hold your son accountable. After everything that I said, all you can do is tell me that I caused enough trouble for today. Meanwhile, your son is causing trouble in people's lives," I responded.

I was pissed and just walked to my car and drove off. I guess I know why Deshaun is such an asshole; he gets it from his raggedy ass momma. Once I arrived home, I changed my flight to Italy for the next night. I was determined not to allow Deshaun to make me miss the opportunity to go on a dream trip.

The night that I found out that my relationship with Deshaun was a lie, I cried all night. I was devastated. The pain was insurmountable. I was hoping that I never made anyone feel the way that I was feeling at that moment. I started to think about Alonzo and how I treated him at the end of our relationship. I asked God to forgive me if I ever made Alonzo feel the pain that I was feeling. This moment made me cognizant of the fact that my life was a lie, and it was reflected in my relationships. I wasn't who people thought I was, and I was in relationships with people who were just as fictitious as my life.

I should have seen the warning signs with Deshaun. He was always working, he said that he did not have any family, the address on his license was different from the address that I thought he was staying at, and he had absolutely no social media accounts. I could not believe that I had attracted this type of person into my life. I felt like I needed to cleanse my soul, but I did not know how to do that. I remembered what that football player Samuel said to me. He said to ask God for help. And that is just what I did. I asked God to cleanse my mind, body, and soul. I asked God to remove any and everything in my life that was not of him. I wanted to start anew; I wanted to start over.

Chapter 9

Exploration of Foreign Territory

There are times in life when you become so absorbed with everything that is going on around you, that you neglect the things that are going on within you. I had not taken time to just stop and think. I had always been around people, plotting, and trying to figure out my next move. I had not taken the time to think about real long-term plans. I felt like Italy was my time to be alone and explore a foreign land, and to explore another foreign entity; myself. I had done so many things that were out of the norm for me, and I just did not recognize myself. I had become someone that I did not like much. I was dedicated to becoming a better version of myself.

Initially, I had my reservations about flying to Italy alone. First, I had never been on a flight for so long; further, I had never gone overseas. But I asked God for strength and said to myself, it's time for me to just live my life. I was not going to let my anxiety about flying nor my broken heart stop me from having a once-in-a-lifetime experience.

I slept for most of the flight to Italy. I guess I was exhausted from my spirit being crushed and from crying like a baby while getting very little sleep. But when the plane landed, I really felt my pains, worries, and sadness vacate my soul. I wanted to get to the hotel, get washed, get dressed, and get out. My first stop was in Venice, Italy.

My first course of action was to get something to eat after I left the hotel. I told my taxi driver to drop me off, where I would have a lot of food options. As I rode in the taxi, I was able to truly take in my surroundings. I was in awe. I felt like I had gone back in time. I was mesmerized by the picturesque city with its historic architecture, winding canals, and marvelous bridges. The taxi driver dropped me off in an area that was packed with people, many of whom were tourists. I immediately began to walk towards where all of the tourists were walking. The next thing I knew, I was crossing bridges, and my eyes were trying to take everything in. As I walked past the restaurants, my nose captured the alluring aromas of true and authentic Italian foods. One restaurant captivated my senses as I watched the chef in full chef attire with the white chef hat and apron to match. He was hard at work, rotating food as flames gracefully danced around the pots and pans. Soon, I was dining outside of the restaurant overlooking the Grand Canal as couples rode by on gondolas. I indulged in the best seafood pasta that I had ever eaten in my life. The seafood pasta was comprised of a variety of seafood such as shrimp, scallops, mussels, clams, and even squid. The noodles, which were made from scratch, pleased my palate. During this meal, I was introduced to a Hugo Spritz. A Hugo Spritz consists of prosecco, lime, mint, seltzer, and elderflower liqueur. The drink has a sweetness to it, and it's also refreshing. I was in heaven. I had my two favorite things, food and drinks.

After dinner, I continued to walk and watch the boats full of tourists ride by, and after seeing far too many gondolas, I decided to jump on one. There was an area near the water where people could wait for the next gondola to arrive so that they could get on. Luckily, I was the only person in line at this particular location. When a gondola docked, and tons of people got off, I had a moment of feeling embarrassed about requesting to get on alone. After all of the people left, the gondolier operating the gondola was so kind to me and did not make me feel ashamed. He had an inviting smile as he reached his hand towards me so that I could board the gondola. At that moment, I realized that the only person that was critical of me was me; no one cared that I was alone. I decided to free myself of self-judgment and embrace who I was and where I was.

The sun was setting as the gondola peacefully glided through the canals of Venice. The water shimmered as it reflected the lights from the buildings of this ancient city. Never in my life did I think that I could experience a romantic moment alone. This was an intimate fairy-tale moment that I experienced by myself. For the first time, I realized that being alone does not mean that you are incomplete. I realized that no other person can ever complete me; I complete me. I spent two full days in Venice, eating and drinking while enjoying my own presence. I felt a sense of accomplishment.

After Venice, I took a beautiful train ride to Sorrento. During the train ride, I had the chance to see the beautiful terrain of Italy. During some parts of the ride, there was greenery as far as the eye could see. There were beautiful mountains and bright blue skies. I thought about how lucky the people who lived here were to have such serene surroundings. Also, I thought of the rich history of Italy and the people who lived there thousands of years ago. I thought about what these people saw every day, and how they lived their lives. I was having a moment of gratitude, which I had not taken the time to experience in a while.

Once I arrived in Sorrento, I was amazed by its beauty. I was also surprised by the tight, narrow streets that the taxi driver navigated through at what I felt were high speeds. Each time I took a taxi somewhere, the taxi driver was ripping and running as if they were so familiar with the streets, that they could drive with their eyes closed. I shopped alone, ate alone, and drank alone. Everything I did was solo, and it felt good. I felt like a grown and mature woman. I didn't need anyone, and I didn't want anyone. I was learning to like myself, by myself.

After being in Sorrento for one day, I was ready to go to Capri, Italy. I could not wait to hit the beach and do some more shopping. I had to take a boat from Sorrento to Capri. As I was boarding the boat, there was nothing but couples. I was starting to fall into the space of judging myself again, but I quickly tried to pull myself out of my critical thoughts. I just kept saying to myself internally, "I am complete all by myself." Then, a black male entered the boat. I did not see many black folks in Italy, and it was refreshing to see someone who looked like me on the boat. I started looking for his companion, but no one accompanied him. He was about my height, 5 feet 7 inches, thin, had a lighter complexion, and had a short dark Caesar haircut that was fitting for Italy. His dark black hair laid across the top of his head, forming a multitude of waves that could make anyone seasick. This guy was full of personality and seemed so excited. He greeted everyone with a "Yall ready for some fun?" Everyone on the boat shouted, "Yeah." We were automatically drawn to each other because of obvious reasons. We were both black, alone, and clearly from the United States.

The ride from Sorrento to Capri was majestic. I gazed upon the crystal blue waters as our boat propelled us further into the Mediterranean Sea. I sat back in the boat as I saw the amazing colorful houses and structures cascading down the enormous mountains above the wondrous sea. What I was experiencing externally mirrored what I was experiencing internally. My spirit was filled with contentment and peace, and so were my eyes.

Once we arrived in Capri, we were told that we had a few hours before returning to our boat. This was perfect for me because I was looking forward to hitting the beach and then eating. I immediately walked to the black sand beach. I sat down on my chair under my umbrella that was stationed next to the chair. I took off my sundress so that I was only wearing my red and white two-piece bikini set. I plopped my wide-brim straw sunhat on with my sunglasses and closed my eyes as I listened to the hypnotic sound of the ocean waves colliding into the seashore. I put in my earbuds and started listening to a new album that came out from a female rapper named Hazy. She was very raunchy, but I liked her flow, and her beats were always fire. I was listening to her with my eyes closed, and then I felt a shadow over me. I looked up, and there was the black guy from the boat. I pulled my shades to my nose to look at him and took one of my earbuds out of my ear. "Hey," I said.

"I don't think I had the chance to formally introduce myself; I'm Tyrell," said the man.

I was slightly annoyed. I was totally in a vibe, and he was ruining it for me.

"What are you listening to? You should be listening to the ocean. Can I see your earbud?" Tyrell asked.

I don't know why, but I slowly handed Tyrell one of my earbuds. He placed it close to his ear without inserting it into his ear.

"Dang girl, you got some ratchet ears," Tyrell said.

I just burst out into laughter. I knew that my choice of music was not always the classiest, and Alonzo would tease me about the music that I listened to.

"Go to your music app; I want to show you something," Tyrell said in an excited tone.

Then Tyrell requested to see my phone. Out of curiosity, I gave it to him. Tyrell typed something into my phone.

"This is a song that describes you perfectly," Tyrell explained.

Then I began to hear the song from back in the day about a man who saw a beautiful girl, and he talked about how his life wouldn't be complete without her in it. Tyrell actually started to sing the song. I was impressed by Tyrell's vocal skills; his voice possessed so much soul, I could tell that he grew up and sang in the church.

"Okay, I hear you. You can sang," I said in an enthusiastic tone.

"I just had to speak to you outside of the group. If you don't mind me asking, what are you doing for the rest of the day?" Tyrell asked.

"I'm going to take a taxi to where the shops are a little later. How about you?"

"So am I. If you don't mind, we can take a taxi together."

Once I finished sunbathing, Tyrell and I took a taxi to where the shops were. Tyrell asked if he could treat me to lunch. I was totally okay with that. Laying on the beach had me exhausted and hungry. During my lunch with Tyrell, I learned that he was an on-air personality for a popular radio station in Miami. I also learned that Tyrell was hilarious and had a joyful and inviting spirit. I felt like I was talking to my homeboy. Tyrell was in his mid-twenties and was a free spirit. He epitomized living in the moment.

After eating lunch and shopping at multiple shops, it was time for me and Tyrell to get back on our boat and head back to Sorrento. Tyrell was like, "I heard they party hard in Capri; let's stay here and hit up some clubs." I had been enjoying Tyrell's company so much that I concurred without any reservations at all. I was ready to let loose and be completely free. Tyrell's free spirit was contagious. Our carefree attitudes caused us to miss our boat ride back to Sorrento. But that did not bother us at all. We bought some more clothes and shoes for our anticipated night at the clubs.

The clubs in Capri were upbeat, and the energy was magnetic. Tyrell and I went to two clubs, and live music was played at both clubs. Neither of us knew any of the music, but the music had a rhythm that we could vibe to. We danced closely, and Tyrell made me feel like we were the only ones in the clubs each time we danced. He twirled me around, he held me with his firm grip, and the way that he could move his body was very alluring. I could not remember the last time that I had this much fun. Furthermore, this experience was so freeing because I was not trying to be Tyrell's girl, there were no motives on my end, and we were just having unadulterated fun.

That night, Tyrell and I went to the room that Tyrell had booked at the last minute. Out of respect, he ensured that there were two separate beds in the room. But Tyrell did not have to do that because I wanted to end the night with him beside me. I desired to have sex with Tyrell, and that is what I did. It was what I wanted. No strings attached, no expectations of a relationship, nothing other than two adults having enough courage to do what they both wanted unapologetically.

The next morning, I did not really know what to expect, but Tyrell was consistent. As the sun was coming up, I was awakened by his warm embrace. We stayed up so late, and when we tried to get up and get ourselves together, we would ultimately fall right back to sleep. Then, eventually, I got up and took a shower. I was trying to be as quiet as possible as I was tip-toeing around the room, quietly, sifting through bags and my purse to put on some of the new clothes that I purchased the day before. At one point, I bent down, and I passed gas. It literally slipped out. It was not loud, but I was hoping that Tyrell did not hear it as I looked over at him with his eyes still closed. Then Tyrell opened his eyes slightly and said in true Tyrell fashion, "I heard your booty blow me a kiss." I just burst into laughter.

"You were not supposed to hear that," I said.

Tyrell just laughed, hopped out of bed, and started getting ready.

The boat ride back to Sorrento from Capri with Tyrell was beautiful. During this ride, Tyrell was lying back, and I was lying on his chest, enjoying the waves of the ocean as our boat glided through the beautiful waters. I did not see much of Tyrell after reaching Sorrento as I was preparing for my departure. My last encounter with Tyrell was when he came to visit me at my hotel before I checked out. We shared a long, intense, and passionate kiss before saying our goodbyes. He accompanied me to my taxi and that was it. It was like a beautiful dream. This trip taught me that regardless of the chaos going on in my life, I could always choose joy. My Italy trip brought me inner peace and joy that cannot be explained; it can only be experienced. It was the reset that I so desperately needed.

Chapter 10

What Goes Around Comes Around

When I got back to the United States, I felt revived and ready to take on the world. But there was a part of me that had some anxiety about going back home. Home was the host of all the pain and heartbreak that I had left behind when I went to Italy. But I kept in mind that my lease was ending, and I had signed a lease for a new and much more beautiful apartment. I was ready to say goodbye to my past and make a grand entrance into my future. However, when I pulled up to my apartment, it was a gut punch that made me realize that I was back in reality. It was sickening. I had my phone in airplane mode since my departure from Italy and never took it off until I got in front of my apartment. Dreading going into my apartment, I decided to look through my phone. There was a part of me that wanted to know if Deshaun tried to reach out to me. It's funny how no matter what a person does, you want to believe in the best in them and not the worst. I did not receive any calls or text messages from Deshaun at all. To my surprise, I did have tons of missed calls from Grace and my mother. I figured that I would get my luggage in the house and give them a call once I got settled in.

When I got to my apartment, the key to my door would not work. I checked the keys on my key ring to make sure I had the right key. It was certainly the right key. I was really concerned at this point. I then went to the leasing office. When I walked into the office, I told the lady at the front desk that the key was not working for my apartment. The lady said, "Oh yes, Karma, we have been trying to get in touch with you. Your apartment was burglarized. We replaced your door. We think that the burglary happened yesterday; well, it was discovered yesterday morning, because one of your neighbors, Ms. Mary, noticed your door cracked and then pushed the door in a little and saw your apartment destroyed. Ms. Mary immediately contacted the police. Your neighbor told us that you had left the country and would not be back until today."

Thank God I saw my neighbor, Ms. Mary, before leaving the country and told her that I would be in Italy. She was trustworthy and always looked out for me. The lady in the apartment office began looking at a piece of paper on her desk and said, "We connected with, let's see here, Grace because she is also on the lease; the lock change came with the new door. Grace said that she had been trying to connect with you, but your phone was going straight to voicemail." The lady eventually pulled out a new key to my apartment and handed it to me.

As I was going to my apartment, I immediately began calling Grace. Grace seemed really happy to hear from me.

"I am so happy to finally hear from you. Ms. Mary told me that you were in Italy," Grace said.

"Yeah, I was in Italy; I can't believe that someone robbed me. I am afraid to go into the apartment."

"I called your mom, hoping that she could contact you. Your mom was pissed and said that she had no idea that you had gone to Italy. Girl, you have to let folks know when you are leaving the country."

Grace was right. I should have been smarter, but I was not in the right frame of mind before I left. Further, I thought that I would be going to Italy with Deshaun, the man that I thought I loved, but I was wrong about that. Before opening the door to my apartment, I told Grace that I would call her back.

I unlocked and opened my apartment door, and my apartment was in total disarray. All I could do was smirk; karma had come around and bit me in the ass. Every high-priced bag, shoes, and clothes were gone. Things were thrown all over the place. I went straight to my jewelry box; the jewels I had stolen from the rich and famous were gone, I ran to the safe where I put the money I had earned while working with Aiko, but the safe was gone. I started crying and became so nervous about my future that I became nauseous and went running to the bathroom to vomit. Then I had a moment; I remembered specifically asking God to remove any and everything from my life that was not of him before leaving to go to Italy. I wanted to start anew; I wanted to start over. I learned at that point that you have to be careful what you ask for.

So many things were going through my mind. On the one hand, I saw this as a way for me to start over because nothing good had been coming to me. On the other hand, my mind went straight to Aiko. I felt that Aiko was involved in my burglary. She was the only person outside of Ms. Mary and Deshaun who knew that I was leaving town. Deshaun was already living a lavish life; he had no reason to break into my home.

Ms. Mary was like the neighborhood watch person. She lived alone and was an older, frail woman. Ms. Mary's interests included church and looking out for her neighbors. She lacked both the physical capability and the moral willingness to commit a burglary. My mind kept going back to Aiko telling me that I needed to get rid of the items that I had kept from our business trips. She did not want anything to be traced back to either of us. It wasn't Aiko's style to wreck a home that she was stealing from, but I felt that Aiko was trying to throw me off. I was infuriated that Aiko would betray me in this way.

As I was walking through my house, I looked down and saw the engagement ring that Alonzo had given me amongst the disorder of random things thrown all over my floor. The diamond shined, and the platinum on the ring was just as flawless as it was when Alonzo first put it on my finger. I asked God, what he was trying to tell me. Once again, I was reminded that I had asked God to remove everything from my life that was not of him, and the thief took everything I had possessed in a dishonest way, and the one thing that they missed was my engagement ring from Alonzo. Was this a sign from God?

When someone breaks into your home and steals your things, it's a type of violation that is maddening. I did not even want most of the things that the burglar left behind. Knowing that this awful person touched everything in my home as they decided what was valuable enough for them to take was disturbing. At this point, I was so convinced that this awful person was Aiko. I could not even stay in the house. I felt even more sick and guilty about how I had violated people in this same way. I may not have wrecked their homes, but I did take belongings they worked hard for and things that weren't mine to take. I vowed to myself that I would never allow myself to get so lost that I would do things to intentionally hurt others. My grandmother would tell me that what you do to others will be done to you.

I left the apartment and went to a hotel, and on my way, I finally called my mother back. I was hesitant about calling her because I did not want her to try to convince me to come back to Buffalo. I just did not need any additional negativity. I knew that my mother was going to be 100% honest with me, and I felt so fragile at this point. I called my mother, and when she answered, she immediately said in an elevated voice, "Where have you been?" I explained to my mother that I had gone to Italy. My mother said, "You can never leave the country and not tell me. I was worried sick about you. When Grace called me and said that your apartment had been broken into and that she was trying to reach you, I almost had a heart attack. Then Grace told me that a neighbor told her that you were in Italy. How could you tell your neighbor that you are leaving the country and not your mother?"

My mother's ridicule just raised my anxieties, and suddenly, I had to pull over to throw up. I was throwing up as I was on the phone with my mother. Of course, when I was done, I was telling my mother that I was going to call her back. My mother proceeded to say, "Were you throwing up? When was the last time you had your period?" Shit, I thought. When was the last time I had my period? I had been so busy planning for Italy, running around doing God knows what, that I had totally lost track of when I had my last period.

"I'm good mom. I have to go," I anxiously said.

I went to a pharmacy to get a few pregnancy tests before going to the hotel. I went to the hotel and felt so alone, scared, and sad. I longed for the presence of my true friend, Grace. I called Grace and requested that she meet me at the hotel. It seemed like Deja Vu. The last time that I took a pregnancy test, Grace was right by my side. Grace did not ask any questions; she simply said that she was on her way.

When Grace got to the hotel, I was relieved. Grace came to the hotel with shirts, pants, bras, and panties for me. She knew that my house was broken into and that I probably didn't have time to do any laundry. Grace was very thoughtful in this way. I was so grateful. I hugged Grace so tightly and thanked her. I told Grace about me dating Deshaun and about how he was married with kids. I told her the entire story about how I found out about his marriage and children. Then I told her that I thought that I was pregnant with Deshaun's child. Grace was not judgmental at all. She simply told me that she was going to be there for me no matter what.

My nerves were off the charts. All of the Zen that was infused into my spirit during my Italy trip had fled my body, and my soul was in a state of distress. I was literally shaking as I took the pregnancy test. I thought about all of the partying and drinking that I did in Italy and feared how I may have harmed my baby. The few minutes that I had to wait for the results seemed like a lifetime as I swam through the waves of my thoughts.

Grace and I sat quietly, looking at the time on our phones. When my phone alarm went off, Grace and I knew it was time for us to see the results. I took a look at the pregnancy test, and I was pregnant. I started taking deep breaths to try to calm myself. Grace wrapped her arms around me and said, "It's alright baby; everything is going to be alright."

I cried out, "What am I going to do? This can't be right."

"What are you going to do?" Grace asked.

I immediately stopped crying to think. I had not had a chance to think about what I was going to do. Nothing in my mind, body, or soul told me to do anything other than to have my child. "I am going to have my beautiful baby," I told Grace.

"There you have it. Now, it's time for you to get ready to be a mommy, and I am going to get ready to be an Aunty."

We hugged, I wiped my tears, and my sadness became mixed with excitement. I had always longed to have children, and I was being given another chance to bring life into the world. I was not going to make a selfish mistake by getting an abortion to protect Deshaun and his family. After losing me and Alonzo's baby to a miscarriage, there was no way that I was going to get rid of this baby.

Telling my mother that I was pregnant was very hard. The day that I called my mother, her spirits were upbeat, and she was excited to hear from me. I said to my mother, "Mom, I have something to tell you."

With concern in her voice, my mother said, "What is it, Karma?"

"I need you to hear me with your heart and not judge me like the world will. If there was ever a time that I needed my mother, it's now".

With a distinct sense of concern in her voice, my mother said, "Baby, tell me. Tell me what you need to tell me. I won't judge you. I promise."

In tears, I said, "Mom, I'm pregnant. The father's name is Deshaun, and he is married. I didn't go into the relationship knowing that he was. He told me that he was single with no kids. I can't believe this. Not only is he married, but he also has children. Mommy, I feel like I was scammed. But I already decided that I'm keeping my baby no matter what Deshaun says. In fact, fuck Deshaun."

After revealing this truth, I let out a deep cry. I could hear my mother on the other end of the phone, trying to conceal her cry.

My mother then proceeded to say, "When I had you, I wanted a child. However, spite played a major role in me having you. Because your father and his wife desperately wanted me to terminate my pregnancy, I was determined to have you. And when your father and his wife had a miscarriage, oh, how I celebrated and threw my celebration in their face by naming you Karma. Don't be like me. I want you to do what's best for you, but my wish is that you have this baby out of love and the desire to be a great mother. Don't worry about revenge and never use your child as a weapon. I had to learn this the hard way. Enacting Karma on the father of your child is not your job. God, will orchestrate Karma whether good or bad."

"I would never use my child as a weapon against Deshaun. But Mom, what if he gets away with this without any repercussions? I don't see him being a father to my child. What will be his punishment?"

"His punishment ain't none of your business, and his Karma ain't never gone be your job. Allow life to take care of this Deshaun guy. You need to let him know that you are having a baby, but don't have any expectations."

This was a lot for me to digest. My mother then announced to me that she was going to come to Los Angeles and help me out for a while. I was surprisingly happy about this. I needed as much support as I could get at this point.

Once my mother arrived in Los Angeles, I moved into a new apartment. I had no idea how I was going to pay for this upgrade. During this time, I was in the process of renewing my nursing license. I was hoping to find work as a nurse in a work-from-home capacity where I could give recommendations to my patients over the phone via a Nurse's Line for a healthcare insurance company. But in the meantime, I was struggling. One day, I was cleaning out my purse, and the check that Grace had written to me for her portion of the rent at our previous apartment fell to the floor.

"What is this?" my mother asked as she picked up the check.

"A while back, Grace had written me a check for her portion of the lease and bills at the apartment we shared. I refuse to cash it."

"Girl, are you crazy? You better cash this damn check."

"But Mom, I am not a charity case, and Grace wrote me this check after apologizing for practically calling me a broke loser."

"Girl, this ain't charity; this is what you are owed. Stop letting your pride get in the way of everything. Cash that damn check you struggling, and I am over here helping you out, and you have access to all of this money."

My mother always had a way of talking sense into me. I cashed the check, and this check literally saved me financially until I was able to get a job.

The moment that I had been dreading, calling Deshaun to tell him that I was pregnant. I waited until after I had my first prenatal appointment to get confirmation from a physician that I was pregnant before contacting Deshaun. I called his cell phone and received a message that his phone was no longer in service. I told my mother. My mother said, "Let's go by his house, and I can hand deliver the message that he is having a baby; you can stay in the car." My mother was so old school. I told my mother that I did not feel comfortable with her doing this, but she insisted.

My mother and I headed to the home that Deshaun shared with his wife, kids, and mother. When we arrived, I saw a for-sale sign in the front yard. I was shocked. I guess Deshaun wanted to make sure that I had absolutely no access to him. After seeing this, I told my mother that I'd rather not. I told my mother that I would much rather go through the court system. Then, out of nowhere, I saw the lady whom Deshaun called mom come outside and start walking towards my car.

"That's Deshaun's mother. We should go!" I said.

"No, we ain't goin nowhere." My mother got out of the car and started walking towards the woman, which prompted me to get out of the car as well. Within seconds, it was like all three of us were in a standoff.

Deshaun's mother looked at me and said, "I recognized your car. I just want to make sure that you ain't comin over here to stir up trouble like you did the last time; my son is going to put a restraining order out on you if you keep comin round here."

My mother walked towards Deshaun's mother as if she was going to give her a good ole' fashion ass whoopin. Deshaun's mother took a few steps back and was clearly shaken.

My mother started twirling her index finger around as she held one hand on her hip. "Let me tell you somethin, my daughter ain't stirin up shit. But I hear that your son is the one doing all the stirin. My baby is pregnant by your lying ass son."

Deshaun's mother stood there in shock and asked me, "How far along are you?"

"I am eight weeks pregnant."

The look of hatred and fear left Deshaun's mother's face and was replaced with a look of sympathy and concern.

"I'm Ms. Eleanor, and I will be sure to get this message to my son."

"Yeah, you need to get more than a message to your son. You need to get some good sense into him too," my mother said.

"Listen, I ain't gone take much more of you bad mouthin my son."

"Your son ain't shit," my mother yelled out.

"Listen, I ain't tryin to argue with yall. If it's true that you are pregnant by my son, he needs to know this. And I'll be the one to let him know."

"Well, are you going to get your son out here?" my mother asked.

"No, he is not home right now but just give me your number so that we can at least stay in touch."

Ms. Eleanor and my mother exchanged numbers. I was not sure what was going to happen in the future, but at least it seemed like Ms. Eleanor wanted to open the lines of communication between her and my mother.

About a week went by with no word from Ms. Eleanor or Deshaun. To keep my mind off of Deshaun, I occupied my time with reality television, my mother, and my job search. My mother was obsessed with daytime talk shows, but I wasn't. Usually, when she was watching her daytime talk shows, I would either be out and about or in my room watching reality television. One day, I decided to be a good daughter and watch one of my mother's favorite daytime talk shows with her, and it didn't hurt that my favorite female rap artist Hazy had just started on the show as one of the hosts. After watching the show, the news came on, so I just started watching the news. I quietly fantasized about Aiko finally getting caught stealing from someone and it being reported on the news. I was still bitter because I knew that she robbed me while I was in Italy. Then I heard my mother say, "That's my girl right there." Between looking at my phone and watching the news, I looked up to see who my mother was talking about. There was an anchor man and an anchorwoman.

"Mom, who are you talking about? Who is your girl? I'm your only girl," I said in a joking matter.

"Laura Pennington," my mother said in a cheerful tone.

I started watching the segment that Laura began doing on single mothers. This segment caught my attention since I knew that I would fall into this category after having my baby. Laura was talking about a program in the Los Angeles area for single mothers that helped them with getting things that they needed for their babies, such as cribs, toys, food, and even diapers. Suddenly, I stared into the television closer, this female anchor seemed familiar, but her name was not ringing a bell for me. Suddenly, it dawned on me that the female anchor who had caught my eye was Deshaun's wife. Laura Pennington was the woman that I had seen outside of Deshaun's house when I confronted him about him standing me up for our trip to Italy and lying about being married.

"Oh, hell naw," I blurted out.

"What's wrong?"

"That's Deshaun's wife," I said.

Laura was just as beautiful as she was the day that she was standing outside of her house with Deshaun and his mother. I could see why my mother would refer to her as "My girl." Laura was beautiful, smart, and extremely talented.

"Hold up, I'm about to look this woman up," I said as I frantically googled Laura Pennington on my phone.

My search then commenced. My search of Laura Pennington revealed that she had been a news anchor at the station for ten years and that she came from a prominent family. Her father was an ex-NBA player named Julius Nash, who was a commentator on a sports network and a billionaire because of business ventures outside of sports. My search confirmed that Laura had three beautiful children and a loving husband. Laura was well-respected in her community. I even watched a news segment that she covered on stay-at-home fathers where her own husband, Deshaun Pennington, was featured. I was flabbergasted. I knew that Deshaun wasn't a sheriff, but I did not think that he was a stay-at-home father. This angered me even more to know that Deshaun was spending his wife's money when he was entertaining and spending time with me. What a fucking fraud.

Months went by, and depression set in; my mother eventually suggested that I get therapy. I was lucky enough to get a work-from-home job in the health insurance industry, so I had health insurance. I really did not have any excuses not to seek help. Plus, I wanted to get help. I wanted to introduce my baby to the best version of myself. Further, I needed to remove the stressors from my life because, ultimately, stress is what caused my last miscarriage. Overall, I believed that therapy would give me an outlet and provide me with the tools that I needed to remain calm during the storm that I was in the midst of.

This time in my life was very trying. But my mother was so caring and nurturing. She catered to me and took good care of me. My mother would tell me each day, "No matter what you are going through or how bad things may be; you have to get up, wash up, get dressed, and get out." And this is what I did each day. My mother made me get up and get myself together every day. I ate, I went to therapy, and my mother took me to church. The sun began to peek through the dark cloud that had been hovering over my soul.

Chapter 11

Babies And Circumstances Change Everything

I did not make much of a fuss about being pregnant, especially over social media. I did not want to hear all of the questions that people had. But when my sweet baby girl Trinity was born, I had to share it with the world. She was the most beautiful baby I had ever seen. She had a head full of black curly hair and the longest eyelashes. She was a little brown princess. When I posted Trinity on social media, Tyrell, my fling from Italy, immediately texted me saying, "What up?" I responded, "It's not yours." Tyrell responded with the laughing emojis and said, "Cool, congratulations." There was no way that Trinity belonged to Tyrell; I was unknowingly over a month pregnant when I arrived in Italy. Everyone said their congratulations, even Alonzo. It was crazy, how we did not have a baby together but managed to have babies with other people shortly after we ended our relationship.

Although Trinity was my everything, I was also her everything. She required so much of my time and attention. Thank God my mother was so helpful, but being responsible for a person's entire life without another parent is tough. I really resented Deshaun during the first few months of Trinity's life. In fact, I would go as far as to say that I hated him. It was like he got away with everything unscathed, and here I was putting together the pieces of my life. Deshaun didn't have to experience any of the realities of being the caregiver of a new life. I was starting to put things in motion to get child support from Deshaun, and then one day, I received a text from an unknown number. The text read, "This is Deshaun. I know you probably don't want to hear from me. I would really like to see the baby. Please let me know if this is a possibility." This text message sent my mind racing in a million different directions. I was upset that Deshaun had not checked on me throughout my entire pregnancy, but then I thought that he must have had a change of heart and wanted to make amends. After several texts back and forth,

I agreed to meet Deshaun in a public setting at a diner. I did not completely trust Deshaun because I didn't really know Deshaun.

I'll never forget the day that I was scheduled to meet with Deshaun. Trinity was three months old. I was sitting at a diner, prepared to see Deshaun for the first time since the day that I angrily came to his house unannounced to confront him about standing me up and living a double life. Grace was supposed to come to the diner to support me, but she was running late. As I sat at the table with Trinity nestled in my arms, I could not keep my eyes off the door, waiting for the moment that she would meet her father for the first time. I don't know if I was holding Trinity so tightly because I feared Deshaun losing his mind and harming Trinity or if it was because I myself was nervous. As I continuously looked up at the door each time it opened, I finally saw a man enter with the same bald head, beard, and face as Deshaun, and he walked towards me with a woman. As I looked closer, I realized that this was not Deshaun at all. This guy nearly looked as if it could have been Deshaun's twin. But, when the man spoke, it was clear that he was not Deshaun.

"Hello, Karma," the man said.

I immediately pulled Trinity closer to me and became extremely afraid. "Who are you?" I replied.

"I'm Don, I'm Deshaun's brother."

"I'm Jasmine," the woman said.

"What's going on?" I said cautiously.

The woman, Jasmine, seemed to be trying her best to put me at ease, "So sorry, Deshaun could not make it. We are here to give you an opportunity to be able to move on with your life without the hurt and pain associated with Deshaun along with hefty compensation." I sat there in silence. "You will be compensated handsomely, all you have to do is never bring up Deshaun, his wife, or his children," the woman said in a low tone. Then the lady looked at me with a hardened look and said, "Most importantly, you won't be bringing up your child in association with the Pennington family in any way, including in association with Deshaun. You have 48 hours to get back to me."

The woman, Jasmine, gave me a card and walked away. The guy, Don, walked behind her. I took a look at the card that Jasmine gave me and confirmed my instincts that Jasmine was a lawyer. After Jasmine and Don's departure, Grace came running into the diner.

"Girl, I am so sorry, I did not miss it, did I?" Grace asked.

"Yeah, you didn't miss much; Deshaun and his family are offering me money to basically disappear from their lives. Deshaun's punk ass didn't even show up. His brother and a lawyer came instead."

"So, are you going to take the money?" Grace asked while staring at me in suspense.

"I don't know; I have a lot to think about."

I had a lot of things to consider. My mother told me to just take the money and move on with my life. I was thinking that as well; however, at this point, I wanted both Deshaun and his wife, Laura, to suffer. I wanted Deshaun to suffer for treating me like I was nothing and as if I meant nothing to him. I wanted his wife, Laura, to suffer for not sympathizing with me as a woman. I wanted them both to suffer for thinking that they could put a price on me and Trinity. I was offended. My mother kept telling me that it was highly likely that Deshaun would not be a part of Trinity's life, so take the money so that Trinity could be taken care of financially. I felt so conflicted. Eventually, I made a conscious decision to stop drowning in my feelings and to begin swimming in my intellect. Essentially, I had to put aside my feelings in order for Trinity's future to take the forefront. I was being offered enough money not only to take care of Trinity for the rest of her life but also to send her to college. I would never get that much money from child support. Taking the money would be the right decision for me and my child.

I got back to the lawyer Jasmine and told her that the only way that I would agree to sign the document in exchange for the money was if Deshaun and his wife were present during the signing, along with me and Trinity. I said that I would not sign anything without their presence. I felt that it was important for Deshaun to face the outcome of his actions literally. Furthermore, I felt that it was important for his wife to come face to face with what her husband's negligent actions produced. I could not allow them to make us disappear without coming face to face with our existence. I needed them to feel our presence and for a humanistic experience to transpire rather than solely a financial transaction. I was good with taking the money in exchange for Deshaun and his wife having to leave the situation with some sense of sympathy or even remorse.

The day that I arrived at the law office to sign the paperwork regarding me keeping the identity of my child's father a secret was a sad one. My mother accompanied me to the law office. The woman

Jasmine, whom I met at the restaurant, was the only person that I saw in a conference room that a secretary walked me, my mother, and Trinity, to. Jasmine shook my hand and asked me and my mother to have a seat as I placed Trinity's car seat on the conference room table. Jasmine looked into the car seat and smiled at Trinity.

"So where is everyone?" I asked Jasmine.

"Well, let me go over a few things first."

Then I heard the conference door open and saw a very familiar face. This was the face of a man that I once loved. The man who created butterflies in my stomach. The man that I had made love to time and time again. This man was Alonzo. My mouth literally dropped. My mother was looking in the other direction and playing with Trinity as she was taking her out of the car seat.

"Oh, Jasmine, I didn't know that this room was occupied; sorry about that," Alonzo said as he immediately exited the room without even looking in my direction. Alonzo had not seen me at all. It's crazy because here I was, trying to be seen, trying to have my baby be seen, and I was in plain view of the love of my life, and he didn't even notice me. Before I could wrap my mind around what had occurred, Deshaun and his wife Laura walked through the door. Deshaun acted as if he could not look into Trinity's direction. I made sure that Trinity was facing both Deshaun and his wife.

Sometimes, facing the truth is harder than hiding the truth. When Deshaun's wife, Laura, looked at Trinity, her eyes filled with tears. Laura had to come to the realization that Trinity was here, and she belonged to her husband and no amount of money would take that away. Laura sat down for about a minute before she excused herself from the room while bursting into tears.

Once Deshaun actually looked at Trinity, his eyes were fixated on her. I wondered if he was thinking that Trinity reminded him of himself or if she reminded him of his other children. During this time, Jasmine shuffled through papers. Suddenly, Deshaun walked over to Trinity without laying an eye on me.

"May I hold her?" Deshaun asked.

I handed Trinity to her father, and she immediately began to smile. Deshaun held Trinity and smiled as he began talking to her, calling her a pretty little lady.

"You have a pretty baby," Deshaun said to me.

"We have a pretty baby," I replied.

This was hurtful because even at this special moment, Deshaun was unable to claim Trinity as his own. When Laura came back into the conference room, Deshaun quickly put Trinity back in my arms and sat next to Laura. As Laura sat, she did not say a word. This was weird for me because I was accustomed to seeing Laura on the news being professional, poised, and confident. Seeing her in this element where she was distressed, saddened, and uncomfortable was a strange sight. Before we knew it, we were signing the paperwork as I was thinking about how I was going to get a chance to see and speak to Alonzo before leaving the law office. Once Jasmine handed me my lump sum check, I was ready to just move on.

Patience is important, especially when you get the chance to see your first love for the first time in a long time. I made sure that my mother and Trinity were the last to leave the conference room. I had asked Jasmine to give me and my mother a moment and she left us behind as she closed the conference room door.

"Mom, did you see Alonzo walk in here?"

My mother had a puzzled look on her face; she looked at me as if I had completely lost it.

"No, are you alright?" my mother asked.

"Mom, Alonzo came into this room for a quick second and spoke to that lady Jasmine; he didn't realize that the room was occupied; I guess he was trying to have a meeting in this room."

"Are you sure?"

"Yes, I need you to take Trinity to the car and wait for me. I am going to see if I can speak to Alonzo really quick before I leave."

My mom acquiesced and walked out with Trinity in her arms.

As I approached the reception desk to ask to speak to Alonzo Rodgers, I was excited and nervous at the same time. I had no idea how he would receive me. Would he embarrass me by requesting I leave? Would he give me a hug? Would he not even show up to the front desk? I had meticulously played out every scenario in my head. My heart was about to jump out of my chest.

"Hello, I know that you just saw me, but I am now here to see Alonzo Rodgers," I said to the receptionist.

"Is he expecting you?" the receptionist asked.

"Not really. Please tell him that Karma is here to pay him a visit." I said this with a smile on my face. I figured that Alonzo would at least get a kick out of my play on words if he did not appreciate my visit.

I sat in the waiting area for what seemed to be forever. Suddenly, Alonzo's tall frame entered the space. He was more distinguished and striking than he had ever been. He was wearing a tailored-made dark blue suit that fitted him perfectly with a white shirt and red tie. His shoes were shining. He looked like his hair was freshly cut, and his mustache and goatee were perfectly shaven. Even his beautiful black skin glistened. When Alonzo laid eyes on me, it was as if he had seen a ghost.

"Karma," Alonzo said as he walked towards me with his arms extended to embrace me with a tight hug. Alonzo's big, strong arms wrapped around my body, and he held me as if he did not want to let go. I felt that I was in the perfect place at the perfect time. I thanked God for creating the perfect yet awkward scenario to reunite me and Alonzo.

"You look incredible," Alonzo said.

"You're looking good yourself. What are you doing here?"

"I was about to ask you the same question," he said.

"It's a really long story."

"How about we talk about it over dinner tonight? I am going to text you. I have a meeting that I need to be in right now. But I would love to catch up over dinner."

"Absolutely, I am looking forward to tonight," I replied.

Things are never as bad as you play them out in your mind. I was determined to make amends with Alonzo. I really wanted him back in my life.

It's funny how one dinner date can change the course of your life. Well, that's definitely what happened the night that Alonzo took me to dinner after my crazy day at the law office, accepting money from Deshaun and his family. I met Alonzo at a beautiful steakhouse. He arrived wearing the same dark blue suit that he had been wearing earlier that day. I cleaned up a bit. I slipped on a tight black dress that hugged and accentuated all of my best attributes. The dress was short, my butt was sitting round and pretty, and my breast squeezed together, exposing the perfect amount of cleavage, just the way Alonzo liked.

When Alonzo greeted me, he hugged me so sweetly and so firmly. His embrace made me melt in his arms. We sat down and made some small talk, but the first real thing that I said to Alonzo was sorry. I told Alonzo that I was so sorry for the way that I left him and that he did not deserve to be treated like that. I explained to him that I was so wrong for blaming him for my miscarriage. Alonzo stopped me from talking when I started talking about the miscarriage. Alonzo explained to me that he had been doing some work on himself and reading a lot of self-help books. Alonzo admitted that he could have done a better job communicating with me and that there were things that he wished that he could have done differently.

I needed to understand how Alonzo ended up in Los Angeles. Was he single? How old was his baby? I wanted to know it all.

"Alonzo, what in the world are you doing in Los Angeles?"

"Well, the law firm that I was working for relocated their headquarters to LA. It was a hard decision to leave Buffalo. But I did what I needed to do for my career. And don't you go thinkin that I followed your ass to LA either," Alonzo said as he was laughing. "But it's nice to see you," he continued.

"I hear that you had a baby," I said.

Alonzo's expression turned to one of annoyance. "I never had a baby. I was dealing with a girl who was going around saying that she was pregnant by me and even posted it on social media. You know I don't be on social media like that. I was pissed that the girl would post that she was expecting a baby with me while tagging me in the post. Everybody was reaching out to me and saying congratulations. I didn't know what the hell was going on. Long story short, I got a paternity test while she was pregnant, and the baby was not mine."

A part of me was really relieved that Alonzo did not have a baby. "Are you dating anyone now?" I asked.

"I have gone on some dates, nothing serious. I have only been in LA. for about two months. I am trying to get adjusted," Alonzo explained.

This was all the information that I needed. No significant other and no child.

"Do you want to talk about why you were at the law office today?" Alonzo asked.

I knew that he researched my entire situation related to Deshaun. Although I had anticipated the topic coming up, I still felt embarrassed and anxious when it came to the subject.

"Yeah, I was dealing with a liar who never told me he was married, and I got pregnant, but I don't regret Trinity."

"Between me and you, that guy you were dealing with, and his wife are making sure that their past looks squeaky clean because their family has some big things in the works. But you stay away from them and never look back. You are too good to be associated with them."

At that very moment, I realized that no one had ever propped me on a pedestal so high that they felt that certain people were not worthy of my presence. This night was special because Alonzo and I had some difficult conversations that we did not get a chance to have in the past. We stayed at the restaurant so long that we were the last ones to leave before it closed.

Many dates came after Alonzo, and I reunited. I remember Grace, Dane, Alonzo, and I went out on a double date one night. It was perfect because Grace had an opportunity to catch up with Alonzo. This dinner was a great opportunity for me to spend time with Dane. Dane and I had never really spent a substantial amount of time together. Once we were all seated, we began talking and laughing. Talking about the good times in Buffalo. Dane started talking about how he went to Buffalo and how it was cold as hell when he was there, but he enjoyed the food. We were getting along very well, and the conversation and drinks flowed. The only person not drinking was Alonzo. The next thing I knew, I felt hands on my shoulder, and someone whispered, "Hey bitch." I turned around, and it was a ghost from the past. I looked up, and there was Terry Tea staring me in the face. The same Terry Tea who would tell Aiko and me about his oral escapades with Grace's husband, Dane. Terry Tea hugged me.

"Gurl, you lookin good," Terry Tea said in a gleeful tone.

In a shocked and shaky voice, I replied, "Hey, how you doin?"

Terry Tea looked directly at Dane and said, "I'm good. I didn't know that you knew my friends Dane and Grace."

"Yeah, I know them. And you look great by the way," I replied because I could not think of anything else to say.

Terry Tea continued to look directly at Dane and said, "Thank goodness I don't look like what I've gone through. I am exhausted. I was up with my boo all night last night. I almost didn't make it out to dinner, but I decided to SUCK it up."

Terry Tea then looked at Grace, "Grace the Face, looking as lovely as ever. You and I both know what it's like to SUCK it up don't we Gracie Pooh?"

Grace did not say a word. However, Grace's facial expression displayed her irritation and frustration.

Well, I am going to HEAD out and let you all enjoy your meal. Oh yeah and Dane, keep your HEAD up baby," Terry Tea said.

This was the most awkward experience ever. This encounter was definitely one of the top three most uncomfortable moments of my life. During the conversation, Dane just wrapped his arms around Grace and looked in the opposite direction, off into the abyss, and Grace looked directly at Terry Tea during his subtle yet savage ambush on Dane.

"Let me get back to my dinner, those mussels I ordered aren't going to SUCK themselves out of the shells. Bye, loves," Terry Tea said before sashaying off to another section of the restaurant.

I was 100% sure that everyone, including Alonzo, caught on to the subliminal oral sex references that Terry Tea was throwing towards Dane. It was clear that Terry Tea was trying to make it very clear that he and Dane were intimate.

"Wow, that dude is wild," Alonzo said, breaking the awkward silence.

"Hey Karma, I have to go to the ladies' room; come with me," Grace demanded.

I was trying to keep my cool; I was dreading having to go to the bathroom with Grace. I knew she had questions that she wanted me to answer.

"What the fuck was that?" Grace said angrily once we got into the bathroom.

"I don't know what the fuck that was."

"What do you know, and for once, I need you to be 100% honest with me," Grace pleaded.

"What? I don't know anything,"

"Stop lying to me, Karma, I know you. I know when you are lying to me."

Guilt started to set in. "I only know Terry Tea on a social basis."

"What do you know about this Terry Tea and Dane?"

"I don't know anything."

"Fuck, Karma, stop lying to me!" Grace yelled and then lowered her voice as a woman walked out of one of the bathroom stalls. We both stood quietly until the woman washed her hands and exited the restroom.

I just told Grace that Terry Tea had told me that he was sexually involved with Dane. I explained to Grace that I found out about this when she and I were not on speaking terms. I even mentioned how

Grace blew up on me when I said that she and Dane were moving too fast; it would have been foolish to bring that information to Grace's attention. I continued to explain that I was so happy that she and I were on good terms that I did not want to jeopardize it by bringing up Terry Tea and Dane's sexual relationship and losing my best friend again. Tears literally poured down Grace's face.

"Did you ever think that you would jeopardize our friendship by withholding such important information from me?" Grace asked.

I just stood there speechless.

"I knew that you knew something over a year ago when I came to your apartment and told you that I hired a private investigator and found out that Dane was cheating. Your response was to let Dane know that I was aware of his affair with a man. I gave you the benefit of the doubt and believed that you mistakenly said that Dane was having an affair with a man. You had an opportunity to be honest with me and didn't.

"I'm sorry, Grace; I didn't want to make things worse between us and make you angry at me."

"Well, just to let you know, Dane is no longer seeing Terry Tea despite what Terry Tea was trying to imply a minute ago. Dane and I are stronger than ever, and we have decided to continue to work on our relationship."

The only thing that I could say was, "I'm sorry."

"I thought that we were better than that Karma; I thought we were sisters," Grace yelled before collecting herself, drying her tears, and storming out of the ladies' room.

I just stayed in the ladies' room for a while because I intensely regretted not telling Grace about Dane and Terry Tea. I felt that I was not the friend that Grace deserved. I felt that I had betrayed my very best friend. Once I collected myself, wiped my tears, and fixed my make-up, I returned to the table. By the time I got back to the table, Dane and Grace were gone. Alonzo was sitting there alone.

"What was that all about?" Alonzo asked.

"I really fucked up."

I explained the entire situation to Alonzo, and he simply said, "You did what you thought was best; it will be okay." Alonzo encouraged me to mend my relationship with Grace, but I did not know if we would ever get back on track.

Within three months of Alonzo and I reuniting and dating again, I thought that it would be good for him to actually start spending time with Trinity. We were spending more time together, and I needed Alonzo to get comfortable with the idea of me having a child. Furthermore, I needed to see how Alonzo interacted with Trinity so that I could determine if he could be a permanent fixture in her life. I was protective of Trinity and did not want her to ever experience the heartache that I have had in my life. I did not want anyone, including a man, to walk out of her life and for her to have to feel that type of pain.

There is no committed relationship with me without a committed relationship with Trinity. I decided to have a heart-to-heart conversation with Alonzo about meeting Trinity. One day, Alonzo and I were on the phone. Alonzo had just finished telling me about his crazy day. After Alonzo unleashed the trials and difficulties that had plagued him throughout the course of his day, I decided to welcome him with the opportunity to meet my most cherished blessing, Trinity.

"I have been thinking; you and I have been getting serious, and it may be time for you to meet my baby Trinity," I said.

Alonzo had become incredibly quiet. With each second that passed, the quietness seemed to afflict pain on my soul. Finally, Alonzo ceased the silence by saying, "I have to be honest with you Karma; although I love you, I don't know if I can trust you."

"You can trust me; you have to trust me if we are going to move forward."

"Yeah, Karma, that is easy to say. Trust can't be promised or solicited; it has to be earned. I don't want to meet your daughter until I can trust you. Remember, you left me the last time; I did not leave you. Worst of all, you left me at the worst time, after Aunt Betty died and after we lost our baby. I did not think that I could trust anyone after that, let alone trust you. I need time."

I was so surprised by how that conversation went. I thought that Alonzo and I were moving in the right direction, but I had to respect the fact that my lack of transparency and consideration for him in the past led him to feel as though it would not be wise to jump back into a committed relationship with me.

My mother coming to Los Angeles to help me out during a tough time turned into her relocating to Los Angeles. Since my mother moved to Los Angeles, I relied on her a lot. She and I were living together, and she was a huge help when it came to caring for Trinity.

When my mother invited both of my siblings to my house for her birthday, I could not make much of a fuss about it. I never really got along with my siblings, but I was willing to take one for the team. My mother thought that it had been far too long since the last time we were all together in the same space. My sister Celine was scheduled to arrive with her husband Todd and her teenage daughter Rhea. My brother Matthew was going to arrive with his new wife, Jackie. We had all grown up, and I was hoping that everyone would be able to behave maturely.

My decent-sized apartment had become a gathering space for the first time ever. I had never had so many people in my apartment. When my sister arrived with her husband Todd and thirteen-year-old daughter Rhea, I greeted everyone with a hug. My sister gave me an insincere embrace as she always did when we hugged. Her husband hugged me and then Rhea had her eyes rolled up in her head before she even hugged me. Rhea had such an attitude. I felt that Rhea's disposition directly reflected how my sister Celine felt about me. My mother always said you can tell how someone feels about you by the way that their children treat you.

When my brother Matthew entered my apartment with his wife Jackie, they barely spoke to me at all. As we all sat at the dinner table talking and eating, I looked at my mother; her expression was that of gratitude.

"Not to be in your business or anything, but where is Trinity's father?" Asked Matthew as Trinity sat in her high chair eating her food.

I was seriously annoyed by Matthew's question. I knew that he did not really care and that this was just one of Matthew's attempts to embarrass me and make me feel less than.

"Let's focus on this moment and us all being together," my mother interjected, saving me from Matthew's attacks as she had done so many times before.

"Momma, Karma has a mouth and a brain of her own; let her decide if she wants to focus on this moment or answer Matthew's question," Celine replied.

"Trinity's father is minding his own business, which is something that you both need to be doing," I replied to both Matthew and Celine.

Suddenly, Matthew stood up as if he were going to give a profound speech, "Are we going to address the elephant in the room, Momma? You always feel the need to protect Karma. That's why she has ended up the way that she is. She is always waiting for you to rescue her, and you do every time. So much so that you uprooted your entire life to help Karma here in California. That's why Karma can't get her shit together. Karma only cares about herself. She is irresponsible; hell, she probably doesn't even know who the father of her baby is."

"That's it, that's enough," my mother screamed as my sister Celine sat there with a grin on her face. It was as if both Matthew and Celine had planned this ambush. I had enough and felt it was time for me to stand up to my older siblings. I allowed them to berate me my entire life, but not today. I looked Matthew in the eye, and said, "First of all, you don't know enough about me to assess what my life had turned out to be. You have never really been a brother to me." Then I looked at Celine and said, "Celine, you have never really been a sister to me." I then stood up, walked behind my chair, and proceeded to push my chair into the table and addressed both Matthew and Celine, "You both sit high on your proverbial thrones and look down on me as if I am a peasant and you have done this my entire life. I want you all to understand that you are no better than me. And I also want to remind you that you are at my house."

"No, we are at my mother's house," Celine yelled out.

"Bitch, I pay all the bills, and I have personally paid the rent for the remainder of the year, so before you speak, at least know what the fuck you're talking about," I replied.

"Last I recall, black and blue does not look good on you, so I suggest you watch your mouth before I whip your ass," Celine yelled.

At this point, Celine's daughter Rhea stood up from her chair as if she was going to confront me.

"Everyone, stop, please stop, this is not getting us anywhere," my mother cried.

Then the doorbell rang. All I could think was, "Who the hell is this?" My mom opened the door and there were two male police officers standing at the door. One officer was tall, thin, and white and the other was shorter, heavier, and black.

"Is Karma Robinson here?" the tall police officer said.

"Yes, what seems to be the problem?" my mother asked.

Initially, I thought, "I know we weren't loud enough for the police to be called." Then my life began to flash before my very eyes. I walked over to the door, "I'm Karma Robinson, how may I help you?"

"We need to speak with you, can we come in?" the shorter police officer asked.

I turned to everyone in my house, and they all looked shocked, frightened, and concerned.

"Yes, follow me."

I walked the police officers to Trinity's room, which was away from everyone who was in the apartment. I was petrified. All I could think about was if the police had already spoken to Aiko. I envisioned this day many times in my head, and I always said that I would keep my cool and deny everything. I would never admit to going into the homes of the rich and famous and stealing some of their most prized possessions.

"We want to talk to you about some burglaries," the tall officer said.

I began to experience heart palpitations, and my palms were getting sweaty. The shorter officer then began asking me a series of questions. "What is your date of birth? How long have you lived in this apartment? How long have you lived in LA? Was your previous apartment burglarized? Do you have any idea who burglarized your previous apartment?" As I began answering questions, I realized that the police were there questioning me about the apartment burglary that occurred a year earlier while I was in Italy at my previous apartment. I was wondering if the police had finally caught Aiko. When the police finished their questioning, I said to the officers, "Out of curiosity, why are you coming to me a year later?"

The shorter officer said, "Well, the situation is still under investigation, so we can't give you details, but we think that we have recovered some of your things, and when it's possible, we will ensure that we get them to you."

I was relieved. It definitely did not seem like the police suspected me of any wrongdoing. As the officers were leaving my apartment, I noticed that the only people left in my apartment were my mother and Trinity. Everyone else had left, and I was grateful for that. I did not care if I ever saw Matthew and Celine again.

My mother was on a mission to bring all her children together. My mother made another attempt to reunite her children, this time at a restaurant for breakfast before my siblings and their families went back home to Buffalo. When everyone finally got to the table, there was an awkward silence. My mother was the one starting most of the conversation. Then I saw Celine's husband Todd nudge her, and Celine said, "I just want to apologize for my behavior yesterday. Sorry for disrespecting you, Momma, and yelling in your house. Sorry Karma for making threats towards you and overstepping my bounds."

"Celine, I accept your apology, but I feel that you are constantly trying to disrespect me. Literally, you just disrespected me by apologizing to Mom for disrespecting her in her home. Sweetie, you were in my home not Mom's."

"Okay, let's cool down. Celine, come on, what did we talk about?" Todd said.

"My apologies, Karma, I will do better moving forward. I will work on being more respectful," Celine said.

"I just want to know why the police were at your house," Matthew said before he began laughing hysterically.

"The police were at my house because I was robbed, and they needed more information. That's what I hate about you, Matthew. Your default with me is to always assume and hope for the worst. That's why I told you the other day that you were never a brother to me. You never tried to look out for me. My pain has always been your joy. That's fucking sick," I said.

Matthew's huge smile turned into a slight grin as he tried to remain collected as shame began to enter his consciousness.

Matthew's wife, Jackie said, "Karma, I have not spent a lot of time with you so there is a lot that I don't know; however, Matthew and Celine, moving forward, do you all think that you can have open and honest conversations with Karma without being sarcastic or brutal. You all need to understand that you are being cruel when you don't exercise compassion when trying to have honest conversations."

For the first time, my siblings, hell, even I had the opportunity to see how my siblings' behavior towards me was seen from the lenses of people who did not grow up in our household. To see my sister's husband Todd, actually encourage her to apologize, and to hear Matthew's wife, Jackie, speak about how cruel my siblings were to me was refreshing. I did not feel completely alone; for once, someone other than my mother stood up for me in their own way.

Shortly after the breakfast gathering with my siblings, my siblings, and their families returned to Buffalo. I was happy to see them leave but I was happy that they visited. In a weird way, I was able to get some closure. I stood up to my siblings for the first time, and I felt that my siblings would be able to do some self-reflection that would allow them to become better people.

I have a gift of knowing when change is going to come. Although I never said it out loud, I knew that my mother would be leaving my apartment to venture out on her own soon. My mother had been such a great help to me. But recently, I was back working, Trinity and I were financially secure because of the legal agreement that I signed with her father, Deshaun. Plus, my spirits were up. One day, my mother was sitting in front of the television watching the news after one of her talk shows went off as she normally did. I sat down next to her.

"I want to talk to you," my mother said.

"Sure, what's up," I replied.

"Well, I wanted to let you know that I'll be moving out soon."

"Where will you be moving to?"

"I have been seeing someone for the past few months. He has a beautiful house in the Valley, and we have decided to move in together."

"Okay, Momma. I see you. Got you a whole man. Do you know him well enough to move in with him?"

"Yes, his name is Larry, and he has one adult daughter. He is nice, generous, intelligent, caring, kind, and a gentleman."

"Well, I support it."

Then, the news got my attention. The news was talking about the rapper Lil Pharaoh. Over a year prior, Aiko and I went to his house during one of our heists and I took his diamond necklace, a very distinct diamond necklace with a Pharaoh medallion. The only jewelry I never gave Aiko to cash in with her connection was Lil Pharaoh's medallion necklace and the actress Michelle Thompson's 8-carat emerald-cut pink diamond engagement ring that she got from a famous basketball player. Both items were unique and were stolen when my apartment was burglarized.

The man reporting the news said, "Rapper Lil Pharaoh went to social media over a year ago pleading for whoever stole his $200,000 necklace to return it to him for a handsome reward. No one ever came forward. But recently, there was a break in the case. A man named Carl Davis was wearing Lil Pharaoh's custom-made necklace at a club where Lil Pharaoh was celebrating the release of his new album, and the authorities were contacted. Officials searched Davis's Belleview Apartment, where they found what they believe to be millions of dollars in stolen items, including an engagement ring that belongs to critically acclaimed actress Michelle Thompson. Authorities are still trying to determine if Davis acted alone or if he had accomplices. Davis faces several charges."

I realized why the police showed up at my door, and I also realized that this Carl Davis guy robbed my apartment and unknowingly took items that I had stolen from Lil Pharaoh and Michelle Thompson.

"What a damn fool, stealing a man's chain and wearing it in his face. These kids nowadays are batshit crazy. Wait, Belleview, isn't that your old apartment building?" My mother said.

"Yeah, it is," I replied.

"He's probably the person who robbed you," my mother said as if she had just solved a world problem.

"I know, right," I said.

I felt guilty and I felt relieved at the same time. I felt guilty because I knew this Carl Davis guy would be punished for items that I stole, and I felt relieved because I was not being charged with any crimes. I also felt bad about instantly blaming Aiko for robbing my apartment. I should have never assumed the worst of Aiko; I should have talked to her. Although I did not want Aiko back in my life, I felt bad about secretly blaming her for robbing me.

When love is true, it will come back to you. Although Alonzo was initially apprehensive about meeting Trinity, he eventually came around. It took many months for Alonzo to finally decide that he felt that it was suitable to meet her. Alonzo asked to meet me for a picnic and asked if I could bring Trinity. I was excited about this. I wanted to move forward with Alonzo and hoped to marry him someday. I was excited the day that Trinity and I met Alonzo at the park. I was curious about how Trinity would interact with him. It was not like she had a lot of males in her life. Trinity was about ten months old. She was already walking; Trinity was advanced in everything. As I walked towards Alonzo, he was sitting on a huge picnic blanket on the grass with sandwiches, fruits, applesauce, juices, and wine. Alonzo stood up and hugged me, and he reached out his arms to Trinity, and Trinity literally fell into his arms. Trinity then began to lay her head on Alonzo's shoulder.

"Hey, Trinity, beautiful name for a beautiful baby," Alonzo said.

I was impressed that he put so much thought into what to bring to the picnic to make sure that Trinity had plenty of food to select from. I felt like we were a little family. Trinity was crawling and walking around eating everything that she could put her hands on, as Alonzo and I talked.

"This is a big step for you, and I want to let you know that I really appreciate this, and I want you to know that I love you and that I never stopped loving you," I said.

Alonzo lovingly touched the left side of my face, gently kissed my lips, and said, "I love you, and I never stopped."

My heart just melted. When Alonzo and I first started dating, he had a hard time expressing his love. This man had come a long way. From this day forward, the love that I had for Alonzo grew. Over the following months, Trinity began calling Alonzo "Dada" and, eventually, "Daddy." In a way, I felt that Trinity brought Alonzo and me closer together. I felt like my life was starting to come together.

Chapter 12

Same Man, New Life

People evolve, and so does life. In such a short time, Alonzo and I were not the same people we were when we lived in Buffalo. Alonzo had become a successful attorney. I was a mother and a nurse. I was still working from home and providing patients with advice over the phone for an insurance company. This was not an exciting career; however, it was paying me and keeping me occupied. I wanted to get back into acting so badly or at least do something in entertainment, but nothing was working out. Then, one day, I was speaking to one of my nurse friends, Chrissy. She told me that she interviewed with a legendary older black actress named Diana DeCosta to be her personal nurse. Diana DeCosta was an award-winning actress and had a reputation for being a total bitch. Chrissy told me that due to some personal issues, she was unable to take the position and wanted to know if I was interested. Chrissy knew that Diana needed someone to start as her personal nurse as soon as possible and had recommended me. This job would require me to work on the set of a show that Diana co-hosted.

I will never forget the day that I interviewed for the role of Diana DeCosta's personal nurse. Diana's assistant called and was really "matter of fact" and "straight to the point." I was to meet Diana at the studio where she filmed a show with three other women called Our Perspective. My mother loved this show. The job required me to work on set. One of the women who hosted the show was Hazy; she was my favorite rap artist. I was listening to her throughout my entire trip in Italy. My Italy fling Tyrell said I had ratchet ears for listening to Hazy because of her raunchy lyrics. The other host was a very conservative Afro-Latina female named Ana Alvarez. Ana Alvarez hosted a national news program in the past. She had a straight-to-business type of attitude. Ana Alvarez was extremely beautiful, with her lush dark brown hair hanging loose inches past her shoulders. Ana was undeniably the leader of the show. And finally, a legendary black female comedian named Wendy Knight was also a host. Wendy Knight was on the short side. She always wore her hair in a shoulder-length bob and wore long, beautiful nails. I was excited about having the opportunity to work in the presence of these amazing women.

When I drove up to the studio, security allowed me through the gates once I told them who I was and who I was there to see. Once I arrived at the building, the assistant met me, immediately took me into a room, and told me to hold tight and that Diana would be joining me shortly. The room was like a little apartment. There was a beautiful, soft white couch with white fur pillows. The décor was beautiful, with silver and gold fixtures. The room smelled heavenly fresh. On the opposite side of the room were soft, comfortable white office chairs and a smaller conference table. Fresh, colorful flowers surrounded the room; they were meticulously placed on each table within the room. I decided to take a seat at one of the white office chairs. Before I could completely get comfortable, I heard the door open and close. A breeze and a figure literally flew by me.

"Hello, my dear. Your name?" I heard a voice say.

That breeze that flew by me was Diana DeCosta; I was star-struck. I was in the presence of greatness. I was speechless.

"Hello, my dear," Diana repeated.

Once I was able to snap out of being star-struck, I responded, "Hello, I'm Karma Robinson."

"Let's get straight to it. You will be my personal nurse, but you will not be announcing that to anyone, I don't need anyone thinking that I am sickly. People will know you as my 2nd assistant. I had a mild heart attack a few weeks ago, and I am diabetic. Not to mention, a bitch is old, so I would feel comfortable with a medical professional keeping an eye on me. I don't want anyone here to know about it. There have been rumors in the blogs, and I have denied them all. I need you to be available while I am here at work, checking my blood pressure and sugar levels. Never talk about my medical condition or check any of my vitals in front of anyone unless I have a medical emergency, and you need to save my life. Do I make myself clear?"

"Yes, Ms. Diana," I replied.

"Never refer to me as Ms. Diana. Diana DeCosta will do."

"Yes, Diana DeCosta."

I could not believe it. I was able to get the job so easily. I would be working with Diana DeCosta. I knew my mother would be so proud because she loved the talk show Our Perspective and she loved Diana DeCosta as a movie star.

While working 4 hours a day, I was paid a little more than I was being paid working full time as a nurse taking phone calls all day. This was amazing. I would be able to get exposure to the celebrities that were on the show. My optimism had me imagining meeting directors or actors who would help me land my first big role on television or in a movie.

Working with Diana DeCosta on the hit talk show Our Perspective for only half a day allowed me to be able to spend a lot of quality time with my daughter Trinity and my man Alonzo. By the time I got my gig with Diana DeCosta, Trinity was getting older, and Alonzo and I were discussing marriage. My mother had moved out with her boyfriend, Larry. During this time, Trinity and Alonzo were spending a lot more time together in my small apartment. Alonzo constantly reminded me that Trinity needed a yard to play in. We were really talking about purchasing a house now that I had a job that I absolutely loved.

I never really celebrated my birthday growing up. My mother was a single mother who made sure her children had the essentials. She always made sure we dressed nicely and ate well. My mother never splurged on frivolous gifts and birthday parties. For our birthdays, we were lucky to get a cake. After our first year together, Alonzo asked me what I wanted for my birthday. I told Alonzo that I never had a birthday party, but I was not sure if I wanted one as an adult. I did tell Alonzo that I would not mind going on a trip and celebrating. My man Alonzo came through like he always did. One day, Alonzo told me to pack my bags and that he was taking me on a trip. He would not tell me where we were going, but it would be a quick weekend trip.

When Alonzo and I arrived at the airport, he told me that we were going to St. Thomas in the Virgin Islands. I was so excited. I had never gone to St. Thomas, and I thought that it would be a good getaway for both of us. When we arrived in St. Thomas, the skies were blue, and the sun was shining upon my existence. Alonzo had a driver pick us up from the airport. As the driver was maneuvering through the streets of St. Thomas, I was anxiously awaiting to see where we would be staying during our romantic trip. I was speechless when the driver pulled up to a beautiful white home with two pillars in the front and a circular driveway. Alonzo and the driver grabbed our luggage from the trunk as I slowly walked up to the house in awe.

"How do you like it, baby?" Alonzo asked.

"I love it; I can't wait to see the inside."

Once we walked inside the home, there was an elegantly designed white sectional that wrapped around the living area, where there were huge French doors that opened to the circular-shaped swimming pool. The ceilings were high, and the dining room area was exquisite, fit for the queen that Alonzo treated me like. I walked up the winding staircase and saw our beautiful bedroom that had rose petals on the bed positioned meticulously to form the shape of a heart. This reminded me of when Alonzo took me to Niagara Falls, Canada, and proposed to me years prior. The rose petals were shaped like a heart on our hotel room bed that day as well. I did not want to get my hopes up, besides, I had to continue to gain Alonzo's trust before he would consider marrying me.

"The bed is for later; for now, get dressed and ready for dinner," Alonzo said in his sexy voice.

Although I was tired from traveling, I asked no questions and got ready for dinner. Alonzo and I ate at a beautiful restaurant and returned to the home that Alonzo rented. I could not wait to explore the island the following day.

When Alonzo and I arrived back to the home, it was just getting dark. I was already planning all of the things that I would be doing to Alonzo to show him how much I appreciated him.

"Surprise!!!!" was all I heard when Alonzo and I walked into the house. I almost peed my pants. I looked around and the first people that I saw were my mother and Trinity. I couldn't believe it. I was so confused. Then, as I further accessed the room, I saw Grace. I was so happy to see Grace, although I knew we had some things that we needed to work through. I almost broke down in tears when I saw my cousin Debra from my father's side of the family. I had not seen her in years; she was the cousin who would take me to see my paternal grandparents. There were a few friends there who worked with me from the healthcare Insurance company, including my friend Chrissy, who helped me get my new job working for Diana DeCosta. Tears surged out of my eyes and down my face, I turned to hug Alonzo, and he was down on one knee with a ring box in his hand with an enormous diamond ring protruding out of it.

"Karma, you are my dream girl. I want to give you a dream life, and I am asking you, will you be my dream wife?"

"Yes, yes, yes," I yelled as Alonzo slid the engagement ring on my finger."

This ring was much different from the first engagement ring that Alonzo had gotten me. As I looked around, there was not a dry eye in the room. I could not believe that Alonzo had gone through so much trouble to make my birthday so special. There was a DJ, tons of food, and people who meant a lot to me. We all partied that night; I felt so much gratitude and elation. I was even happy about seeing Grace. I had not seen her since our double date encounter with Terry Tea. Grace was happy to see me, and she embraced me, and I had a chance to apologize to her. Grace apologized to me for taking her troubles out on me. Grace and I did not have time to have a deep discussion about our argument during the night that we went on a double date with our men. However, us seeing and loving each other was a step in the right direction. In totality, I could not have asked for a more perfect night.

My birthday celebration was amazing. After my birthday/engagement party, Alonzo and I had the house that he rented to ourselves. It was amazing. I spent time with my family at lunch and dinner the next day. Before leaving, my cousin Debra wanted to meet me for breakfast. I met my cousin Debra at a coffee shop right off the beach. Debra was just as youthful and beautiful as the last time I saw her. I was excited to speak with her and to catch up. Debra informed me that my biological father was terminally ill. Debra explained to me that my father was dying of cirrhosis of the liver. Apparently, my father had been suffering from alcohol abuse for years. I had a weird feeling as Debra was relaying this information to me. Instinctively, I felt burdened and saddened by the news. I was burdened because this news was an inconvenience; I was supposed to be celebrating my birthday weekend and engagement. I felt saddened due to my lack of sorrow for having a dying father. Also, Debra told me that my sister Jennifer, who was six years younger than me, really wanted to meet me and that my father wanted to see me as well. Debra giving me this information had me swarming with emotions. I secretly longed to have a sibling that I felt actually loved me and who I loved equally. I especially longed to have a little sister. I was always jealous of people who had great relationships with their siblings. On the other hand, I knew that I needed to protect myself. Things were going so well in my life, and I did not want to invite any bad energy or drama into my space. I told my cousin Debra that she downloaded a lot of information on me and that I needed to allow the information I was provided to marinate before making any decisions.

After my fantastic birthday weekend, I returned to work. I always checked Diana DeCosta's vitals before she hit the stage of the show. After checking her vitals, I would essentially be on standby. I would often times stand behind the stage or I would sit in the audience and actually watch the show. On this particular day, the show was packed with audience members, and there were no extra seats, so I decided to stand off to the side of the stage. I wanted to keep an eye on Diana DeCosta because she said that she was not feeling well. Before the show started, I went to grab her some medicine and water. As I was bringing Diana her medicine and water, I walked by Laura Pennington. I felt like someone punched me in the stomach. What the hell was she doing here? I tried to keep my cool and act as normal as possible. When I walked by Laura, I acted as if I did not know her. I had not seen Laura since the lawyer's office when she and her husband or the father of Trinity had me sign the paperwork to essentially ignore the reality of Deshaun being Trinity's father. I discreetly provided Diana with her water and pills. Diana handed me back the water, and I ran to the side of the stage.

"Welcome to Our Perspective. We have a great show for you today, but before we get started, we would like to welcome our guest host, Laura Pennington from WSLC News in Los Angeles," Diana DeCosta announced.

Laura walked on the stage in all of her splendor. Her beautiful, long black hair flowed down her back and floated as she walked towards the couch that the ladies sat on. Her beautiful, flawless chocolate skin was accentuated with makeup that seemed to have been applied by the best makeup artist. All of her curves were faultlessly displayed in her professional business attire. Laura was poised, distinguished, and breathtaking.

During the show, Laura Pennington's father, an ex-NBA player turned billionaire, came to the stage to make a huge announcement. Laura Pennington and Julius Nash announced that Julius Nash would be running for President of the United States. It all made sense. I was offered so much money because Julius Nash needed to make it seem as if his family was perfect since he would be running for office. Julius Nash spoke about his ambitions of becoming president and how he could translate his business savvy into the White House. I was in shock and extremely uncomfortable. I could not wait until this day's show was over. I could not believe that I was paid off so that Julius Nash could appear to have the perfect family. Nonetheless, I was preoccupied with more pressing matters. My ailing father constantly weighed on my thoughts.

Making the decision to return to Buffalo to see my dying father and little sister was tough. But Alonzo promised that he would go with me and support me. When I arrived in Buffalo, my father was at the hospital where I once worked as a nurse. It was the same hospital that I was working at when I had my miscarriage. Alonzo and my cousin Debra went to the hospital with me. Walking through the hospital floor felt surreal. I almost felt like I was floating. I was overwhelmed with anxiety and fear. Once I went into my father's room, I saw him lying there, frail and sickly. I looked at the whiteboard across from my father's bed and saw his name, Eric Jamison. I instantly got even more anxious because I did not know what to call this man. Do I call him Dad or Eric? I just stood over him, assessing his condition. I was a nurse, so I knew that he was in bad shape. The tubes, the noises, and the environment, just made me start going into nurse mode. I began looking at his vitals to further assess his current state. Then, our eyes locked. My father's eyes had opened, and he was locked into me. I just blurted out, "Hi Daddy, it's me, Karma." I could feel Alonzo's grip around my shoulder get a little tighter, letting me know that he had me.

In an effort to assemble his ego, my father mustered up enough strength to say in an earnest tone, "I know a child of mine when I see them."

I did not know how to respond to that. I had never seen this man in my adult life. But there was a part of me that was so happy that my father referred to me as his child.

"As you can see, I don't have much time left. I wanted to see you to tell you that I'm sorry and I wish I could have done things right when I was well. But I wanted to say I'm sorry before I have to say goodbye for good," my father said as his bottom lip was curled and quivering while a single tear ran down his dry brown face.

At that moment, I went back to being a child. My childhood wish had come true, my dad wanted me. He really wanted me. A warmth overcame me. But soon, the adult me replaced the feeling of warmth with the feeling of anger. I was so happy to hear my father say that he was sorry, but at the same time, I was angry that he had not done it sooner. I knew that we did not have time to really connect due to his illness. Further, I feared that my visitation with my father would likely open wounds within me that would leave permanent scars. I started to wonder if I was making a mistake.

"Daddy, you're up," I heard a voice say.

"Hey Jennifer, I have someone I want you to meet. This is your sister Karma," my father, Eric, said.

Jennifer looked at me and started hugging me tightly. I was in shock. I hugged Jennifer back as I tried to absorb everything happening to me. After Jennifer's embrace, she looked at me and said, "You are so beautiful. I have seen you on social media, and you are even more beautiful in person."

I was in shock that she had even looked for me on social media. The last time I tried looking for Jennifer on social media, I did not see anything. Debra would post things with Jennifer in it every now and then, and that was all I saw of my little sister. As I looked at her, I instantly saw so many similarities between us. She had my brown-colored almond-shaped eyes; my mocha-colored complexion, and her hair was the same texture as mine when it was in its natural state.

Looking at Jennifer made me take a closer look at my father lying on his deathbed. Jennifer and I both had our father's eyes and complexion. I could tell that the little hair that our father had left was the same texture as me and Jennifer's. The two to three-inch soft and loose grey curls were sparsely spread across my father's balding and aging head.

"I am so happy to see you; the last time I saw you, you were so little; you grew into a beautiful young lady," I said.

"I hope that you two can become close and be there for each other," my father said in a tone that was infused with pain and weakness.

Meanwhile, my cousin Debra was sobbing in the corner of the hospital room. I think that Debra longed for the day that my father could have his two daughters together in the same place surrounded by love. But even Debra knew that this would be the first and last time that this would occur.

When I left the hospital that day, all of the questions that I had for my father began to flood my brain, and all of the things that I wanted to say to my father came to my mind. The next day, Alonzo took me back to the hospital to see my father, but he would not wake up for the entire three hours that I sat in his room. I even tried to nudge him a bit, and nothing. I never got the chance to ask my father the questions that I had or tell him how his absence impacted my life. I did not think that I could ever really forgive my father. When his life ended, so did the possibility of me getting the answers and closure that I thought I needed.

The phrase, "Where's the good in goodbye?" often comes to mind when I reflect on the finality of a moment – especially the finality of life. Although I did not have a relationship with my father, at the end of the day, he was still my father. A day after my last visit with my father at the hospital, he died. On my father's passing day, my sister Jennifer invited me to our father and his wife Linda's house. When I arrived at the house, it was somber. Jennifer greeted me right away and began introducing me to members of the family. My heart really hurt for my little sister Jennifer. It was interesting to see the anguish that she was experiencing and how she and I had experienced our father totally differently. As Jennifer was introducing me to family members, I asked about my paternal grandfather. I knew that my paternal grandmother had died years prior, but I found out that my paternal grandfather had died just a month earlier. This saddened me because I had no idea, Debra didn't even tell me about this. I guess I was not important enough to tell. Jennifer introduced me to her mother, Linda.

"Ma, this is Karma," Jennifer said. Linda looked disheveled and extremely sad. There were bags under her red eyes, I could tell that she had been crying. Linda's hair was cut into an unkept pixy haircut. Her thin, straight strands of hair held curls that were falling, and her edges were coarse due to sweating. When Linda looked at me, it seemed as if her mood went from despair to anger. There was tension generated from the energy that Linda was giving me. Jennifer also seemed a little uneasy while introducing us.

"Give me a minute; let me check on my guests," Linda said, walking away.

"I am so sorry, Karma; my mother is really taking all of this hard," Jennifer explained.

"It's okay, I understand."

Alonzo and I spent most of our time at the house, sitting side by side. I eventually got up to get something to drink. This is when Linda approached me.

"May I speak to you for a moment?" Linda asked.

"Sure."

Linda brought me into what appeared to be a guest room in the house and closed the door.

"I need to talk to you and make a few things clear. Jennifer has always known about you because of Eric's cousin Debra, and that was against my wishes. I would appreciate it if you would just go and never come back. Jennifer does not need you in her life. She has gone through enough and does not need anyone manipulating her or playing with her emotions. And don't expect to get anything from Eric; he left you nothing. Don't get any warm and fuzzy feelings because Eric was at the end of his life and not in his right mind when he requested to see you. He never considered you his child. I am not trying to hurt your feelings, but I am trying to spare your feelings in the long run. Move on, little girl, and stay away from Jennifer!"

Linda's words hurt my heart. I stormed out of that room in tears and began walking straight to the front door to leave. Jennifer grabbed me by the arm.

"Are you okay?" Jennifer asked.

I could not formulate my thoughts, let alone words; I just continued to walk. Alonzo ran after me. When I got outside to the porch, Alonzo just grabbed me, and I sobbed in Alonzo's arms like a child. I let everything out right then. I had no idea I had so much pain pent up inside of me. I cried because of the loss of my father. I cried because I could not resolve things with my dad. Most of all, I cried because just when I thought I would at least be accepted by my father's side of the family, I was rejected again. I was being ostracized for my existence. This felt worse than the time that Debra brought me to my paternal grandparents' house, and my father stopped by and shamed them for having me there.

"What happened? Was it my mother?" Jennifer asked.

"I just have to leave," I replied.

"Please don't leave Karma, please don't leave," Jennifer said with hurt in her voice and tears in her eyes.

"I'm sorry, Jennifer, but I have to go."

Alonzo and I left. I never made it to my father's funeral. I just decided to try to move forward and not allow Linda's words to hurt me. Damaged people will try to damage you, and I was determined not to carry Linda's burden by allowing Linda's pain to become my pain. I granted Linda's wishes and did not return any of Jennifer's calls or messages when I returned to LA.

After my traumatic trip to Buffalo, I was ready to get back to work. While I was out of work, Laura Pennington had been co-hosting Our Perspective. Laura Pennington impressed the producers so much that there were rumors circulating that she would get a permanent hosting role on the show. Laura was only supposed to co-host the show for a week while Ana Alvarez, the Afro-Latina host, negotiated her contract. Ana Alvarez refused to show up to work until all the kinks in her proposed contract were ironed out. The ratings were higher in the absence of Ana Alvarez, and Laura had undeniable chemistry with the other hosts. Laura Pennington was so good on the show that Ana Alvarez's contract was not renewed. This really sucked for me. I tried to stay out of Laura's way, and Laura acted as if I did not exist, which was fine with me; I was no stranger to feeling invisible to others.

One day I reported to work as normal, and Diana DeCosta wanted to speak with me privately immediately. I was scared out of my mind. She did not seem like her normal self. I was wondering if I was about to see the bitch side of Diana DeCosta that I had been warned about. Diana got me into her little apartment/dressing room and immediately slammed the door.

"Sit, my dear," she said.

"Is everything okay?" I asked.

"I don't know, you tell me, my dear. What the hell is going on between you and Laura Pennington?"

"What do you mean?"

"Don't play with me. Answer my question, what the hell is going on with you and Laura Pennington? I need to trust you, my dear. If you are not honest with me, I can never trust you. You need to let me know why Laura wants you out of this building, never to return."

I took a deep breath, contemplating what I should say and what I should not say. I was trying to figure out if I should call Alonzo for legal counsel. I did not know what to do. Then, my spirit told me to do what was in my heart. "Diana, what I am about to tell you cannot be shared with anyone because there would be legal ramifications. If you reveal anything, I'll be in a situation where I could lose everything." Diana began to look concerned and empathetic. "What I am about to tell you is the truth." Tears began to fall from my eyes. "Over two years ago, I was dating a guy. He told me that he was single. After I found out that he was married and broke the relationship off, I found out that I was pregnant with my daughter Trinity. Laura and her husband Deshaun had me sign a Non-Disclosure Agreement where I am not to share with anyone that Laura's husband is the father of my child. In exchange for signing the agreement, I was compensated financially. This is the money that I use to care for my child. This is why I am begging you never to tell anyone about this."

"Wow, it's okay, sweetheart, but it does not surprise me at all. Laura's father is running for president, and he is a billionaire; the family had to appear to be perfect."

"So does this mean that I am going to lose my job?"

"No, my dear, Laura Pennington is negotiating her contract, and I found it strange that as a part of her negotiations, she requested that you not work for me or for Our Perspective. What Laura does not understand is that I'm the HBIC around here and that I call the shots." By the way, HBIC stands for Head Bitch in Charge. I was happy that Diana had my back like this.

Planning a wedding and dealing with Laura Pennington's demand for me to be banned from my job was a lot. I was determined to remain positive and continue to look forward to being a wife and having a family with Alonzo. Alonzo had already told me that he was going to adopt Trinity, which warmed my entire soul.

Alonzo proved time and time again that he was the man that I needed. He took care of me, and he took care of Trinity. His motivation to provide for us was evident in the way in which he searched for homes. If the school district was not up to par, no matter how perfect the home was or how perfect the price was, Alonzo wouldn't even consider it. It was not long before Alonzo found the perfect home with a pool in Bel Air. It was a beautiful modern white house with black trim. The house even had a pool house just like in a popular sitcom I watched while growing up. This house was a far cry from the homes we lived in in the past. This house was similar to the homes that Aiko and I robbed, so when we purchased the home, I made sure that we had the best alarm and surveillance system money could buy. Once we moved into the house and I still had not found a venue for our wedding, it became clear we could have the wedding at our home. In my mind, I thought that this would be the perfect time to show off my home and save money. The home had a massive yard that would be perfect for a wedding.

One day, while at work, a special guest was on Our Perspective. His name was Roman Hart. Roman Hart was the creator and executive producer of one of the most popular reality show franchises on television. I loved reality television and was a huge fan of Roman Hart. I knew that I needed to stay under the radar because Laura Pennington was gunning for me. Further, she was still negotiating her contract with the show, and I was hoping that she would just forget about me. Ultimately, I really wanted to at least say hi to Roman Hart, even if it got me in a little trouble.

Tensions were high the day that Roman Hart showed up to the studio. Diana was particularly nervous, and I did not understand why. She was a Hollywood actress, for heaven's sake. I even had to give Diana her anxiety medicine that day to calm her nerves. It was weird because I had never seen her like this before. Right before Diana was supposed to get ready to hit the stage with her co-hosts, she said in a frantic tone, "My reading glasses, my reading glasses, I think I left them in the car. Karma, please get them." Without any question, I started to dart out of the room and towards the parking lot. Suddenly, a shining diamond pendant in the shape of a crown caught my eye. I bent down to pick up the pendant. When I looked up, I saw Laura Pennington walking in my direction with her head down, looking at her phone while speaking to her assistant. In a frenzy, I opened the first door I saw and slipped into the room before Laura could actually see me. As I turned around with the diamond pendant hanging from my hand, I looked into the eyes of the one and only Roman Hart, who was buttoning up his shirt. I had mistakenly walked right into Roman Hart's green room. There were three other people in the room who just looked at me in shock. Stunned, I just stood there.

"Oh shit, you found it; thank you so much," Roman Hart said as he took the diamond pendant dangling from my hand. "I literally just noticed it was missing," Roman Hart continued.

"Roman Hart, I am your biggest fan, I know you probably hear that a lot. But I really just admire your fearlessness and your ambition; I just want to tell you that you are amazing," I said.

Roman Hart lit up. "You like my work, huh?"

"Oh yes, absolutely."

"Well, I was just speaking with my team about my next move; as a fan, what is something that you would like to see on television in the reality TV space that you haven't seen?"

I just blurted out, "You should do a reality show of this show. All kinds of crazy shit happens behind the scenes of a daytime talk show."

The room was blaring in silence. Roman Hart's face was expressionless. "That's fucking crazy," Roman Hart replied.

I could literally feel my body overheating from embarrassment. I thought, how could I come up with such a stupid idea?

"That's so fucking crazy that it's genius. What is your name?"

"Karma Robinson."

"Karma, that's an interesting name. How do you envision this show?"

"Well, I see you following the cast throughout their day-to-day, including filming in their homes. I see filming in the prep room prior to each show. I can even see filming during the cast's discussions, re-capping conversations with guests.

"I like it!"

"Excuse me, Mr. Roman Hart, I have to get something for my boss, but it was truly a pleasure speaking with you."

I was so excited as I bolted towards Diana's car to get her reading glasses. By the time I got back into the building, the show had started, and Diana's glasses were in my hand.

I waited patiently for the commercial break so that I could give Diana her glasses. As soon as the break started, I ran to the stage with Diana's glasses. Diana was pissed.

"What the hell took you so long? Did you manufacture the goddamn glasses yourself," Diana whispered.

"I am so sorry. I ran into Roman Hart, and we began talking for a few seconds."

"So, do you work for Roman Hart, or do you work for me? Go, we'll address this after the show," Diana whispered.

I looked up, and Laura Pennington was staring in me and Diana's direction with a slight smile on her face. I thought that I had surely fucked up this time, but how many opportunities would I have to speak with Roman Hart and pitch him an idea.

I nervously waited for the show to end. Diana entered the dressing room/small apartment as I sat on the sofa. Diana just looked at me and shook her head. Diana sat next to me and said, "Karma, I'm going to have to let you go."

"Why, I know it took me a while to get your glasses, and I will never let it happen again," I pleaded.

"No, Karma, it's not just that. Laura Pennington has finalized her contract for Our Perspective, and it has been agreed that you can no longer work for me. Your salary comes from the show, not from me directly, so we have to let you go."

"How can the show put something like that in Laura's contract? My fiancé is a lawyer, and we will sue."

"I don't think they were stupid enough to put this in her contract, and I am not even supposed to be telling you this. I just feel that we have built a great rapport, and it was only right for me to tell you the truth. Before you leave, I just want to let you know that I fought for you; I fought hard. And I have not and will never tell anyone about Laura's husband being the father of your child. I will take that to the grave. You just make sure that you take care of that baby of yours."

I was devastated. I started to feel powerless, and that Laura Pennington had more control over my life than I did.

Coming home to tell Alonzo that I had lost my job after we had just purchased our dream home was one of the hardest things that I have ever had to do. Plus, we were planning a wedding. I had most of Trinity's money in a trust fund since I knew that I was stable and could take care of all of my responsibilities without spending Trinity's money on anyone except for Trinity.

"Hey baby, how was your day?" I asked when Alonzo walked through the door.

"It was actually one of the best days. It's days like this that reassure me that law is my passion. How about your day?"

"I got let go today!" I blurted out.

"What?" Alonzo yelled out.

I just burst into tears, and Alonzo immediately grabbed and consoled me. I was trying to tell him what happened, but the sounds of me hyperventilating between each word that spilled from my mouth made it difficult for Alonzo to comprehend what I was trying to tell him.

"Don't worry about it; it's all going to be alright. I promise it's going to be alright," Alonzo said. Once I was finally able to compose myself and tell Alonzo everything, he said, "Would you like to go the legal route and sue, or do you want to search for another job?"

"Well, something amazing happened at work today. I met Roman Hart, and he asked me for a show idea. I suggested a reality show based around Our Perspective, and he absolutely loved it."

Alonzo just stood there in deep thought and said, "Message him on social media, tell him what happened to you today. If he liked your idea as much as you say he did, he may have something for you."

"Yes, this is a great idea; what do I have to lose?" I said.

"Remember, Karma, you have nothing to lose. We are still going to get married, and we are still in a great place financially, so don't worry about money." Alonzo always had a way of easing my fears.

I reached out to Roman Hart via social media, gave him my number, and waited patiently. I waited for about two weeks and never received a response. I decided to move on and start applying for jobs. But I absolutely loved my job at Our Perspective and was so bitter and angry about my unfair removal from the show. I yearned for Laura Pennington to suffer for what she did to me. I anonymously contacted news reporters and paparazzi, telling them that Laura Pennington's husband was unfaithful and had a child out of wedlock. Nothing seemed to be catching any steam. I finally was able to get a job for another healthcare company as an Advice Nurse working from home. I was so depressed. Then, one day, I received a call.

"Hello, I would like to speak to Karma?" a voice that I did not recognize said.

"This is Karma."

"Well, hello, this is Roman Hart; how are you?"

"Oh, my goodness, I am great, Roman Hart. How are you?"

"I'm fine; I would like to meet with you at my office. Are you available in about two hours?"

"Of course I am," I replied.

Roman Hart had provided me with an address for me to meet him. After I hung up with Roman Hart, I was excited and nervous. I had literally just started my new job; I had only been working the job for about one week, and I was already leaving early, but I sincerely felt as though I did not have a choice. I said to myself, "I have to follow my dreams," I was going to take this meeting, and whatever happened with my new job, was just going to have to happen.

The drive to meet Roman Hart was nerve-wracking. I was kicking myself because I never asked Roman Hart what we were meeting about, which resulted in me not feeling prepared for the meeting. I felt that this meeting could be life-changing.

Once I arrived at the office building, I told the security at the front desk that I was there to see Roman Hart, and within minutes, someone came to greet me. I was taken to a floor of the building that was so pristine; every morsel of the space sparkled as if there was a cleaner that shined everything hour after hour. There were awards in glass cases and pictures of all of the reality franchises that Roman Hart had created. I was led into a conference room where Roman Hart sat at the head of the conference room table, and four other people were in the room. Roman Hart greeted me with a hug and introduced me to everyone who was around the table. I was so nervous that I did not hear all of the introductions. All I heard was something about them being producers. Roman Hart proceeded to say, "Thank you so much for reaching out to me. I had my people reach out to Our Perspective to get your contact information the day after I was a guest on the show. No one seemed to know who you were. Fast forward to yesterday, I was speaking with a friend about a new show that I would be starting, which was your idea. I was telling my friend that I wish that I could find you so that you could get the credit that you deserve for giving me such a great idea. Then as I was casually looking through all of my messages on social media, I saw yours. I never forgot you or your name. Karma! I know how to listen to God when he speaks to me. I felt that your message was a sign. So, explain to me why you no longer work for Our Perspective?"

"Laura Pennington did not want me there. We have a history that I can't talk about because I signed an NDA (Non-Disclosure Agreement)."

"Juicy, is there a way that you can disclose the information in the NDA without implicating yourself? Is there any way that someone else can reveal what is hidden in the NDA?" Roman Hart asked.

"I have to talk to my lawyer about that."

"Well, Karma, I have good news. My production company will be working with the network to do a reality show with the entire cast of Our Perspective. I want to accredit you with co-creator and executive producer titles. Do you have any experience producing?"

"No, I don't have any experience, but I can't work for Our Perspective because of Laura Pennington."

"No, sweetheart, you won't be working for Our Perspective; you will be working for "The Real Perspective," which will be the name of the reality show under my production company. The executive producer job will be a one-year trial; since you don't have any experience in this space, I am confident that you will be fine. But I need you to discreetly bring Laura Pennington's secrets to life. Laura has agreed to allow the cameras into her house. We can really make some reality TV show magic."

I agreed, and Roman Hart told me that he would be sending me a contract to sign electronically. I felt vindicated. I felt like I was getting my power back from Laura Pennington.

The first day of production was exciting. I could not wait for those bitches to see me. There was a pre-production meeting with the cast so that they were introduced to everyone who would be working on the new reality show, The Real Perspective, not to be mistaken with the daytime talk show that the ladies already worked on, Our Perspective. I was already sitting at the conference room table when the first person from the cast walked in. I could not have planned it better; Laura Pennington was the first cast member to walk into the room. She looked at me as if she had just seen a ghost. Then I saw Diana DeCosta and Hazy walk in behind her.

Diana walked over to me and gave me the biggest hug, "How are you? What are you doing here?" Diana asked.

Before I could respond, Wendy Knight said, "Damn, this cat has nine lives, Karma; I thought you got canned, well welcome back."

"Karma is the co-creator and one of the executive producers for this show, and I don't want to hear about anyone not wanting to work with her; she is here to stay, and all of you have signed your contracts agreeing to work with the staff and production for this show, so I hope that this is clear," Roman Hart stated.

Laura Pennington sat back in her chair with her arms crossed, I could literally feel her anger as she tried to terrorize me with her facial expressions of fury.

"Y'all fucked up for that," Hazy said as she laughed. "What is going on between you two?" Hazy asked while looking back and forth between me and Laura Pennington.

"I have no issues, I am only here to do my job," I replied.

Laura Pennington continued to sit silently. I loved how the tables had turned.

After about a month on the job, I hired a private investigator to determine what Deshaun Pennington, the father of Trinity and husband of Laura Pennington, had been up to. What I have learned is that people are who they are, and I was willing to predict that Deshaun's trifling ass was up to no good. He was by far the most deceiving and dishonest person I had ever met in my life. I knew that when Roman Hart told me that my executive producer job would be a one-year trial, he was letting me know that it was up to me to bring the best out of this show. Diana

DeCosta was the only person outside of my mother, Grace, and Alonzo who knew that Laura Pennington and her husband paid me off never to reveal that Deshaun was the father of my child. I certainly did not want that to come out, but I definitely wanted something salacious about Deshaun to be revealed during the show. Roman Hart wanted me to dig up some dirt. I was determined to bring out my proverbial shovel and do some deep digging.

For the most part, I stayed out of Laura Pennington's way as an executive producer. I must admit, I spent more time with the cast than required. My job depended on the success of the show, and I was going to be as involved as necessary so that the show would be an absolute success. I spent a lot of time with Diana and Hazy. Hazy was interesting as hell. She was dating a football player named Jordan Williams, who she had suspected was cheating on her; she drank hard and partied even harder. She was amazing for reality TV. She confided a lot with Diana DeCosta because Diana was like a mother figure to Hazy. Diana always provided Hazy with sound advice. I was just keeping my fingers crossed that something would come through on Deshaun because Laura Pennington was boring as hell on the show. She and Deshaun put on this act of being the perfect family. They did not bring any excitement to the show. They were so stale and so fake. Their storyline was focused on Laura's father, ex-NBA player turned billionaire Julius Nash, running for president of the United States, and then when her father dropped out of the race due to a lack of support, Laura's storyline was even more dull. I really needed some material on Deshaun, and I needed it quickly. Wendy Knight was funny as hell. Her quick wit and humorous nature brought the fun out of the other cast members.

While working a hectic schedule for The Real Perspective, my wedding day was approaching fast, and Grace was right by my side. Since my engagement/birthday party in St. Thomas, I had been back in contact with Grace. We were working on rebuilding trust, so I asked Grace to be my matron of honor. Grace and I had gone through a lot together, but we were like sisters, so it was only natural for us to come together for such a momentous occasion in my life. She told me that she and Dane were working on a baby. I was happy for Grace. I still did not trust Dane, but he was not my man so if Grace was good, I was good.

Soon, I discovered that everything is all good until it isn't. One day, Grace revealed to me that she and Dane recently had a threesome. Grace told me that she did not like it at all, but Dane enjoyed it. Grace's existence seemed to be centered around making Dane happy. I asked Grace if the threesome was with a man or a woman, and to my surprise, she said a woman. I was in full shock. I asked Grace how they selected the woman for the threesome. Grace said that they paid a woman and did not provide details about how they selected her or where they got her from. Grace stated that they brought the woman home one night; Grace said that she tried to partake, but the chemistry was not there. Before she knew it, she said this woman was straddling Dane, and it was as if Grace wasn't even in the room. Grace said, "The way that Dane looked at her, touched her, and how he was engrossed in her entire presence was nothing like anything I have experienced with him. I felt more like a spectator than a participant."

"Do you think that Dane and this woman had been together before the threesome?" I asked.

"I don't know; in fact, I don't know what to think anymore."

I felt so sorry for my friend. Here she is helping me plan my wedding while her heart was aching due to her inattentive and insulting husband. I did not give Grace any advice at this moment, and I was not judgmental. I just listened and told Grace that I would be there for her. I was trying to be the friend that Grace has always been to me.

Life always seems to throw you curve balls. One night, I was preparing for bed when I got a call.

"Hello, Karma?"

"Yes," I replied curiously.

"This is Linda, your father's wife. Do you have a moment to speak with me?"

I was not excited about hearing from Linda. Our last encounter left me feeling broken and devastated.

"What's going on?" I replied.

"I know that I am probably the last person that you want to hear from, but your sister Jennifer is going through a lot. Of course, she lost her father, but I think that she was expecting to gain a new relationship with you, and when that didn't happen, it sent her into a downward spiral and deep depression. She is so depressed that she won't even talk to me, her own mother."

"So, what do you want me to do about that, Linda?"

"I am first asking you to forgive me for all of the ugly things that I said to you after your father died. I was grieving and not thinking straight. I just ask that you reach out to Jennifer, talk to her, and try to get to know her. Maybe you both will realize that you are better off being distant sisters, or perhaps you both will build a wonderful relationship. Either way, I am asking that you reach out to her and see what happens."

"I'll think about it," I said. I had a new job and was planning a wedding. I did not know if I had the time or mental capacity to forge a new relationship with my sister.

My mother always gave me the best advice. I told her about Linda requesting that I reach out to Jennifer, and my mother said, "Extend her the same grace that you would want someone to extend you." My mother had really evolved since I was a child. I instantly started thinking about my friend Grace and how I had not been the best when it came to her, and Grace had forgiven me time and time again. My mother asked me to think about Trinity; if Trinity needed someone's help, I would want that person to help Trinity in every way possible. My mother told me that Linda is a desperate mother, taking desperate measures to help her only child. This was all that I needed to push me to reach out to Jennifer.

For some reason, I was tense about reaching out to Jennifer. Jennifer was such a sweet girl, and I knew that a part of me was jealous of her because our father seemed to love her so much, and he didn't even acknowledge me until he was on his deathbed. Logically, I knew that I had no reason to be upset or bitter towards her and I did not want to make her a casualty of my broken heart. I decided to reach out to Jennifer with a clear mind and an open heart.

After pacing back and forth in my bedroom for a couple of minutes, I called Jennifer and there was an answer on the first ring.

"Hello, Jennifer."

"Karma, I can't believe you're calling me."

"Yeah, I wanted to reach out to see how you were doing."

"First, I just want to apologize for my mother's behavior; I figured that you would never want to talk to me again after your interaction with her."

"I just needed some time that's all. I wanted to reach out, to invite you to my wedding. It will be at my house."

"I would be honored to come to your wedding. I haven't been to a wedding since I was about twelve years old, and I have never been to California."

Without completely thinking I blurted out, "Maybe you can come to California a week or so before my wedding so we can hang out. I can show you around."

"Wow, I would love that, but I have been tight on money."

"Don't worry about it, I can purchase your airline ticket, and you can stay with me."

"Oh really, I'm so excited; you have no idea what this means to me."

The conversation with Jennifer really made me feel good. I was proud of myself for completely opening up my heart to Jennifer, and my soul told me that I could have a great relationship with her.

I have learned that the energy you release is the same energy that you receive. It's just that simple. I worried about what type of energy I would attract by hiring a private investigator to see if Deshaun was cheating so that it could spice up Laura Pennington's storyline. I had nearly become obsessed with the success of the show. Further, it was very important that Laura Pennington paid the consequences for trying to destroy me. After about two weeks, the private investigator said that he was unable to find anything on Deshaun. The private investigator said that Deshaun was squeaky clean and recommended that I close out the case. I told the private investigator to look harder and continue his investigation. I figured that if the private investigator was doing his job right, he would at least figure out that I was the mother of Deshaun's child. I told the private investigator to continue for at least two more weeks, and he agreed.

Diana DeCosta had tons of personality; she was a gorgeous older woman but did not have the best sense of fashion. One day, Diana was looking at social media and was down because of the comments that people were making about the way that she dressed.

"Karma, do you think that my sense of style is as bad as social media makes it out to be?"

"No, but I do think that you could spruce things up a bit."

"I have had the same stylist for years, and she has been so preoccupied with her new family. I think that she has not had the time to keep up with the latest fashions. Do you know any stylists?"

The only person that I could think of was Terry Tea. I had Terry Tea's number but had not spoken to him since me and Alonzo's double date with Grace and Dane, where Terry Tea made all of those subliminal oral sex references towards Dane. Although Terry Tea was messy, he was an exceptional stylist who would bring some spice to the show. Before I could completely think out this idea, I said, "I know one of the best celebrity stylists; his name is Terry Tea." I instantly thought, "Fuck, I should not have done this." If Grace watches the show and sees Terry Tea, she may think that I have absolutely no loyalty.

"Great, let's call this Terry Tea right now. I am in desperate need, my dear."

I called Terry Tea and had him on speakerphone. "Hey, Terry Tea, this is Karma."

"Well, hello, stranger," he replied.

I rushed to get straight to the point. "Terry Tea, I am the executive producer on a reality show, and Diana DeCosta needs a celebrity stylist. It will also offer an opportunity for you to possibly become a friend on the show."

There were a few moments of silence, "Hell yes, tell me when to start and where to start, honey," Terry Tea said.

It was done. I knew that Terry Tea would provide the spice that the show needed. I knew that I would keep my job after Terry Tea started on the show, but I was not sure if I would keep my friend Grace.

The reality show was up and running. Each day of filming got better and better. One day, I received a call from the private investigator. He wanted to meet with me. I met him outside of a mall. He hopped into my car. "I've uncovered some things that I thought that you would be interested in." The private investigator handed me a large envelope full of photos. These photos showed Deshaun going into a woman's house, him holding hands with a woman, and him kissing on a woman. I looked closely at the pictures and realized that the pictures were of someone that I knew. I had to gasp for air. The pictures were of Ana Alvarez. Ana Alvarez, who had her co-host job on Our Perspective taken by Laura Pennington. I was floored. I had no idea how Ana Alvarez and Deshaun would have hooked up in the first place. Further, I was wondering what lie he told Ana Alvarez to get her to have any interest in him at all. I was shocked by this news, and I was elated at the same time. I almost felt guilty about how excited I was.

I had to be really strategic about how I was going to ensure that the pictures were exposed during taping. I had to make sure that no one suspected that I had anything to do with it. I came up with a brilliant idea that I told no one about, not even producers. I knew that Hazy and Laura were not the best of friends. Laura often criticized Hazy for the type of music she performed and about her lifestyle. Laura always looked down on Hazy, whether it was live on air during a taping of Our Perspective or during the taping of the reality show The Real Perspective. I made sure that the pictures were mailed to Hazy anonymously. It was a beautiful day when Hazy came to me and another producer with the pictures.

"Hey y'all, I got these pictures in the mail of Laura's husband Deshaun frolicking around with Ana Alvarez," Hazy said.

"Well, this is reality television, and it is your duty to make her aware of this. At the end of the day, Laura needs to know," I said.

"Well, I'm going to talk to Diana first to see what she thinks," Hazy replied.

"That's a great idea; go to Diana's house tonight so that you two can talk about it," the other producer said.

Hazy seemed conflicted. "Listen Hazy, you have nothing to feel bad about; this has nothing to do with you. You are doing nothing wrong. Deshaun is wrong. Providing Laura with this information isn't bad, but withholding this information from her would be awful. Trust me, if this show does not expose this, something or someone else will," I said.

"You are right," Hazy responded.

I knew that Diana DeCosta knew about Deshaun and me having a child together; she was the only person I worked with who knew about this. At first, I worried that Diana might reveal my secret, but she assured me that she would never tell anyone. One thing about Diana DeCosta was that she was one of the most loyal people I have ever met. I knew that my secret was safe with her. Still, I relied on Hazy to reveal Deshaun, and I was counting on Diana to refrain from interfering with that.

Hazy had a way of adding sauce to everything. She had a spunk about her. Hazy was about 5 foot 4 inches tall; she wore a short haircut. Oftentimes, Hazy would allow her short loose jet-black wavy hair to descend upon the side of her face with a part along the right side of her head. She had a petite frame. Hazy's eyes were brown, and her complexion was that of a beautiful bronze. Hazy was stunning but had the propensity of being entitled and sometimes flat-out rude. This is why Hazy was the perfect person to deliver the message to Laura that Deshaun was cheating.

Hazy and Laura tolerated each other, and the reality show made them spend more time with each other than they normally would. Laura was very judgmental of Hazy. Laura would tell Hazy that she needed a man like Deshaun, who is going to love her and care for her. What a hypocrite, I would think. Hazy would listen to Laura while rolling her eyes from time to time. Sometimes, Hazy would make smug remarks during her and Laura's conversations. But I could tell that Hazy receiving those pictures of Deshaun cheating made her feel that Laura was no better than her.

Hazy arrived at Diana's house dressed like a private investigator. She was wearing black sunglasses, black gloves, a short black trench coat, and black high heels with a large envelope in her hands that concealed the pictures of Deshaun and Ana Alvarez together.

"How much do you like tea? Because I have a tea kettle full that is whistling and piping hot, I even have some honey to stir in it named Ana Alvarez?" Hazy said as soon as Diana opened her front door. Hazy told Diana about how she received pictures of Deshaun and Ana Alvarez anonymously in the mail. Then Hazy revealed the pictures to Diana. Diana had to gasp for air.

"Darling, that tea is scorching hot; I think you burned me with it," Diana said.

Then, at the perfect time, Laura texted Hazy and said, "Hey girl, I am reaching out because I would like to invite you and Jordan out to dinner. I think that it would be a good opportunity for Jordan to bond with Deshaun. Deshaun is the perfect example of what a committed man looks like, and Jordan needs an example like Deshaun in his life."

Earlier that day, another producer convinced Laura that she and Deshaun needed to mentor Hazy and her boyfriend Jordan. This was the perfect setup. Hazy quickly responded and agreed to meet Laura and Deshaun. Diana told Hazy that she needed to tell Laura what was going on with her husband, Deshaun, and Ana Alvarez. Diana told Hazy, "No woman wants to be the last to know about something like this. You would be doing her a disservice if you didn't tell her. Being unaware of an issue doesn't eliminate the issue. Tell Laura what is going on." I was pleased to see that Diana was talking some logic into Hazy so that she would not feel guilty.

The day that Hazy and Jordan were scheduled to have dinner with Laura and Deshaun was a big day for production. The cat was going to be let out of the bag. The restaurant was perfect. First, Hazy and

Jordan arrived and were seated as they waited for Laura and Deshaun. After about 20 minutes of Hazy and Jordan waiting, Laura arrived and greeted them.

"Where is Deshaun?" Hazy asked.

"Well, Deshaun's mother was just admitted into the hospital. She'll be fine, but he needed to be with her."

"Well, I wish we knew that because we could have rescheduled," Hazy stated.

Then Laura took a deep breath and said, "I thought it was important for me to show up because I really want to be a mentor to you, Hazy. Jordan, you will meet Deshaun, but I think that he could be a good mentor for you. Hazy, you and Jordan have such a volatile relationship, and I am not trying to overstep my bounds, but infidelity is very unhealthy for any relationship."

"What about infidelity in your relationship? Or let me rephrase that, has there been infidelity in your relationship?" Hazy asked Laura.

Laura had a look of shock on her face, her eyes widened, and her mouth was slightly open. "Deshaun and I have had our share of issues, but we have moved past that, and because we have had our share of issues, we are stronger than we have ever been."

Hazy rolled her eyes and said, "How do you define strong? What I have learned is that a house can be built super strong, but if an even stronger tornado twirls into the house, the house will be destroyed. The house was never weak; it's just that the tornado was stronger."

"What I have learned is that no matter the strength and destruction of the tornado, you can always rebuild, and sometimes what you rebuild is better than what you had before," Laura replied.

Hazy said in a low voice, "Well bitch, get your work boots, lumber, and power tools ready."

"What?" Laura asked.

"Oh, nothing. But what if you keep rebuilding, and tornadoes come and destroy what has been built every couple of years or so? When do you pack up and re-build elsewhere?"

Laura was in deep thought and then said, "Well, if you love the location of the house enough, you just keep rebuilding."

"I guess we are similar, I have chosen to rebuild, but I want you to stop judging me for it. Jordan and I have some other engagements. We will meet up again when Deshaun is available."

Jordan was completely confused; he had no idea what was going on. At this point, Hazy had not told Jordan about the pictures because she wanted his authentic reaction to be shown on television. Hazy left the dinner without revealing the pictures to Laura. Hazy told production that she really wanted Deshaun to be there. As the executive producer, I saw a great opportunity. I figured this saga could drag on for at least two episodes of the reality show. I knew that this would be riveting television.

Laura was a very ambitious woman. She had multiple businesses, from a clothing boutique to a coffee shop and a youth mentorship program that focused on teaching children the art of public speaking. Laura's newest venture was a book that focused on creating and maintaining a healthy marriage. Laura had planned a huge party to celebrate the release of her new book. Production insisted that Hazy reveal the pictures at the party; however, Hazy refused. Hazy wanted to reveal the pictures at the rescheduled dinner with her, Laura, Deshaun, and Jordan. I had contemplated getting Diana to reveal the pictures, but she just said, "Darling, this ain't my fish to fry." I was under more pressure from Roman Hart to do what I needed to do to get someone on the cast to reveal the pictures to Laura. I knew that Laura's children, parents, and closest friends would be at this book release celebration. The more I thought about it, the more I realized that it would not be a good idea to reveal the pictures at this event. I may have been ambitious, but I wasn't heartless.

Laura's book release party was just what I had imagined it to be; the ambiance was breathtaking, and the guests included the elite from film, television, and sports. I was really focused on production. I needed the cast to bring out their best during this event. Laura made a speech about her relationship and how she and Deshaun had to overcome many obstacles to get to the place that they are in today. Laura continued to vow that her book would be able to assist anyone in a relationship, whether it's a married couple, a couple that is dating, or a couple that is engaged. Everyone at the party seemed so happy and so proud of Laura.

Eventually, Ana Alvarez showed up at the event looking absolutely stunning. Hazy had invited Ana Alvarez as her plus-one when she was contemplating revealing the pictures at the event. The producers quickly ushered Ana Alvarez over to the cast of the reality show. The cast had their own section that they were sitting in. I looked at Hazy, and she looked extremely frustrated. I did not know if it was because she and Jordan were going through issues, and that was the reason why he did not attend the event. Eventually, Laura and Deshaun made their way to the table where the cast was. Deshaun's arm was wrapped around Laura's shoulder so tightly.

"Hey ladies, I hope you are enjoying yourselves," Laura said.

All of the ladies said, "Yes."

"Where is Jordan?" Deshaun asked Hazy.

It was like Deshaun flicked a switch in Hazy's soul; she instantly looked angry. Hazy had been drinking pretty heavily that night. "He's probably out doing what no good men do. You know what I'm talking about, don't you, Deshaun?" Hazy said angrily.

"Hey, it's not my fault that Jordan's not here," Deshaun responded.

"You have a lot of misdirected anger, Hazy; instead of getting mad at my man, go get yourself a new man. In all seriousness, you can have a happy and healthy relationship like Deshaun and I," Laura said. Laura had been trying to bring out more of her personality recently because production had told her that she was not very entertaining. Being so unnecessarily sassy was out of the norm for Laura, which further ignited a raging fire in Hazy.

"Oh really, a happy and healthy relationship like this," Hazy said as she opened the envelope full of pictures of Ana Alvarez and Deshaun. Hazy spread the pictures across the table, and each girl, Diana, Ana, Wendy, and even Laura, began to pick them up and look at them. My heart dropped; this was absolutely perfect. I was waiting for Laura to punch Deshaun or for her to throw a drink at Hazy or to drop-kick Ana. But Laura did none of this. She picked up a picture and looked at Ana and Deshaun with eyes that were filled with disappointment, embarrassment, devastation, and fury. Laura threw down the picture that she was holding and yelled, "Why?" Laura literally ran out of the building.

Wendy had a look of disgust on her face and said to Deshaun, "While your wife was writing a book about yall's relationship, you were out here making a fool of her." Then Wendy looked at Hazy and said, "You couldn't find a better time to show these pictures?" Hazy said nothing.

Diana Decosta looked at Ana and Deshaun and said, "You both ought to be ashamed of yourselves."

The next thing I saw was Laura's family and friends, looking in the direction of the cast table, including her children and Deshaun's mother. Some participants of the party went running after Laura, and soon Deshaun went running after Laura as well. For the first time, I saw Laura as a human, not as the wife of my child's father, not as the beautiful television personality, not as a cast member, not as a spoiled rich girl, but as a human. I felt awful. I thought that this moment would make me feel vindicated. I also thought that I would get the revenge that I had longed for because I felt abandoned by Deshaun, and I felt that Laura enabled the abandonment of not only me but that of my child.

Soon, the party was over, and production was wrapping up. Nearly everyone left the party. As I was leaving, I realized that I had left my purse inside the venue. I went back into the venue, and to my surprise, I saw Deshaun's mother, Ms. Eleanor.

"I guess you bring trouble with you wherever you go," Ms. Eleanor said as she briskly walked by me.

I didn't bother to respond. Soon, I found my purse sitting on a chair and as I grabbed it, I saw Laura standing in front of me.

"Do you have those pictures?" Laura asked.

I actually had the pictures in my hands. "Yes," I replied as I handed Laura the pictures.

"You know, Deshaun was in the car denying that these pictures were of him so much to the point that I was questioning what I had seen. I had to come back here to get the pictures tonight. It's crazy how you can do everything for someone, and they can mistreat you like this." Then Laura burst into tears.

Instinctively, I embraced Laura as tears began to fall from my own eyes. We both knew what it felt like to be hurt by this man.

"I am sorry if I did anything to hurt you because of the actions of Deshaun," Laura said.

"No need to apologize to me, it's not your fault, and it never was your fault," I replied.

"To think that he would have an affair with Ana. Was Ana seeking revenge on me for taking her job? I don't know what to think," Laura said.

That night, life taught me an important lesson. Sometimes you can spend so much time trying to expose the villain that you yourself become the villain. What Deshaun was doing was going to come to light eventually. I contributed to Laura being embarrassed in front of her parents, her peers, her friends, and most importantly, being embarrassed in front of her children because of me hiring a private investigator to expose Deshaun. I felt terrible. Further, consoling Laura after this catastrophe made me feel inauthentic.

The Monday following Laura's Saturday book release celebration was the cast's first day back on the set of the daytime talk show. The tension was super thick. The reality show, The Real Perspective, would be filmed during preshow prep for the daytime show Our Perspective. It seemed that everyone was distant from Hazy. Hazy was not shy, and she was going to address an issue when she identified one.

"Let me first say before the start of the show, I am sorry, Laura, about how things ended up at your book release this weekend. But I don't apologize for exposing the truth. I could have done it in a different way, but it had to be brought to light. You never seize the opportunity to air my dirty laundry, and I have always respected your input. But the night of your book release, I just lost it because I felt that you and Deshaun were acting like elitists, and I felt that you both were looking down on me when you all had issues as well."

Laura simply said, "I have nothing to say to you Hazy."

Wendy Knight chimed in "Look before either of you hold a grudge, perhaps you should hold a conversation. You both are hurt, and you both are guilty of hurting each other. You all need to speak privately, come on everyone, let's go." Wendy stood up and waved for everyone to leave the room. When the cast left, the production, including me, Hazy, and Laura, were in the room.

Hazy sighed and said, "Someone anonymously mailed me the pictures of your husband and Ana. I was initially reluctant to show you, but you kept attacking me and Jordan's relationship. Part of it is my fault because I made you feel too comfortable, and I know from experience that familiarity sometimes breeds disrespect. You kept treating me like I was a naïve, stupid little girl who was allowing a man to stomp all over her when you had the perfect relationship. When I found out your relationship was not perfect, I must admit, a part of me was relieved. I felt that I was not alone. I was agitated by the fact that you were acting like you and Deshaun could be a part of the rescue team for me and Jordan's relationship when your ship was sinking just as fast as mine."

Laura looked agitated and defeated. I could tell that Laura did not want to really speak because I was present. I excused myself and later listened to the conversation. I heard Laura tell Hazy that she never meant to make Hazy feel that she was looking down on her and Jordan and that she apologized for making her feel that way. Laura proceeded to say that it was incredibly cruel for Hazy to reveal the pictures at her book release celebration in front of her guests and family. Laura let Hazy know that she knew that Hazy had every intention of exposing the pictures during the event. Then Laura began to get angry, and her tone changed. Her voice was stern and slightly elevated as she said, "I know that Deshaun is not perfect, but Ana wanted to get back at me for taking her job, and Deshaun fell right into the trap. See Hazy, you and so many others are spectators wishing that you could cultivate a winning team like the one that Deshaun and I have. We may not win every game, but baby, we are going to win the championship every time."

Hazy replied, "Okay then, LeBron, win all the championships, hell become MVP, I don't give a damn. But let me tell you this, you can't truly have a winning team if one of your star players is a cheater."

That day, the ladies went on to host Our Perspective without a hitch. You could not tell that so much turmoil was going on behind the scenes.

Time always flies when you have a lot to do and a short time to finish. My wedding was literally a week away, and as promised, I flew my sister into town to spend time with her before my wedding. When I picked my sister Jennifer up from the airport, she looked like someone who had just been let out of a bubble and allowed to see the big world for the first time. Her spirit was filled with joy and excitement, and it showed on her beautiful face that reminded me so much of my own. Jennifer was amazed as we were driving through Los Angeles with the palm trees standing tall parallel to the street.

"Wow, this place is just like in the movies. I can't believe I'm here. It's beautiful. Karma, do you miss Buffalo?"

"Hell no, the only thing that I miss is the food," I replied.

When we pulled up to my house, Jennifer seemed to be in shock.

"Oh, my goodness, this is your house. This is my dream house," Jennifer exclaimed.

As we walked in, we were greeted by Alonzo and Trinity. "Hey Jennifer, so happy to see you," Alonzo said as he hugged Jennifer.

"So, you are my beautiful niece," Jennifer said to Trinity.

Trinity walked up to Jennifer and gave her a hug. By this time, Trinity was two years old. I walked Jennifer to the room that she would be staying in so that she could get comfortable. Jennifer settled onto the bed and caressed the blankets, seemingly captivated by their softness. "Sis, can I tell you something?" Jennifer asked.

"Of course,"

"The day that you called me and asked me to come to Los Angeles for your wedding, I was really depressed. I was upset about losing Dad, I was upset at my mother for running you off, I was lonely, I didn't have many friends, and I was ready to end it all. Karma, I had a handful of pills in one hand and a bottle of liquor in the other. Then you called. After talking to you, I saw a glimmer of light and had something to look forward to. I got myself some help, and I have been in therapy ever since. I still have my battles, I still have bad days, and I still have a long way to go, but I'm here. And I just want to thank you for being kind to me when you really don't have to."

I was in total shock. I literally had goosebumps going up my arms as Jennifer told me her story. At that moment, I realized that my mother was actually the person who saved Jennifer's life because if it wasn't for her talking me into calling Jennifer, Jennifer would have probably killed herself. And what's even more ironic is that Jennifer's mother, Linda, wanted my mother to have an abortion when she was pregnant with me. The baby that Linda wanted dead ended up saving her only child's life. Life is truly unpredictable.

While Jennifer was in town, I figured that I would bond with her. We went shopping, out to eat, and sightseeing. I asked questions about our father. Jennifer told me stories about her and our father and her mother going on family trips and about how our father was always there for her. When Jennifer sensed that I was getting sad, she would immediately stop and ask me about how I grew up. Jennifer even discussed our father's alcoholism. She told me that when things were good, they were really good, but when things were bad, they were really bad. Jennifer explained that our father suffered from depression, and there were times when he went on drinking binges, and she would describe the intense smell of alcohol that permeated through his pores. Jennifer explained that sometimes, our father could be verbally abusive to her mother, but he would not behave in this way towards her. Many of Jennifer's stories about our father made me angry at our father. For instance, Jennifer told me that she got a nose piercing when she was sixteen years old, and her mother, Linda, was furious. Jennifer said that her mother punished her and would not allow her to hang out with her friends for a month. Jennifer said that our dad went out and got a nose piercing just like Jennifer's to show solidarity. Jennifer said that all her mother could do was laugh, and her mother promised to stop her punishment immediately if our father promised to take his nose ring out. Our father granted Jennifer's mother's request. Although this story was sweet, it was hurtful to me because our father never did anything for me. This was a lot to deal with as I prepared for one of my life's biggest days. Further, Alonzo and I had family and friends coming into town. We had a lot that we needed to do and the last thing that I needed was any emotional strain impacting me negatively.

Three days before the wedding, Alonzo and I had gotten into a huge argument. I had a lot to prepare for the wedding, and Alonzo was not as active as I needed him to be. Alonzo kept telling me that he had been working a lot of hours and offered to pay someone to help me but insisted that he did not have time to help. My argument was that I worked crazy hours as well, but I had been able to plan and execute when it came to the wedding. Alonzo said that his assistant at work could help out, but he completely refused to assist. I was okay with the compromise; however, I was still very upset by Alonzo's disinterest in planning the wedding.

I left work early the day before the wedding because I was sick. I had chills and a fever. I could not believe that I was this sick the day before my wedding. I think that my sickness was stress-induced. I pulled up to the house, and Alonzo's car was parked in the driveway. I was so happy about this because I needed help. I really needed someone to help take care of me. I first went to the kitchen to start to make myself some tea. I heard a banging sound coming from Jennifer's room. I thought that this was strange. Then my woman intuition started to set in, and I thought to myself, "Oh hell no." Alonzo's car is in the driveway; he is home early, and I hear banging coming from the guest room that Jennifer is in. I nearly ran to the room and turned the knob, and to my surprise, the door was not locked. I opened the door, and I saw Jennifer naked, bent over the bed, and the next thing that I saw was a complete shock. I could not believe my eyes. It was Todd, my sister Celine's husband.

"Todd, what the hell? Get yo ass out of there," I yelled as I slammed the door.

I walked upstairs to my room, looking for Alonzo. Alonzo was lying in bed sleeping. "Alonzo, what are you doing home?" I asked as I was shaking Alonzo awake. Alonzo was hot to the touch.

"I feel awful; I am coming down with something. I left work early and just went to bed," Alonzo replied.

"I'm sick too, but did you know that Celine's husband is here in our house?"

"Yeah, Celine and Todd came into town this morning and met your mother here at the house since she was watching Trinity. Your mom and Celine went shopping. Todd was tired, so he decided to stay here."

"Okay, well, I caught Jennifer and Todd downstairs fuckin in the guest room," I said.

Alonzo suddenly sat up straight, waiting for me to spill the rest of the tea. "Wait, what?" Alonzo said.

"Yes, did you see Todd and Jennifer together? Did they seem like they knew each other?"

"Actually, I did overhear Jennifer and Todd say that they worked at the same place a while ago," Alonzo explained.

This wedding was already starting off to be a mess. About an hour after I got home, my mother, Celine, and Trinity were coming to my house with shopping bags. As soon as they walked through the door, my mother started to explain that Celine and Todd had come to my house because they had come to town too early to check into their hotel, and Todd was sleepy and needed rest.

I just responded by saying, "Oh, was rest what he needed?"

Celine gave me a dry hug. "Is Todd up yet?" Celine asked.

"Well, he was definitely "up" earlier!" I said in the most sarcastic way possible while putting a lot of emphasis on "up."

Suddenly, a nervous Todd came walking out of the guest room opposite the guest room that Jennifer was staying in.

"Hey baby, were you able to find what you were looking for?" Todd asked Celine.

"Yes, and I even found something for you," Celine said.

Todd kept looking in my direction as if he was begging me with his eyes not to tell Celine that I had seen him and Jennifer having sex. I wasn't going to say a thing. I was not going to let anything ruin my wedding.

Unfortunately, later that day, Alonzo and I were both in urgent care. We both had some type of viral infection and were given steroid shots along with antibiotics. The steroid shots made us both feel so much better. I was so thankful for Alonzo's assistant because she wrapped up all of the last-minute things that I needed her to wrap up, including the last-minute RSVPs and seating arrangements.

After finally settling in after getting treated at Urgent Care, I decided to sit outside next to the pool and drink some tea before heading to bed. My mother, Todd, and Celine were still at my house helping my mother care for Trinity and catching up. Eventually, Todd came outside and sat next to me at one of my patio tables. "Please, Todd, not tonight," I calmly said.

"Karma, let me explain," Todd said.

"Todd, the only person that you need to explain anything to is Celine. But don't tell her shit until my wedding is over."

Todd continued and explained that he and Jennifer worked together in the past. While at the company, he had an affair with Jennifer. Todd said that he was impacted by layoffs at his company and that his affair with Jennifer ended at that time. Todd told me that he and Jennifer had a strong sexual attraction, and once my mother and Celine left the house, one thing led to another. "Please don't tell Celine; she does not need this type of pain," Todd said.

"First of all, please spare me the details and trust, I won't say a word." I was at a place where I did not want to interfere in anyone else's relationship. Celine already hated me, and she would hate me even more if I told her that her husband had sex with my half-sister.

After talking to Todd, I knocked on Jennifer's door; I had not seen her since I saw her and Todd having sex. Jennifer slowly opened the door.

"I'm sorry, Karma," Jennifer said in a low voice.

"Listen, after the wedding, I need you to go back to Buffalo and continue getting the help that you need. What were you thinking, having sex with my sister's husband? How can I trust you?"

"I know Karma; I feel so bad. But Todd and I have a history. Todd was my boss, and we were heavily involved. I was in love. Eventually, Todd was fired because of the affair, and he stopped talking to me. I told one person about me and Todd hooking up, and that person went straight to Human Resources. Next thing I knew, Todd was fired."

"What in the world? At any point did you know that Todd was married to my sister?"

"No, I swear. I didn't know until today. I knew that he was married, but he said that he and his wife were separated."

"Wow, the story that Todd told me was a little different. But you deserve better Jennifer. You deserve a man who prioritizes you, not someone incapable of making you number one." I was hoping that Jennifer would heed my advice. I knew that she was already going through a lot, and I did not want things to become even more complicated for her by entertaining Todd's no-good ass.

Alonzo and I slept in the same bed the night before the wedding because we were too sick to follow any traditions. On the morning of our wedding, neither of us was 100%, but we felt a lot better. I went to the other end of the house while he stayed on the opposite end in an effort for us not to run into each other prior to the wedding.

My wedding day was absolutely beautiful. The sun was shining; there was the perfect breeze, and it was not too hot and not too cold. This was perfect because the wedding ceremony took place outside in my yard. My hair was mostly up, and loose curls hung from my head. My wedding dress was a princess gown that sparkled from top to bottom. I wore a beautiful veil that shimmered as much as the dress. The diamond necklace that lay across my chest was elegant, along with the diamond earrings that dangled from my ears. I looked like a princess. Trinity was wearing a replica of my dress; she was the most beautiful flower girl I had ever seen.

The wedding party was small. I only had Grace standing beside me, and Alonzo had his brother Darnel. Yes, this is the same Darnel that I slept with in high school who filmed us having sex. But by the time Alonzo and I got married, that was water under the bridge. Darnel was so far removed from me that I wasn't bothered.

As I was walking down the aisle, I was so happy. The white chairs were lined up on either side of the aisle that led to the gazebo that was decorated in white roses, and there stood Alonzo. Alonzo was so handsome; he wore an all-white suit. The closer I got to Alonzo, the more I noticed the tears trickling down his face as he tried his hardest to hold the tears in. I saw my friends, co-workers, and family. My mother had the biggest smile on her face as she stood next to her boyfriend, Larry. I saw Diana from Our Perspective. Because I was Diana's assistant/nurse in the past, we had formed a real bond. I genuinely loved her. But what I was not expecting to see was Terry Tea standing right next to Diana in all his splendor. I thought to myself, "Oh shit." Terry Tea must be Diana's plus one, and I probably missed it because Terry Tea's real name ain't no damn Terry Tea. Plus, Alonzo's assistant put together the last-minute seating arrangements, so I didn't even get a chance to notice Terry Tea being a guest at my wedding. My recommendation for Terry Tea to be Diana's stylist has resulted in Terry Tea being at my wedding and being in the presence of Grace and her husband, Dane. And how will Dane and Terry Tea interact with one another while Grace is present? And will Grace think that I did this on purpose? All of these thoughts were running through my head as I was walking down the aisle to become Mrs. Rodgers. I looked at Grace, and tears were coming down her face. I didn't know if she was crying because she was so happy for me or because Terry Tea was at my wedding. Then I decided as I was walking down the aisle, I was not going to let anyone, or anything interfere with this moment. I was going to stay focused and embrace every second. I was going to marry my king, and he and I deserved for this moment to be solely about us.

Alonzo and I exchanged vows. I have never been good at expressing my feelings, but I took the time to truly write what was in my heart. Alonzo started his vows by saying. "Karma, today, I feel like God has blessed me beyond measure. The love that I have for you is unconditional; it's pure, and it's just visceral. Although there was a time when life separated us, our bond was so magnetic that we were able to find our way back to each other. I know that I am the luckiest man on earth. When I first met you in that snowstorm in Buffalo, I knew that you were the one for me. I love the way that you love. I admire your perseverance, tenacity, and most importantly, your warm spirit. I feel blessed that with you comes beautiful Trinity. Trinity, I am not only gaining a wife today, but I am also gaining a beautiful daughter in you. I promise you both that I will always love and care for you all the days of my life. And Trinity, I hope that you are ready to become a big sister because I plan for us to have a big family." The guest burst into a gleeful chuckle. "But really, Karma, I want you to know that I will be an unwavering constant in your life. I will fight for you, when necessary, I will fight with you whenever you experience an uphill battle, and together we will fight the odds and be an example of what true love looks like." When Alonzo finished his vows, there was not a dry eye. I wiped my eyes and proceeded with my vows, "Alonzo, the way that we met and the way that we were reunited was divine synchronicity. You have always taken care of me, and now that you take care of my baby Trinity, I am forever grateful and extremely blessed. Even on our bad days, I love you. I'd rather experience a bad day with you than experience a good day without you. When we were apart, I felt something missing inside of me, but now that we are together, I feel whole. I love you and I am overjoyed to become your wife and amazed by your commitment to being Trinity's father. I love you for what you have done for me, and I love you for everything that you will do in the future." I meant every word of my vows.

After the ceremony, it was time to get ready for the reception. Alonzo and I went to the pool house to just take everything in as our guests went to the part of our yard that held a tent where the reception would take place. We both felt better than the day before and we were both happy that we were finally experiencing our wedding day. Then, I heard a knock at the door. Alonzo and I were slightly annoyed; we both thought that it may have been his assistant or the wedding planner. Alonzo opened the door, and it was my older brother, Matthew. Alonzo had only met Matthew briefly in the past, and he looked totally shocked to see Matthew entering the pool house. Matthew shook Alonzo's hand and proceeded to say, "Hey Karma, you look absolutely beautiful today."

"Thank you so much," I replied.

"I just wanted to let you know that I am disappointed. Not only am I disappointed, but I'm pissed," Matthew said.

In a very frustrated voice, I asked, "Why?"

"Because you should have asked me to walk you down the aisle."

Alonzo walked to Matthew and said, "Listen, man, this is Karma's day, and she doesn't need any negativity. I'm going to have to ask you and your energy to leave."

For the first time, I saw Matthew look intimidated. Alonzo was so tall compared to Matthew that he towered over him. Matthew looked up at Alonzo and said, "Look, man, I'm trying to have a conversation with my little sister."

"Well, the conversation that you are having with my wife is now over," Alonzo replied.

Matthew walked out of the pool house and apparently left my house because I did not see Matthew for the rest of the day, and this was fine with me. Matthew was nothing but a big bully, and Alonzo handled him in a way that protected me. To have a man by my side who was going to protect me made me feel a sense of safety that I had never experienced before. When Matthew left the pool house, I hugged and kissed Alonzo and said, "Thank you for handling Matthew. He is such a punk, and he thought that he could ruin my day. I guess he wasn't prepared for you."

Alonzo looked at me and simply said, "I got you, no matter what."

The reception was beautiful; there were ice sculptures, chicken, Lobster, and steak. Walking into the reception took my breath away. My colors were blush pink and cream. The combination of blush pink and cream was everywhere from the light fixtures to the tablecloths and centerpieces. The centerpieces that sat at each table were clear tall flower vases that held beautiful fresh pink and cream roses. The huge rose pink and cream five-tier cake had pink and cream flowers trickling down the side of it; this cake nearly stole the show. As Alonzo and I walked into the reception, everyone seemed so happy. All we heard was cheers and people telling us how we were a beautiful bride and groom. I looked over at Grace and she did not seem very happy. She had a slight smile on her face. I looked around, and I did see Dane, but right as I saw Dane, I got a glimpse of Terry Tea looking directly at Dane.

I was trying to discreetly avoid Grace during the reception. At one point during the reception, I remember telling my mother that I needed to use the bathroom, and then I heard a voice behind me say, "I'll take you; that's a matron of honor's job, to help the bride go to the bathroom, right?" Grace said.

"Oh, Grace, where have you been hiding all night, yes, please help me with the bathroom," I replied.

The walk to the bathroom was so awkward. We were both quiet. When I got into the bathroom, Grace assisted me. Before I could wash my hands, Grace said, "I see Terry Tea was able to make it to your wedding?"

"Grace, I did not know he was coming to the wedding. I invited the lady that I used to work for, Diana DeCosta, and she added Terry Tea as her plus one. I missed this completely because I only know Terry Tea as just that, Terry Tea; I never knew his government name. I'm sorry. No one has bothered you, have they?"

"No, I figured that you wouldn't intentionally do that, but how does Terry Tea and Diana DeCosta know each other?"

At this moment, I had to make a pivotal decision. I had to determine whether I would tell the truth or if I would lie about introducing Terry Tea to Diana so that Terry Tea could become her stylist. I just spit out, "I have no idea how they know each other. I don't want you to worry about any of that. Let's go out there and have a good time. I love you, and I appreciate you being my matron of honor, but most of all, I appreciate you for being my best friend."

Alonzo and I danced and partied, and our guests did the same but with lots of alcohol. We were all having such a great time. I looked around; Terry Tea was no longer eyeballing Dane; his eyes were now on Alonzo's brother Darnel. Darnel and Terry Tea were dancing and flirting with each other. I assumed that Darnel was no longer with his fiancé. I looked at Grace, and she was hugged up with Dane. Everything was working out just right. As the reception was wrapping up, Diana DeCosta grabbed me and embraced me so tightly, and said, "Darling, you are the most beautiful bride that my eyes have ever seen." Diana's words touched my heart.

Then Grace walked up, "Hey Karma, please introduce me to the fabulous Diana DeCosta."

"Of course, Diana, this is my best friend since childhood, Grace."

"Hello, my darling; good to meet you," Diana said.

Then, out of nowhere came Terry Tea, "My Diva Diana, are we heading out?"

Diana proceeded, "Karma was introducing me to her best friend, Grace. Grace, this is my wonderful stylist who was recommended by Karma, Terry Tea."

All I could do was take a deep breath. Diana had to say that I was the one to recommend Terry Tea after I just pretended as if I did not know how Terry Tea and Diana knew each other. I was kicking myself in the ass.

"Yes, we know each other," Grace said as her gaze met mine, heavy with disappointment.

"Well hello Grace the Face, you look gorgeous as always. I saw your husband Sugar Cane Dane running around here earlier. He is such a mess."

I just laughed and grabbed Terry Tea by the arm and walked away with him. "Not tonight, Terry Tea, not tonight," I said.

"What did I do?" Terry Tea asked.

"That Sugar Cane Dane shit, stop it."

"I was just having a little fun. You know that Dane is my sugar daddy."

"Terry, you should be heading out. Thank you for making it to my wedding," I said as I walked away. I was hoping that this incident would not cause severe damage between Grace and me.

When the reception was wrapped up, my mother was at my house getting Trinity ready for bed; she agreed to stay at my house and watch Trinity while Alonzo and I had our alone time. My oldest sister, Celine, was like my mother's shadow. Celine decided to stay at my house to help my mother. I was grabbing something to drink in the kitchen when Celine was sitting at my kitchen table. Celine seemed like she had something on her mind, and it was only a matter of time before she let it out.

"Matthew told me about how he was kicked out of your house because he expressed his disappointment about not walking you down the aisle. I think that was so unnecessary," Celine said.

"Sometimes I feel like you and Matthew have a difficult time grasping reality. You and Matthew have been awful to me my entire life. You both are lucky that you were even invited. You're lucky to be in my home right now. Do you remember what happened the last time I saw you both? You both attacked me and even questioned if I knew who Trinity's father was. I told both you and Matthew that you all had never really been a sister or brother to me," I replied.

"Well, you have not been much of an aunt to my daughter Rhea, that's why Rhea did not show up to the wedding," Celine replied.

Of course, Celine had to deflect someway somehow.

"Rhea acts like she can't stand me; it's hard to create a bond with someone who won't even speak to you. And since we are deflecting, how about you speak to your husband Todd and ask him why he was really let go from his last job," I said.

At this time, Todd left my house and went back to his hotel.

"What do you mean? Little girl, you don't know what you are talking about. Todd was laid off," Celine said.

"Todd was "laid", but he certainly wasn't laid off," I said without thinking.

My mother came out of nowhere and quickly interjected, "Okay, that's enough. Damn, can all of my kids get together, and it not be any drama."

Celine's fury was evident, her fists were balled up, and her lips were tightly closed.

"Celine, go back to your hotel; I'm good. I have everything under control. Thank you for helping me," my mother said to Celine. From this point, I did not care if I never saw Celine and Matthew again. They couldn't even allow me to get through my wedding day without trying to anger me.

It's crazy how you can go from living a dream to being thrust back into reality. Well, that's what happened after my wedding. I did not take any substantial amount of time off work. Alonzo and I agreed to wait until the filming of the reality show, The Real Perspective, wrapped up for us to take our real honeymoon to Hawaii.

About two days after our wedding, Alonzo and I spent two nights at a local 5-star hotel where we worked on a baby, got massages, ate as much room service as we wanted, and relaxed. It was just what we needed after months of wedding planning and not always seeing eye to eye. I did not want our alone time to end.

My first day back to work after the wedding was crazy. Deshaun's new mistress, Ana Alvarez, had a bigger friend role on the reality show. During a confessional conversation, Ana said, "Laura fucked with my job, so I fucked with her husband. She took what was mine, so I took what was hers." Ana was vengeful and bitter. This behavior was out of character for Ana because Ana's brand was comprised of her being conservative and intellectual. I did not know what her angle was, but I knew that the viewers would hate her and that she would not find longevity in reality television with the way she behaved.

Laura was refusing to film with Ana. Production was under pressure to get Laura and Ana in a room to speak to each other. There was already a scene filmed with Deshaun revealing to Laura that Ana reached out to him via social media, stating they needed to meet privately because she wanted to warn him of the hardships that come with his wife hosting a daytime talk show. This was a surprise to me because when Deshaun and I were dating, he had no social media presence. Deshaun said that he went to Ana's house and that they started off as just friends, and eventually, their relationship became romantic. I thought that this was total bullshit. Deshaun never showed Laura the messages on social media; he allegedly deleted them. We needed to get Ana's side of the story on film. I knew that the cast was filming a commercial to raise money for a children's charity. Laura thought that only the main cast would be there, but I made sure that Ana was invited. When Ana walked into the studio where the commercial was being filmed, Laura was in front of the camera filming her scene, and the presence of Ana completely distracted Laura. Laura fumbled her lines and had to start all over again. When Laura finished, she started to grab her things to leave. Hazy grabbed Laura by the arm, "Get off of me. Did you set this up?" Laura yelled at Hazy.

"No, but you can't run from Ana forever; you have to face this head-on," Hazy stated.

"Yeah, at least have a conversation with her, darling. After you both speak, you never have to hear from her again, but you need to hear her side of the story," Diana DeCosta said.

Wendy Knight interjected, "Laura if that bitch is trying to go low, take her down to the deepest darkest depths of hell."

"I am going to have an adult conversation with Ana, and then I am done with this, and I am done with her," Laura said.

Laura asked Ana to speak to her in a dressing room away from the cast and away from everyone associated with the charity. Ana told it all. Ana told Laura that Deshaun reached out to her, and Ana showed Laura the messages that Deshaun sent her on social media. Deshaun reached out to Ana to check on her after it was made official that she would be replaced by Laura. Ana said that initially, she did not know who Deshaun was until she looked at his social media page and quickly realized that he was Laura's husband. Ana said that she was pissed off at Laura at the time, so she invited Deshaun to her house to talk. Ana stated that Deshaun confided in her about issues that he and Laura were having in their relationship, such as a lack of sex. Ana told Laura that this is when the affair began; Ana provided Laura with text messages as well. Laura asked Ana why, Ana had a peculiar explanation. Ana explained that when Laura was filling in for her on Our Perspective while Ana was negotiating her contract, she heard that Laura was telling people on the set that she was going to take Ana's job. Ana told Laura that Our Perspective was her everything; it was her husband, her child, and her life. Ana helped start the show and even selected the co-hosts. Ana told Laura that she did not respect the sanctity of her life's work, so she wasn't going to respect the sanctity of Laura's marriage.

Although Laura put up with a lot of shit when it came to Deshaun, Laura always handled herself with such dignity. Regardless of the situation, Laura always handled herself like a lady. Any other woman would be trying to scratch Ana's eyeballs out of her head, but not Laura. Laura stood with poise and said, "Well, I guess the saying is true, hurt people, hurt people. I just want to let you know that your attempts to hurt me will never heal you. And no matter how many times you sleep with Deshaun, you will never get your job back; meanwhile, Deshaun will continue to come home to me each night until I decide that I don't want him there. So, after all that you have done, I still got your job, I still have my man, and what do you have? If you ask me, you have taken more losses than wins. You have lost your dignity, your respect, and most of all yourself. Your brand is destroyed, your stock has taken a nosedive and you ain't got no job. Basically, you ain't got shit." Laura took one last look at Ana as she turned up her nose, scrunched up her face, and said, "What a clown." Then Laura made her grand exit out of that dressing room and out of the building. Ana just sat there stunned, and her pain was palpable. I guess Ana was hoping to humiliate Laura, but Laura turned the tables and obliterated Ana. Ana was never to appear on the reality show The Real Perspective again. She refused to film from this day forward.

Chapter 13

Success Does Not Always Breed Happiness

Once the reality show, The Real Perspective, started to air on television, it was an instant success. The show exceeded all expectations. Roman Hart was extremely pleased, and he was even more pleased by the work that I had done on the show. I knew that I did not have to worry about having a job next season. Alonzo and I were happy; Trinity was thriving, I had a career that I never knew I wanted, and life was amazing.

Everything for Alonzo and I had been fast-paced for the first few months of our marriage. It was finally time for us to take our honeymoon to Maui, Hawaii. I was so excited; I had never been to Hawaii before, and neither had Alonzo.

Flying into Hawaii and seeing the picturesque landscape was calming and revitalizing. When we arrived at the resort, all I wanted to do was change into my bathing suit and hit the beach with my man. Although Alonzo and I had known each other for years and had been together on, off, and then on again, being married felt different.

After a few days in Maui, Alonzo and I had an overload of the pool, the beach, and lovemaking; Alonzo wanted to drive the Road to Hana. The Road to Hana is a highway of tight winding curves that gives you an amazing view of the Pacific Ocean, waterfalls, and there is even a tropical rainforest in its path. At one stop while on the Road to Hana, Alonzo and I had some of the best barbeque we have ever had in our lives. I had a barbeque pulled pork sandwich that overflowed with pork and sweet and tangy sauce. Alonzo had some barbeque ribs, and the meat literally fell off the bone. At another stop, we had some freshly baked banana bread that melted in our mouths. The scenery and the food were both tantalizing to my senses.

While on the Road to Hana, I wanted to capture as many moments as I could. At one point, we saw a spectacular waterfall. This waterfall was not as massive as the one that I have seen so many times in Niagara Falls. But this waterfall was just as wondrous. Watching the roaring waters falling from the mountainous edge of the falls and catapulting into the misty waters below was spellbinding. I was trying to capture a picture of the waterfall at a particular angle with my phone in one hand and a cup of pop in the other when I lost my balance and fell flat on some rocks. While falling, I squeezed my cup of pop so hard that I punctured holes in it, the top and straw popped off, and I was doused in orange pop. My knee was bloody; I was in immense pain, and I could tell that I had hurt my ankle really badly. Alonzo had to pick me up and carry me to our rental car. He had to drive down the Road to Hana, and it seemed as if it took nearly an hour. I was trying to stay calm, but I was really hurt.

Alonzo took me to a hospital. I hated that I had ruined our honeymoon. When the doctor came into the room to give me my actual diagnosis, he said, "I have good news, and I have bad news, which would you like to hear first?

I instantly said, "Just give me the bad news first."

"You have a fractured ankle. The good news is that you are pregnant."

I was in shock. I know that I had been busy, but not busy enough to not know that I was pregnant. I had absolutely no symptoms like I did with Trinity. Then again, I thought that maybe it was too early for me to experience any symptoms.

Alonzo had the biggest smile on his face as he said, "Karma, we're having a baby," in a joyful tone. After seeing Alonzo's reaction, my shock instantly turned to pure joy. Alonzo had done so much for me and had brought so much joy to my life; I was happy to bring joy to his. We could not wait to get back home to tell everyone, especially Trinity.

When I went to my OBGYN appointment for my sonogram with Alonzo and Trinity, I was so excited to find out if we were going to have a boy or a girl. Alonzo really wanted to have a boy. As I lay on the OBGYN examination table, I could hardly contain myself. My doctor put her gloves on and pulled out the gel that she poured onto my stomach. Everyone's eyes were fixated on the ultrasound screen while the doctor swirled the transducer around my belly. The doctor began to speak, and she had our undivided attention. She proceeded to say, "You are definitely having a boy." Alonzo was elated as he grinned and kissed me on the forehead.

"I wanted a little sister," Trinity screamed.

"Well, I have good news for you. Having a little brother isn't all that bad, but having a brother and sister is fantastic," the doctor said.

Alonzo and I looked at each other in confusion.

"You are having twins, a boy, and a girl," the doctor said.

I nearly passed out.

"Yes!" Trinity screamed.

"Are you sure?" Alonzo asked.

"I sure am," the doctor said confidently as she pointed out which of the little dots on the screen were the boy and which was the girl. After the shock of having twins settled in, Alonzo and I became excited and optimistic about the future. What a blessing to have a boy and a girl. I felt even more blessed when I thought back to my pregnancy with Trinity when I had no support from my child's biological father; in fact, he wanted to erase her from his life. But now, Trinity had a dad who loved her and a brother and a sister who she would love and who would love her back. I was determined to make sure that my children would be taught to have a good relationship. I did not want my children to go through what I had to go through with my siblings, not having my back and not loving me.

My pregnancy seemed to fly by; before I realized it, I was already five months along, juggling work and feeling exhausted. My mother had been caring for Trinity during the day. She wanted to be able to spend more time with her boyfriend Larry, so I decided to register Trinity in a daycare program. Trinity was about three years old. She was extremely intelligent, and she acted like a little grown woman. Trinity had started talking like a sixty-year-old woman in a three-year-old's body. One time Trinity and I were alone in the house, and I was reading a book when she said, "It's so quiet in here you can hear a mouse piss on cotton." Then another time, after Trinity's bath, she told me that she was cleaner than the board of health. Although sayings like this coming out of a three-year-old's mouth were cute and often funny, Trinity needed friends her age. Trinity had literally become the child version of my mother.

Taking the steps necessary to enroll Trinity into daycare was difficult for me. Thinking back, I know for sure that I had some trust issues. I wanted to make sure that my child would receive the best care possible when she was not with me. Alonzo and I did a lot of research and picked what we thought would be the perfect childcare center for Trinity. Alonzo made sure that he was present for Trinity's first day of daycare. During this time, Alonzo was very protective of me, so he was constantly running to the passenger side of the car to open my door and help me out whenever we went anywhere, and this day was no different. Alonzo grabbed Trinity out of her car seat, and we proceeded into the childcare center. The staff were so nice, and they were so patient with Alonzo and me. As I was talking to one of the teachers while holding Trinity's hand, I heard a familiar female voice behind me say, "Karma?" I turned around, and to my complete surprise, there was Aiko holding a little boy's hand. The little boy looked to be about two years old. Before I could say anything, Aiko grabbed me and hugged me so tightly. I literally had not seen Aiko since our heistist days.

"Oh, my goodness Karma, I am so glad to see you. And wow, you have a little girl. How have you been? It's been such a long time," Aiko said.

"I am good, so good to see you. This is my baby girl Trinity, and I am actually expecting twins as well. Is this your little boy?" I asked.

"Yes, it is. Felix, say hello to Karma."

The little boy softly said, "Hi."

"Wow, you are expecting twins. That's amazing," Aiko said.

"Yeah, sometimes it's hard for me to believe that I am having twins. Oh, and this is my husband Alonzo," I proudly said to Aiko.

Aiko looked at Alonzo and said, "Wait, don't I know you from somewhere?"

Alonzo looked confused. "I'm not sure," he replied.

"Wait, you work with my fiancé, Henry, at the law firm."

"Oh yeah, I remember you now," Alonzo replied.

"What a small world. Karma, we have to stay in touch; maybe we can do a playdate with the kids," Aiko said enthusiastically.

"That sounds great, Trinity needs to be around more kids," Alonzo said.

Alonzo thought that networking was very important for his career. Further, Alonzo relied on me to attend various events and to participate in social outings with people that he felt would further his career. I didn't mind. Alonzo had no problem inflating my self-esteem by telling me how beautiful I was and how he loved showing me off. He never made me feel as though I was just his trophy wife. Alonzo also stressed how intelligent, resourceful, and creative I was. He appreciated my knowledge and my contributions to our family.

Alonzo really had the desire to become a partner at the law firm that he worked at. Aiko's fiancé was already a partner, and when Alonzo realized that Aiko and I knew each other, he thought that it was a divine intervention. But on the other hand, I felt like I needed to steer clear of Aiko. I wanted to disentangle the part of my life that linked me and Aiko.

I was dreading Alonzo asking me how I knew Aiko. As soon as Alonzo and I got into the car after leaving Trinity at her new daycare, Alonzo asked me how I knew Aiko. I just explained that we worked together at a restaurant when I first moved to LA, which was the truth. But I didn't want to provide any further details about me and Aiko's past. I guess it's true what they say, you can't run away from your past. As soon as I thought that my past was far enough behind me, it sprinted right into my present in the form of Aiko.

I always looked forward to date nights with Alonzo. We always tried to have a date night at least once a week. On one particular night, I got dressed up and was ready for some alone time with Alonzo. Abruptly, Alonzo said, "Karma, I just wanted to let you know that Aiko and Henry will be joining us." I instantly became annoyed and released a huge sigh of frustration. "What's your problem?" Alonzo asked.

"I am just not in the mood to be on," I replied.

"What do you mean by be "on"?"

"Alonzo, it takes energy to be around other people and to laugh at jokes that aren't funny or muster up conversations when it falls quiet; I just wanted to be alone with you. I just wanted to have a relaxing night and a relaxing dinner."

Alonzo pretty much said that he would cancel with Henry and Aiko. But I had put my own feelings aside and told Alonzo that it was okay to have dinner with Aiko and Henry. I was willing to take one for the team.

Alonzo and I arrived at the restaurant, and Aiko and Henry were already seated. Alonzo and I greeted Aiko and Henry. Henry was a tall, medium-built white man. He had salt and pepper hair that was combed back. He had a warm smile and a friendly disposition. He did not seem like someone that Aiko would date, let alone marry. As we talked during dinner, I learned more about Henry. Henry had been married three times in the past, and he had children that were in college. He was a lot older than Aiko.

Henry seemed to adore Aiko; if he wasn't eating his dinner, he either had his arm around Aiko's shoulder or he would even hold her hand. Every so often, they would kiss each other during conversations.

"So, how did you both meet?" I asked.

Aiko and Henry looked at each other and started laughing. Henry was eager to tell the story. Henry proceeded to explain, "Well, Aiko was with her friends at a party that I was throwing at my house. Aiko and I were flirting with each other all night, so much so that guests thought that we were together romantically. Aiko's friends saw the undeniable chemistry between us, so they dared her to find my bedroom and wait for me there. During the party, I ran to my room for a moment for something, and there she was, Aiko, sitting on my bed. I'm not even going to go into the details of what happened next, but you all can use your imagination."

Aiko looked at me as if she was trying to disguise her embarrassment. I figured that Aiko was in that room stealing shit and not waiting for him.

"Baby, I hate when you tell that story," Aiko said in a playful tone. Then, both Henry and Aiko started laughing.

Alonzo found the story to be amusing; he was spouting out nonsensical phrases like "Yoooo" and "What?," as he laughed in amusement.

Henry suggested that Aiko and I hang out because Aiko had been somewhat isolated since having their child.

"Aiko needs to hang around more mothers. Karma, you and Aiko really should hang out without us men."

Alonzo quickly perked up and said, "Exactly, that would be great. And the kids can get together too."

I just put on my phony smile and said, "That sounds like a plan."

Aiko seemed excited. I still had my reservations about hanging out with Aiko, but I was willing to go along to get along. I felt that I was obligated to help Alonzo in any way possible, and if that meant getting close to Aiko again so that he and Henry could become closer, well, so be it. Connections are crucial for upward mobility in the legal profession.

When life is great, theoretically, you should feel great. Well, this was not the case for me. I had a beautiful and healthy child, my career was booming, I had a husband who loved and adored me, and I was pregnant with twins. I told my doctor that I felt that I may have pre-partum depression, and she totally disregarded me. I just felt sad. I was looking for happiness and had expressed this to Alonzo. Alonzo told me that I just may be overwhelmed with work and tired from being pregnant. As I was talking to him about how I was feeling, Aiko began calling me on my phone. Alonzo looked at my phone and said, “Maybe you and Aiko should hang out so that you can get your mind off of things.” I agreed, and when I talked to Aiko, I made plans to meet her for dinner to catch up. I figured that this would get Alonzo off of my back about hanging with Aiko.

It took a few months for Aiko and I to finally meet up for dinner. Preparing to meet with Aiko for dinner was more stressful than I had imagined. So many memories, both good and bad, were surging through my mind like a tsunami. During the time that Aiko and I were friends, I went from my lowest to a huge high and then down to rock bottom.

I arrived at the restaurant to meet Aiko first. Aiko was running a little behind because her babysitter was late. Once Aiko arrived, she hugged me so tight, as she had done so many times before, and told me that she really missed our friendship. Before I knew it, Aiko and I were talking and laughing like old times. We talked about how we used to party all night and how we would have girl nights at each other’s houses while making pizza and drinking wine. Then things got a little serious, “You know how lucky we are?” Aiko said.

“Do you know the police came to my house and began questioning me about home burglaries?” I said.

Aiko’s mouth dropped, and she looked at me with both fear and curiosity, “What?” she said.

“Yes, I never told you, but I kept a few pieces of jewelry from our heistist days. Then, some guy robbed me when I left the country. The guy who robbed me took the chain that I stole from Lil Pharoah’s house. He was partying at a club wearing the chain. Apparently, Lil Pharoah noticed dude wearing his chain, and the guy was arrested at the club.”

Aiko looked shocked. “I heard about Lil Pharoah’s chain being seen at the club and about a guy being arrested.”

“Yes, so someone else is basically doing time for some of the shit that we did.”

“I always knew that God protected me but after hearing what you said, this only reaffirms this for me. My last attempt at a heist landed me a baby and a fiancé,” Aiko said. Aiko spoke about the night that her fiancé Henry described months earlier regarding how they met. Aiko said that she was never at Henry’s party with her friends. Aiko said that she went to the same hair salon as Henry's ex-wife and that she overheard Henry's ex-wife talking about how Henry was a cash hoarder and kept stashes of money under his mattress. Apparently, the ex-wife thought that Henry might be accepting cash from some of his clients and was doing something suspicious. Aiko said that the ex-wife was also in the salon talking about how Henry was going to throw a party at his house to celebrate ten years at his law firm. Aiko said that the ex-wife ran her mouth so much that she was able to find out the day of the party and Aiko was able to research Henry's address and get all of the information she needed to crash the party. Aiko said that she literally slipped into the party.

During the party, Aiko was trying to find her way to the room to get the money. She stated that Henry walked into the room before she could get the money under the mattress. When Henry walked into the room, Aiko said that she pretended like she was there waiting for him on his bed. Aiko said that she was flirting with Henry all night because she was attracted to Henry and thought that he was sexy as hell, so they had sex right then and right there. Aiko said that after they had sex, she told him that lie about her friends daring her to go to his room, and she thought that she would never see Henry again after they exchanged numbers. But Aiko said that it was like Henry was addicted. The spontaneity, the thrill, and the sheer excitement had him hooked, and a relationship was formed.

I asked Aiko about Henry's ex-wife and if the ex-wife recognized her from the salon. Aiko said that when Henry introduced her to his ex-wife, she recognized Aiko immediately from the salon. Aiko said that for all she knows, Henry's ex-wife thinks it's simply a coincidence that they went to the same salon.

Aiko said that almost getting caught by Henry saved her life. She was trying to find her way out of being a heistist, and every heist became her last heist until she began to run low on money, and then came Henry. Aiko said that her life had changed and that she could never go back to that lifestyle. Aiko said, "I now commit to legit money, and I really mean it." My meeting with Aiko far exceeded my expectations. I thoroughly enjoyed my time with her. I was unable to speak to anyone else about me and Aiko's past, and it was therapeutic to be able to have an open and honest conversation with an old friend, I know that Aiko felt the same.

Work-related events had become a part of life for Alonzo and me. The reunion special for The Real Perspective was taped, and there was a huge party to celebrate the great 1st season of The Real Perspective. I was so excited about it. I was definitely suffering from depression, and very few things excited me, but this celebration awakened my joy. I could imagine myself entering the party with my tall, handsome, and brilliant husband accompanying me while Laura Pennington and her raggedy-ass husband Deshaun looked at us in envy. Alonzo and I were what Laura wanted her and Deshaun to be. The night we were going to the party, Alonzo was lying in bed talking about how he did not feel well and didn't think that he would be able to make it. I was so upset. This would be the first time that the cast, crew, and most importantly, Trinity's biological father could meet Alonzo. I begged Alonzo to accompany me, but he regretfully told me that he was sick, weak, and outright tired. I just asked my mother to come to the house to help watch Trinity and Alonzo while I was gone. Alonzo said, "Just call Aiko and see if she can come with you." At first, I was resistant; however, Alonzo begged me to at least ask because he did not want me driving alone while I was so late into my pregnancy. Eventually, I agreed and called Aiko to ask if she could be my guest at the party. Aiko was completely down for the opportunity; I felt that Aiko had left her old habits behind and would not come to the event to research who her next victims would be.

Aiko came to pick me up in a red luxury two hundred-thousand-dollar vehicle. I wobbled to the car, trying to look as pretty as I could although I was eight months pregnant by this time with a huge belly. I instantly felt out of place. Aiko jumped out to help me into the car, which sat low to the ground. I did not know how I was going to get into the car, let alone how I was going to get out.

"I should have driven my SUV instead; sometimes I forget you are about to have those babies any day now," Aiko said jokingly.

I laughed as I bent down, struggling to get into the car. "Girl, once I get into this car, I don't know how I'm going to get out," I said as I continued to laugh.

I saw Hollywood's elite when Aiko and I arrived at the event. Everyone looked so beautiful, and here I was, looking like a polar bear with swollen ankles. Aiko drove to the valet, and she, the valet, and I were struggling to get me out of the car. As I was being pulled out of the car like a giant whale being pulled from the ocean, I looked up and saw Laura and Deshaun staring at me.

"Wow, Karma, you're gonna pop any day now," Laura said with a giant smile on her face as Deshaun walked off to try to conceal his colossal urge to burst into laughter. I instantly wanted to go home, and I instantly became angrier at the fact that Alonzo was unable to accompany me to the event. The stinging feeling of embarrassment overcame me.

Once we were inside the venue, I introduced Aiko to everyone that I knew, including the cast and crew of The Real Perspective. Then all of a sudden, I heard, "My favorite bitches are back together again." There was Terry Tea. Aiko literally jumped on Terry Tea, and he spun her around, embracing her tightly.

"Terry Tea, it's so good to see you. How have you been? I have not seen or spoken to you in ages," Aiko said.

"Baby, I know, I have been busy, and Karma got me into The Real Perspective working as a stylist for the one and only Diana Decosta," Terry Tea announced with pride in his voice.

Then I heard someone on a microphone calling for everyone's attention. It was Roman Hart. My boss, the icon, my idol, the man who changed my life. Roman Hart started his speech by saying that The Real Perspective was the number one reality show on television and that none of it would have been possible without the vision of a brilliant, talented, courageous woman who has no idea how rare of a jewel she is. Roman Hart continued, "I took a huge risk on this woman. Many told me that I was crazy for taking this woman under my wing, but I saw something special. This woman is a fighter. And honey, in a land full of wolves, she stood tall and did not let Hollywood devour her. And when they tried to swallow her whole, this woman let those bitches choke on her success. Please stand to your feet and acknowledge Karma Rodgers, co-creator and executive producer of The Real Perspective.

I was completely choked up. I waddled towards the stage, and Roman helped me up the stairs that led to the stage and passed me the microphone. My heart was completely full, and I was overcome with emotion. Roman had never acknowledged me in this way; hell, I had never heard Roman speak so highly of anyone. I took the microphone, and I had no idea what to say. Then, my spirit told me to say what was in my heart. "Thank you, Roman, for taking a chance on a nurse from Buffalo, New York, without any experience in reality television at all. I have learned that even when people set out to destroy you, if God has a plan for you, there is nothing that anyone can do to derail God's plan. Not even you can derail God's plan. What is for you, is for you, and The Real Perspective was for me," I said tearfully before hugging Roman Hart and exiting the stage. That speech was for Laura, Deshaun, and anyone else who doubted me or who made attempts to stop my progress. I looked at Laura and Deshaun while giving my speech, and there was a sense of awkwardness that fell upon their faces. I felt vindicated in their presence for the first time. Even though Laura and I had a moment after she found out that Deshaun was cheating on her with Ana Alvarez, I always felt that Laura saw me as being inferior to her. To Laura and Deshaun, I was just that worthless woman who had Deshaun's baby whom they wanted to write away with a check. Now, Laura and Deshaun had to witness Roman Hart standing before Hollywood's elite, talking about how amazing little ole' me was. That moment almost made up for Alonzo not being able to attend the event.

Aiko was truly impressed. I don't think that she knew how impactful my role was when it came to The Real Perspective. Aiko expressed to me that she was really proud of me and that we should be proud of each other for being able to finally make it in Hollywood. We were both able to maintain luxury lifestyles legally, although we never accomplished our goals of becoming Hollywood actresses.

Aiko and I were both kind of hungry after the event, although there was food there. We wanted to really eat, especially me since I was really pregnant. Aiko and I decided to go to the restaurant that we worked at together back in the day. While at the restaurant, we ate and talked like we used to years prior. Time was slipping away and then Alonzo called to check on me; that was my cue to wrap things up.

As Aiko and I were walking to her car, I had an uneasy feeling. The dreariness of the night was unnerving and there was a dark energy that seemed to loom over us. I attributed my uneasy feeling to the eerie atmosphere accompanied by the thick mist and low-hanging full moon. Suddenly, I heard a man's voice say in a low menacing tone, "Aiko!" We both turned around, and there was a tall man wearing dark clothes, a black hat, and black gloves with a gun in his hand. Aiko grabbed me by the shoulders and pulled me in front of her as if she was shielding herself with my body. The man pulled the trigger. Just like in the movies, my life flashed before my eyes. I thought about everything: being a child, my mother, father, baby girl Trinity, Alonzo, and even my unborn twins. I thought about how life would be for Trinity without me, and I hoped that my babies would survive even if I didn't. Then I realized that the man was continuously trying to pull the trigger, and nothing was happening. The gun was jammed. Aiko and I bolted towards her car; for the first time that day, I slid into her car with ease, and Aiko took off.

As Aiko and I sat in the car, I screamed, "What the fuck! You tried to have me killed. What kind of person are you? Who was that guy?"

"I don't know," Aiko replied.

"Bitch, he said your name."

"No, he didn't," she said.

I grabbed my phone to call the police.

"What are you doing?" Aiko asked.

"Bitch, I am calling the police."

Aiko grabbed my phone and threw it out of the car.

"Why did you do that?" I asked.

"Karma, you are not going to mention what happened to anyone, or I will kill you myself. And that would be after I make sure that everyone knows about your heistist days."

"You mean "our" heistist days," I replied.

"No, I'm talking about "your" heistist days. What I will tell you is that the guy who just tried to kill us is dangerous, and I owe him money. He gave me an advance on some money for a heist that I was supposed to carry out. I did not make good on the money. But I will pay him back."

I did not care about anything that Aiko was saying, I just wanted to get home.

I learned a very important lesson that night. I learned that people are inherently who they are. That night, Aiko told me that we were different. Aiko said that I was raised to love, and she was raised to survive, so if her survival meant someone else's death, so be it. Her main purpose was to make it, even if it was to the detriment of others. The blood in Aiko's veins ran cold and I was quickly reminded why my spirit told me to keep her at bay.

When Aiko dropped me off at home, I immediately started locking doors and putting on the alarm. I did not know if anyone had followed Aiko to my house. I was so scared. All of my running around woke up my mother.

"Karma is everything okay?" my mother asked.

"Yes, but Mom, I really just need you to stay here tonight."

"But Karma, I need to go home to Larry."

"Momma, just do me this huge favor; please just stay the night for me."

My mother reluctantly obliged. I wobbled my way up the stairs to my bedroom as Alonzo was coming out of our bathroom.

"Hey baby, how was tonight? I tried calling you, and the phone kept going straight to voicemail," he said.

I sat on the bed and started crying.

"What happened, baby? "What's wrong?" Alonzo asked.

I started to collect myself to determine how I was going to tell Alonzo about what happened to me. Alonzo sat next to me in the bed, holding me, and then I told him about me and Aiko's run-in with the guy with the gun and how Aiko forcibly pulled me in front of her so that I could be her shield from the bullets that were intended for her. Alonzo was infuriated and was ready to go to Henry and Aiko's house. I begged Alonzo not to leave and asked that he not call Henry because Aiko would surely seek revenge. Then Alonzo stopped for a second and began to get into attorney mode. "Why would someone want to kill Aiko in the first place? What do you know about Aiko? Has she been into any shady shit in the past that you know of?"

I knew that it was time for me to come clean with my husband. I could not carry around this secret anymore. "Alonzo, there is a part of my past that I never told you about that involves Aiko."

"What? What were y'all involved in?" Alonzo asked.

"I need you to promise me that you will never tell anyone because I could get into serious trouble."

Alonzo looked confused. "It can't be that bad Karma."

It's bad enough for someone to want to kill Aiko," I replied. I began to tell Alonzo how Aiko and I would essentially prey on wealthy people and eventually get into their homes to steal from them. I explained that I had taken some items from celebrity homes that were eventually stolen from me in a home burglary and that someone else was arrested, charged, and convicted of stealing the items. I explained how Aiko had taken an advance from a guy who would give her money for stolen items; the only problem was that Aiko never made good on the advance, which resulted in the man wanting her dead.

After telling Alonzo about everything, I felt crazy, but I also felt relieved. I asked Alonzo repeatedly if he was lying about not telling anyone, including Henry. Eventually, Alonzo looked me straight in the eyes and said, "I'll lie for you, before I'll tell on you. I'm not going to tell anyone, but you stay away from Aiko. This muthafucka needs to be handled one way or another. I can't let anyone get away with posing a threat to my pregnant wife and my unborn babies."

"What do you mean Alonzo?" I asked.

Alonzo would not say anything other than, "Someone is going to pay for this shit."

The next morning, my water broke, and my beautiful twin babies were born, my baby girl Angel and my baby boy Alonzo Jr. The babies were born a month early and were to remain in the Neonatal Intensive Care Unit until they were able to eat on their own. It did not feel right to be discharged from the hospital and not take home my precious babies.

After the twins were born, Alonzo was so happy. I could not understand why I was not as happy as Alonzo. For some inexplicable reason, I felt off. Everything was going great in my life. I had a wonderful husband, beautiful children, and the home of my dreams. A miracle happened when that man tried to pull the trigger when I was with Aiko, and nothing happened. I should have felt blessed, happy, grateful, and instead, I was sad and anxious. It was as if I was waiting for the moment that the ball would drop, and my world would fall beneath my feet. I could not put the pieces of my mind together to formulate logical, cohesive emotions that reflected how good my life actually was at the time. Imagine the best chef in the world fixing your favorite meal in the best way that the meal could ever be made. Although the meal tastes good, you can't enjoy it because there is something wrong with your taste buds, and you can't figure out what. This is how I felt.

Alonzo and I spent a lot of time going back and forth to the hospital to visit our babies. One visit, in particular, will forever be engraved in my brain. Alonzo and I were on our way to the hospital to pick up our babies. Angel and Alonzo Jr. were finally being discharged from the hospital, and we were so excited and full of anxiety. Alonzo had to stop to get some gas. As Alonzo started to get out of the car, his phone rang, and he answered. The car picked up the call through the speakers, and I heard across the car's speaker Henry, Aiko's fiancé's voice, saying, "It did not go according to plan; it did not go right at all."

I looked outside of the car at Alonzo as he was scrambling to disconnect the call from the car so that he could speak privately on his phone. I was trying to make out what Alonzo was saying, but I could not hear everything. When Alonzo got into the car, he looked sick.

"Baby, what happened? What's wrong?" I asked.

"First, I just want to let you know that I kept my word and that I never told anyone about what happened that night with you and Aiko being approached by the guy with the gun. I also never told anyone about how you and Aiko were stealing from people. But I have to tell you something."

I immediately got nervous. "What happened, Alonzo?"

Alonzo explained that Henry informed him that a large sum of money was taken out of an account that he shared with Aiko, and he asked her about it, and she lied and said that their wedding planner needed it. Henry said that when he talked to the wedding planner about it, she said that she did not receive any large sum of money from Aiko. Alonzo said that he recommended that Henry hire someone to follow Aiko to see what she was up to. Alonzo stated that he figured that Aiko was trying to pay the guy back that was trying to kill her. Alonzo explained that the private investigator that Henry hired would be the perfect way for him to find out who was the guy who nearly killed me while trying to kill Aiko. Alonzo told me that the day before, Aiko had taken out another large sum of money, and the private investigator followed Aiko to a guy who took the large sum of money and then shot her in broad daylight. Because Henry hired a private investigator who was a retired police officer, not only was the man on video shooting Aiko, but he was also apprehended shortly after. Alonzo looked at me with sorrow upon his soul and said, "Aiko didn't make it."

My heart sank and I burst into tears. Although Aiko was willing to sacrifice my life and the lives of my unborn children to save her own, I felt so bad about her death. "Maybe if I had never invited her to The Real Perspective's celebration and asked her to go to our old job, this all would have never happened," I yelled out. I even kind of blamed Alonzo. I thought to myself that if Alonzo had accompanied me to that event that night, none of this would have happened, I would not have had the babies prematurely, Aiko would still be alive, and her son would still have his mother. My heart was hurting so badly. A part of me knew that it was unfair to blame Alonzo; however, another part of me could not help but blame Alonzo.

Chapter 14

The Honeymoon Has Ended

The transitions of life are beautiful, exciting, difficult, and sometimes excruciating. It had been three years since my twins were born, and I was finally beginning to feel more like myself again. After Aiko's death, her fiancé Henry left the firm to focus on raising the son that he and Aiko shared, and Alonzo became a partner at the law firm. It seemed as if the law firm had monopolized Alonzo's time. In the meantime, I had two rambunctious three-year-olds demanding my attention. And Trinity was six years old and had become more independent. In fact, Trinity loved taking care of her little brother and sister. Alonzo Jr. and Angel could not have asked for a better big sister. I hoped that they would stay sweet and continue to love each other. My children had the relationship that I wished that I had with my siblings.

My work life was amazing. The Real Perspective continued to see tremendous success. Unfortunately, the actual talk show from which the reality show spun, Our Perspective, had been canceled. I saw this as a huge opportunity to introduce new talent to the show. Roman Hart, my boss and mentor, felt the same way. I thought of doing some stunt casting by asking Ana Alvarez to come to the show so that viewers could get some resolution regarding the affair between Laura Pennington's husband and the father of my child, Deshaun. Ana Alvarez refused to come back to the show after Laura Pennington ripped her a new one during the shooting of the commercial for the children's charity that the cast filmed years prior. Roman was really pushing for Ana's return; however, Ana vehemently declined. I also had the idea of bringing a man on the show or perhaps two men. Deshaun was on the show often and Hazy seemed to have a different boyfriend every season. But since The Real Perspective was evolving into a show about people in the entertainment industry, it would add some variety to the show by adding men. Hell, maybe the man would hook up with someone or cause an affair. I needed to ensure that the show maintained its entertainment element. I wanted to make sure that the man or men were fine, charismatic, and willing to perform for the camera.

Traveling for my job had become normal and childcare was crucial. I had two nannies, and my mother and Larry would help with the kids when needed if they weren't traveling or spending time with my siblings or Larry's grandchildren. Alonzo and I did not want our children to suffer because of our busy schedules.

During one trip in particular, Roman Hart needed me to fly to New York City. Roman Hart wanted me to scout new talent while he was on his promotional tour. During this promotional tour, he went to an array of shows to talk about his new show that would be airing soon. Roman took me to several radio stations, and during one of the stops, we visited a newly syndicated morning show called The Morning Pickup. When we walked into the studio, the hosts greeted Roman Hart and me. The lady was so sweet, and she had a mouth full of beautiful white teeth with red, glittery, and glossy lip gloss. The man stood up, and he was my height, with his ripped arms that I could see through his white shirt and a beautiful platinum necklace. His short, dark Caesar haircut quickly triggered my memory. "Tyrell, I can't believe this," I said in a tone of shock.

"Karma!" Tyrell replied. Naturally, Tyrell, my fling from Italy, began to embrace me in a bear hug.

"Wow, Tyrell, I guess you haven't left the gym since the last time we saw each other," I said.

"How do you two know each other?" Roman Hart asked.

I instantly got uncomfortable and said, "We have known each other for years."

"We met in Italy," Tyrell said with a sly grin on his face.

Tyrell had become a popular radio show host. I had been following Tyrell on social media, but very rarely was I paying any real attention to what he had been doing for the past few years. Apparently, Tyrell had left Miami radio and had been working on the radio in several different cities before finally landing in New York City on his newest gig.

Tyrell and his co-host interviewed Roman Hart and me, and we had a blast. Tyrell was still full of energy and as funny as ever.

After the interview, Roman Hart said, "We have to get him on The Real Perspective. I don't care how we do it, we have got to get it done. I am sure that Tyrell can do his morning show from Los Angeles a couple of days a week."

I thought that this would be interesting, but I also thought that this would be a little uncomfortable. Still, I was determined to do what it took to ensure that the show was a success. Roman Hart instructed me to make sure that I did what I could to convince Tyrell to get on the show.

Relationships have ups and downs, highs and lows, and my marriage was no different. I had become increasingly frustrated with Alonzo's busy schedule. Further, Alonzo was no longer romantic. Alonzo seemed to lack the lust that he once had for me. There was a time when I could not keep his hands off of me. We still had sex, but it was scheduled and routine. Alonzo was fine with the way things were, and I was not. I begged Alonzo to take me out on dates, but he always complained of being tired. Alonzo loved taking me to social events to show me off, but he rarely took me out where it was just me and him. I never suspected that Alonzo was cheating, but I did feel that our marriage had just gone stale. Things had been this way for over a year. I asked Alonzo to go to marriage counseling, and he refused, so I started going to counseling alone. Counseling really helped me a lot. When going through postpartum depression after having the twins, I went to therapy, and things improved drastically, so I knew the benefits of getting help. But Alonzo just did not see the benefit.

I spared myself loneliness by relying on my friends to spend time with me. Grace and I hung out from time to time. We were not as close as we had been in the past. Partially because I had become domesticated since having the kids and all. Grace was tired of dealing with her husband, Dane. Apparently, Dane had been cheating on Grace for years with both men and women by this time. Grace was working on her exit strategy. Both Grace and I were having issues in our marriages; although hers were much more severe, commonality allowed us to bond.

The success of The Real Perspective had become my number one priority. I began searching for someone else other than Tyrell to join the show in an effort to avoid being uncomfortable. I figured that it would be difficult for us to get Tyrell to become bi-coastal. I did have my eyes on an ex-basketball player who was also a sports analyst for a national show. His name was Kendrick Sims. This guy had magnetic energy. Even if you were not a sports fan, watching him on television was mesmerizing. He had a tall stature with a smooth chestnut pigmentation that radiated a warm glow. The squint in his eyes and the dimples in his cheeks, accompanied by his bright smile, made female viewers adore him, and male viewers idolize him because of his good looks and extensive basketball knowledge. I needed to know more about him.

Roman Hart was interested in the possibility of making Kendrick Sims a part of The Real Perspective cast. I scheduled a meeting with Kendrick, Roman Hart, and myself. We all met at a restaurant in a section that was reserved only for celebrities and the wealthy. Kendrick was even more attractive in person. During dinner, I felt that Roman Hart was very impressed with Kendrick. During our conversation with Kendrick, of course, Kendrick mentioned that he did not know how he felt about being on a show as the only male with a group of women. Roman Hart quickly said, "Tyrell, from the newly syndicated radio show The Morning Pickup, will be joining us." I looked at Roman Hart with a puzzled look on my face.

"Wait, Tyrell, that's my boy. When I played ball in Miami, he was hosting the morning show there. If Tyrell is in, I'm in. But I will only commit to one season. I need to do a test run."

Roman Hart gave me a look like, "Bitch, you got some work to do." I knew that I had to do everything in my power to get Tyrell to agree to join the show. If Tyrell declined the show, then Kendrick would surely decline, leaving me to start from scratch.

Scheming is something that I don't really enjoy doing, but I will do it if I have to. I had come up with a great plan. Grace technically was still married and still living in the house that she and Dane shared, but Dane was never home so she was really living alone. I knew that Grace was creating an exit plan. So, in my mind, I figured that I would introduce Grace to Tyrell, and if they liked each other and started dating, she could become a part of the show, and Tyrell would be interested in spending more time in Los Angeles. This would give her the exposure that she needed to get from under Dane's financial shackles.

Roman Hart had arranged for Tyrell to come into town in an effort to make him fall in love with the city of Los Angeles. He was flown in on a private jet, booked at the most fabulous hotel, given a driver; anything you could imagine that would make Tyrell's visit memorable, Tyrell had. I had a sidebar sit-down conversation with Tyrell at one of the strip clubs that he was entertained at while in town. I told him about the benefits of being on the number one reality show on television and told him how doors in Hollywood would open for him. Tyrell finally stopped me mid-sentence and said, "Listen, I am going to sign on. I want to talk about you. How have you really been? On a personal level."

I started rambling, "Well, I'm fine, I'm a wife, I have three kids."

"Damn, Karma, you make it sound so dull. So, routine. Where's your excitement? Are you happy?"

"I'm happy."

"You are missing something, and your spirit screams that you are missing something. I'm not trying to be in your business or anything, but are you alive, or are you living? I mean, what happened to that spontaneous and full-of-life girl I met in Italy?"

I really felt insulted by Tyrell's words. Then, I became paranoid and wondered if I had become a watered-down version of myself. I knew that my marriage had become boring, and now I was faced with the possibility that I had become boring as well.

"Tyrell, we will get the contract to you soon," I said as I walked away after being bombarded with my own thoughts and Tyrell's perspective of me.

I wasn't sure if Tyrell would sign, but not only did he sign the contract, he signed the contract the following day. Roman Hart was so impressed with me being able to get Tyrell to put ink to paper that he gifted me a diamond necklace. I kind of felt like a fraud because I was not sure about how much of an influence I really had on Tyrell signing on to become a part of the cast of The Real Perspective.

Reality television is just as real as it is fake. The conflicts, the emotions, and the situations are all real; however, the creation of these realities are orchestrated by production. For instance, we were trying to look for ways to introduce both Tyrell and Kendrick to the show. Production decided to introduce Kendrick as Laura Pennington's friend. Laura Pennington's father, Julius Nash, was an ex-NBA player, and so was Kendrick. Although Laura and Kendrick never met, Kendrick would be introduced to the show as a friend that Laura knew through her father. Kendrick told producers that he had only met Julius Nash about twice before. Kendrick started playing in the NBA after Julius Nash retired. Kendrick had no problem with his storyline because he was a huge fan of Julius Nash.

Tyrell would be introduced to the show as Hazy's friend. Since Hazy was a rapper, it made sense for Tyrell to be her friend. The difference between Kendrick and Laura Pennington was that Hazy and Tyrell knew each other a little. Tyrell had interviewed Hazy several times in her career, so this worked out perfectly. I was so excited about the new season of The Real Perspective. My job had become the most exciting part of my life.

My grand plan needed to be implemented to get Tyrell and Grace together. I wanted to help Grace create her own identity outside of Dane and gain financial independence. Being on reality television, even as someone's love interest, could catapult her career in entertainment. Also, if Grace and Tyrell got together, this would make Tyrell want to spend more time in Los Angeles. I started off by telling Grace how a new guy was going to start on The Real Perspective and about him being the host of a syndicated radio show. I showed Grace Tyrell's social media account and told her how fine he was. Grace was definitely interested. There was no denying it; Tyrell was a superstar. I had to tell Grace one more important thing before she decided if she wanted to pursue anything with Tyrell. I explained to Grace that Tyrell was a fling I had when I was in Italy. I explained to her that we only slept together once and that it was never anything serious. Furthermore, it happened so many years ago. I had totally moved on, and so did he. Me divulging this information did not interfere with Grace's interest in Tyrell.

The first day of shooting for The Real Perspective's new season had begun, and I knew right away that the season would be flaming hot. We first shot Kendrick and Laura Pennington having dinner. Kendrick and Laura had only met two days before shooting. Kendrick was single and handsome, and Laura Pennington was and probably will always be breathtakingly beautiful. The sexual tension between Kendrick and Laura was palpable. Kendrick was very sensual in the way that he looked at Laura, the way he talked to Laura, and even the way that he briefly touched Laura's hand when he looked at her wedding ring and asked how Deshaun was doing. Laura's response to Kendrick's seduction was like she had been in the desert without any water for days, Kendrick was a tall, cold glass of water, and Laura could not get enough. In other words, she was thirsty, and it showed. I could tell that Laura had not experienced this type of attention from a man in a long time. Even I was blushing. All of the production knew that something was brewing between Laura and Kendrick, so we had to keep an eye on them at all times.

Sometimes, the energy that I experienced while at work would follow me home. After witnessing the interaction between Kendrick and

Laura, I wanted Alonzo to want me like Kendrick wanted Laura. When I got home, Alonzo was lying in bed watching television.

"Hey baby, I missed you," I said in the sexiest voice I could produce.

Alonzo replied in an indifferent tone, "Miss you too, baby."

"How about I put on something sexy and join you in bed."

Alonzo's eyes lit up as he said, "Yeah baby, put somethin sexy on for daddy."

I smiled and walked into the bathroom, slow and sexy. I showered, put on some makeup, and put on the sexiest lingerie that I had. I walked into the room, ready for Alonzo to take me. Alonzo was propped up on some pillows when I walked into the room. I thought to myself, "Okay, he wants me on top." Then my sexual, high-intensity mood was disrupted by the loud sounds of Alonzo's snores. I instantly became uninterested and went to sleep. I was awakened the next morning to Alonzo rubbing me and kissing me as he was saying, "What happened last night?"

"You fell asleep," I said.

Alonzo then ran to the bathroom to pee and freshen up a little. He came back into the room, and we had the same ole' routine sex that we always had. I was disappointed although I knew that Alonzo had been busy and was extremely tired. I just longed for Alonzo to have a deep, intense desire for me sexually.

Tyrell on The Real Perspective was funny as hell. He always had jokes and kept everything upbeat. One day, we filmed a date that he had with my best friend Grace. I was so happy about this. Grace was introduced to the show as a woman that Tyrell was seeing who was divorcing a hugely successful record label owner. Dane would not allow his name to be used on the show. Nonetheless, the audience could easily look up Grace and discover that she was married to Dane.

I was pleased with how the date was going between the two; there was definitely an attraction there. Suddenly, in the middle of filming, I received a phone call from my mother's fiancé Larry. He called me to let me know that my mother had slipped, fallen, and hit her head before being rushed to the hospital. I immediately dropped everything and rushed to the hospital and reluctantly reached out to my siblings, Matthew and Celine.

After some tests were run, it was confirmed that my mother had a stroke, which resulted in her fall. I was devastated and prayed for her to wake up. Celine was the first of my siblings to make it to the hospital. In typical Celine fashion, she started questioning me. "What happened? Was Momma taking care of your kids when this happened?" she asked. I had to slow Celine down and tell her that my mother was with her boyfriend Larry and not my children when this occurred. I had to remind Celine that my children had not one but two nannies. Then my stupid ass brother finally got into town and entered the hospital room when I was there. He cried like a baby, and once he was able to gather himself, he started his passive-aggressive behavior.

"If it wasn't for Momma being here in Los Angeles under stress all of the time because of the traffic, taking care of people's kids, and all these high prices, she would not be in this situation."

Luckily, Matthew's insults that were targeted towards me were received by my mother's boyfriend Larry.

"Well, your mother doesn't have to drive because I take her where she needs to be. The kids you are referring to are her grandkids, and she loves spending time with them, and she doesn't have to worry about the price of anything because I take care of her financially. She hasn't paid a bill since she has been with me," Larry said.

Matthew looked embarrassed and stormed out of the room. Celine ran after him. At that moment, I really wished I had different siblings. In fact, it made me think of my sister Jennifer on my father's side. She never behaved in this way. And Jennifer actually loved me, and she looked up to me. It sucked being in my family sometimes.

Seeing my mother unresponsive and lying in a hospital bed was agonizing. Alonzo spent hours upon hours at the hospital supporting me. I loved it when Alonzo was there because my siblings had a level of respect for Alonzo, and they did not bully me when he was around. I was afraid of the thought of having a future without my mother.

My mother was the only person on the planet that had my back even before I was born. She protected me, and if I ever needed anything, she was there for me without hesitation. She was my best friend. We spoke every day. She was the foundation for the entire family, even though the foundation was not completely sturdy. I knew that if she did not make it, I probably would never speak to my siblings again. I did take the time to analyze if I would be okay with not speaking to my siblings ever again; I concluded that I would be perfectly fine with them erased from my life. However, the vacancy of my siblings in my life would only sadden me even more because that would confirm the finality of my mother's existence on earth. I was broken.

One night, I was alone, sitting by my mother's bed and dozing off. Unexpectantly, an older lady came into the room dressed in older-style clothes with a bible in her hands. She had an angelic presence. As soon as she walked into the room, I felt a sense of calm covering my spirit. "Hello baby," the woman said to me in a soft, tranquil voice. The lady walked over to my mother and just started rubbing her hand and saying, "My precious baby, it's gonna be alright."

For some reason, I felt the urge to just blurt out to the woman, "Is she really going to be alright?" with tears in my eyes.

The woman turned to me with the softest smile and said, "Baby, she is gonna be just fine." The lady placed the opened bible on my lap and walked out of the room. When I looked down at the bible, the pages were turned to James 5:14-15: "Is anyone among you sick? Let them call the elders of the church to pray over them and anoint them with oil in the name of the Lord. And the prayer offered in faith will make the sick person well; the Lord will raise them up. If they have sinned, they will be forgiven." After I read this, I heard a gasp coming from my mother's mouth and her eyes opened. I yelled for the nurses to come into the room. I tried to find that lady who visited my mother. I asked all of the nurses if there was someone from the hospital's chapel who visited people. No one knew who the lady was; no one saw the lady but me. My mother was able to walk out of that hospital a week later. She was walking with a walker, but nonetheless, she was walking. Eventually, my mother made a full recovery.

When my mother was discharged and came home, she told me how her grandmother visited her while she was in a comatose state. My mother said that her grandmother died when she was a teenager. Then my mother pulled out a picture of her grandmother. A state of shock nearly caused me to collapse. The lady in the picture was the lady in my mother's room that night, without a doubt. The spirit of my great-grandmother visited me and my mother when my mother was hospitalized. I told my mother of the experience that I had, and she said very confidently, "Yep, I know that was her; she told me that I was going to be alright. And she also told me that Karma will come full circle. I don't know what she meant by that." I didn't know what that meant either.

Going back to work was somewhat of a relief after dealing with the ordeal with my mother. Roman Hart was very supportive and allowed me to take as much time off as needed. So much had happened during my absence. One of the cast members of The Real Perspective, Wendy Knight, had a total fallout with Diana DeCosta. I always had a special place in my heart for Diana DeCosta because she was essentially the reason why I was working in the industry. Further, she had grown to be a second mother to me. So, when Diana DeCosta was upset, I was upset, although I needed to remain neutral. During a day of shooting, while I was caring for my mother, apparently, Diana DeCosta invited Wendy Knight to her house for dinner. For some reason, the dinner never arrived, and that's when Diana DeCosta, who was in her late 60's, revealed that she did not cook and has never been able to cook. During the visit, Diana Decosta began talking about how she didn't know why she could never keep a man. Wendy Knight, being the comedian that she was, told Diana DeCosta that she couldn't find a man because she was old and couldn't cook. Wendy Knight said, "You can't be old and not be able to cook, Diana. You mean to tell me that your old ass can't bake a biscuit, fry some chicken, hell flip an egg. Got damn, yous an expendable old ass bitch. That's why you can't keep a man." Wendy Knight was in her 50's and was known for being able to cook well on the show. Diana DeCosta immediately kicked Wendy Knight out of her house, and they had been at odds since. The situation was so bad that Diana DeCosta refused to film with Wendy Knight, which I thought was silly, but Wendy Knight's words were really triggering for Diana DeCosta.

Shooting days were always exhausting for me. During one day of shooting, Tyrell was having a party to celebrate the premiere of a new movie that he was in. He was only in the film for about 1.5 seconds, but Tyrell did not pass up an opportunity to party. Grace accompanied him to the party, and I was elated that my plan to at least get her on the show was working out. Tyrell begged Diana DeCosta to come to the party to resolve her issues with Wendy Knight. During the event, Tyrell brought the entire cast together in an area away from the other guests at the party. Tyrell started off by saying that everyone on the cast looked up to Diana DeCosta and Wendy Knight, and it was important for them to resolve their issues so that they could set a good example for the rest of the cast. Wendy Knight started off by saying that she apologized for the way that Diana DeCosta felt about her comments. However, Wendy Knight ended the apology by saying, "But you still an old bitch that can't cook, but maybe it was not fair for me to say that this is the reason why you can't keep a man. But I call it like I see it. If one plus one equals two, I ain't gone say it equals four."

Hazy had to chime in and say, "Dang Diana, you can't cook. I thought that being able to cook was a prerequisite to getting old," as she laughed hysterically.

Diana DeCosta was so mad that she literally snatched the wig off of Wendy Knight's head and threw it across the room. Everyone inhaled deeply as their eyes widened. All I could think was, "I can't believe these bitches are literally fighting over nothing." I was upset with Wendy for being so damn evil towards Diana and I was disappointed in Diana for stepping off of her throne to morph into a character on reality television. Diana DeCosta was Hollywood royalty, not reality trash and I wanted her to always behave as such. Before things could escalate, the cast and crew began to hold both Wendy Knight and Diana DeCosta back.

After the ridiculous fight between Wendy and Diana, the night was uneventful, but I was exhausted. Although I loved my family, the thought of going straight home after work was overwhelming. I would be leaving one chaotic situation for another. Having three-year-old twins and a six-year-old was pure insanity. I decided to go to a little tapestry bar not far from where we filmed. I wouldn't drive to work when I knew I would be working late. I would get a driver, and this night was no different. So, I figured I'd have a little to eat and a lot to drink.

As I was sitting at the bar enjoying the food and gulping down my drinks, I felt a tap on my shoulder. To my surprise, it was Kendrick, the retired NBA player and new cast member of The Real Perspective. He was so fine.

"Hey beautiful, what are you doing here alone," said Kendrick as he slid onto a bar stool next to me.

"I just needed to decompress after tonight," I replied.

"I feel the same way; I guess great minds think alike," Kendrick said. Kendrick had an enthralling presence. As we sat at the bar talking, he was so engaged. He looked deep into my eyes, he was so attentive, and I had his undivided attention. Kendrick had a seductive way about him. I can't remember everything that he said or everything that we talked about, but I remember how he made me feel. Kendrick made me feel like I was the only person on earth that mattered when he was talking to me. It was special. Eventually, my conscience kicked in, and I started to feel that things were getting inappropriate when I looked down and felt Kendrick's hand caressing my thigh. His strong hand on my thigh while looking into my eyes was enough for him to activate my inner hoe. I abruptly ended our conversation and told Kendrick that I needed to get home. Kendrick was a gentleman, and he offered to take me home. I thought that this would be too risky because of the way that I was feeling. He could have taken me home with him and I would have let him do a lot of things to me that night. But I needed to come to my senses. I thanked Kendrick and told him that I had a driver who would take me home.

After I witnessed how fragile I was when I was at the tapestry bar with Kendrick, I realized that my marriage was in more trouble than I thought. Further, I had a new lease on life after seeing my mother almost lose hers. I wanted to enjoy life because life had become even more precious to me. I decided to talk to Alonzo about our marriage because both he and I deserved to be happy.

One Saturday morning, I asked Alonzo to take me out for breakfast. We went to a cute little restaurant. During breakfast, I explained to Alonzo that I was feeling that we were not spending quality time together and that I felt that this was causing a strain on our relationship. I even brought up the night that I dressed up in my sexiest lingerie for Alonzo and how he fell asleep.

Alonzo listened and said, "Karma, it seems that all you do is complain; you are never satisfied. I can never do right. You never talk about the things that I am doing right. You never acknowledge that I worked so hard to give you the life that you have become accustomed to. You never talk about how I am taking the kids to the park or even on mini trips when you are working crazy hours or traveling for work. I have been juggling a lot to accommodate your career while excelling in my own with added responsibilities at home. I feel like trying to support you and your dreams is always backfiring."

I was so frustrated. "How did this become about you? I am trying to tell you that I am struggling in this marriage because I am not getting the time and attention I need," I replied.

"How about you change your schedule, or you can quit your job, and that way, I will have less responsibility at home, and we can spend more time together. What I don't want is nannies raising our kids. It's important to me that our kids get the quality time that they deserve. So have some sympathy when you see me fall asleep after working twelve hours and coming home to eat dinner with the kids and put them to bed."

I had lost my appetite. I was annoyed that the only resolution that Alonzo could come up with involved me either changing the schedule at my job, which was impossible, or quitting my job. I felt worse after my conversation with Alonzo; no progress was made. In fact, I felt like we took ten steps back.

After everything that I had been going through in my life, with me almost losing my mother and my marriage being in trouble, I needed some retail therapy after arguing with Alonzo during breakfast. I contacted Grace and asked her if she wanted to go shopping with me. Grace was so ready to go shopping. One thing about Grace is that she was fun to be around. What made things even better was that Grace said that she had cooked dinner. Grace asked me to come by her house first, and then we could go shopping. Grace said that she had prepared ribeye, mashed potatoes, and asparagus; Grace made the best garlic mashed potatoes. This was perfect because I had not eaten since my awful breakfast date with Alonzo.

After I threw on some makeup and combed my hair really fast, I told Alonzo that I needed to leave and began to try to rush out of the house. I was so annoyed with Alonzo and didn't want to even be in his presence. Alonzo asked me when I would be returning. I just told him that Grace and I would be shopping and that I would be back later, and I closed the door behind me.

On my way to Grace's house, I was thinking about what I could do to improve my marriage. I really started to think about what Alonzo said during breakfast. Had I been too critical of him? Had I manufactured issues? After all, Alonzo was a good man. He never really did anything to hurt me. I thought that maybe therapy could help us, but I knew that it would be extremely difficult for me to get Alonzo to agree to go to therapy. I promised myself that when I got back home I would apologize to Alonzo because he has always had my back and he has done things that he did not have to do, like adopting Trinity and simply being a great father to all three of our kids. I had to recognize that Alonzo was a far better father to our children than I was a mother. I decided that I needed to be better and that I needed to do better.

When I got to Grace's house and rang the doorbell, the door opened, and as I started to walk in to tell Grace about my day, an unexpected presence interrupted my plan.

"Oh, Tyrell, how are you?" I asked.

"I'm all right."

"Where's Grace?

Tyrell looked sad and said, "Grace had to leave. She got a call that her ex-Dane was in some type of accident, and she ran out the door. You literally just missed her. I'm surprised she didn't text you to let you know."

I then started to fumble around in my purse for my phone. "Dang, I was in such a rush to get out of the door that I must have left my phone at home."

"I was about to leave; I just ate. You can go ahead and make yourself a plate. I kind of lost my appetite after hearing about Dane," Tyrell said.

"Yeah, I don't have much of an appetite either," I replied as I sat on the couch in disbelief.

"Do you know what happened?" I asked Tyrell.

Tyrell said that whoever called Grace said that Dane had a skiing accident and was hurt really bad. Tyrell said that Grace was catching a flight to Aspen, Colorado.

"Well, let me get out of here," I said.

Tyrell grabbed my hand and said, "Before you leave, I just wanted to talk to you. We haven't had a chance to really talk."

I sat down on the couch next to Tyrell. "Talk about what?" I asked.

"I feel that I may have rubbed you the wrong way when I pulled you aside a while back to say that I felt that you had lost your zest for life."

"No, you said, what happened to that spontaneous and full-of-life girl I met in Italy? Making me out to be lackluster."

Tyrell smiled and said, "I didn't mean to offend you, but you don't know how significant my encounter with you in Italy was. I was going through some things at the time. My parents were divorcing after thirty years of marriage, my ex-girlfriend, who at one time was my best friend, had nothing to do with me, and I was feeling all alone in this world. I took a trip to Italy alone because I was trying to get my mind together, and then I met you. You were so nice to me, and it was cool being around you. Then I got back home and followed you on social media. I was crazy busy in my life and wanted to reach out to you but never really got around to doing it. Eventually, I saw that you were pregnant. I reached out to you right after that, kind of thinking about the possibility of the baby being mine, and the thought wasn't all that bad. Thanks for immediately letting me know that the baby was not mine, but I had the realization that I was lucky during the Italy trip and that you were too good to be true. That's what usually happens in my life; I let really good things slip away. Then, when I saw you again, I was expecting to experience the same Karma I experienced in Italy, and instead, I felt that I got a completely different version of you. That's not your fault. I just want you to realize that you are amazing, fun, and full of life. You can't grow out of that. I want you to always keep that side of yourself because that's the side of you that left the biggest impression on my life."

I was in awe when Tyrell said this to me. I had no idea that Tyrell was going through so much when I met him in Italy. To know that I left a lasting impression on someone was revealing to me. But then I started to doubt what Tyrell was saying.

"Are you sure that it wasn't about the sex?" I asked.

"I swear that even if we didn't have sex in Italy, I would still feel the same. It's not like we were going at it every day. It only happened once, and it was great. But seriously, it was your presence that made Italy even more spectacular. I once returned to Italy looking for the same magic but never found it. It wasn't long before I realized that you were the magic. I truly believe that you were the piece that made that trip special for me."

"Wow, thank you, Tyrell, I was going through some things in my life as well, and you made me forget all about my problems back at home. And for me, it wasn't about the sex either. You left a lasting impression on me as well."

Tyrell moved closer to me on the couch. I don't know what it is about you, but I want you. You are so damn sexy," Tyrell said.

Tyrell pulled me close to him and started kissing me passionately, and I reciprocated the passion. Tyrell started taking his hands and putting them inside my pants to gently pull them down. At that point, I stopped Tyrell. "No, this is wrong on so many levels. We are at my best friend's house, and she is dating you."

"Grace's heart is not with me; it's with Dane and you are with me. There is nothing that I want more right now than you."

Tyrell moved close to me again and continued kissing me. A million different thoughts went through my head, and then my mind, body, and soul all came to an astounding consensus of "Fuck it." I wanted what I wanted, and I wanted it now. Tyrell kissed me all over and the look in his eyes was that of sheer desire. The next thing I knew, he had entered my body in such a soft, gentle, yet sexy way right on Grace's huge couch. He was patient, he was loving, and he was really good at what he was doing. I had not experienced love-making this passionately in a while. When we were done, I immediately felt terrible. I felt ashamed, embarrassed, and disgusted. I immediately grabbed my things, and I was preparing for my exit.

"Karma, are you okay?"

"No, I feel so bad right now; we can't ever do this again. We can never let Grace know about this."

"I got you, Karma; I would never tell Grace."

I nearly ran out of the house. I couldn't go home empty-handed, and I needed to collect my thoughts and absorb what just happened between Tyrell and me. I went to Rodeo Drive and walked around aimlessly. I grabbed some things just so that I didn't go home empty-handed. I even grabbed some fast food and sat in the car feeling terrible.

When I pulled up to my house, I sat in the car for a while. I did not know how I would be able to look Alonzo in the eye. When I got into the house, Alonzo was in the kitchen, and he handed me a dozen red roses. Then, when I looked around, there were roses all over the kitchen. Alonzo had my favorite cake sitting on the table. The cake was a fresh strawberry cake from my favorite bakery. "Baby, I thought about everything that you said today, and I am sorry. I am willing to do counseling or whatever it takes to get us both back on track. I shouldn't have gotten so upset with you this morning for simply telling me how you felt. I have to realize that everything isn't litigation and that I don't always have to win. Baby, I heard you, and I am going to do better moving forward."

I felt even worse now. "You didn't have to do all of this. I am sorry, too. You are a good man, and I haven't been the best wife. I need to do better."

Alonzo grabbed me and started to fiercely kiss my lips. The same lips that I had intertwined with Tyrell's. I gently pushed Alonzo away and said, "Baby, I just ate a burger with onions, and I have been out all day."

"No, it's okay, I don't mind. And guess what baby, the kids are gone; they are at the sitters. It's just me and you tonight," Alonzo said.

"No baby, I just started my period," I said, hoping that Alonzo would believe the lie.

"But baby, didn't you just get off of it?"

"I know, right? I think my period is just out of whack. I have a doctor's appointment coming up, and I will talk to my doctor about it. But this is all so nice, baby; I don't deserve it. In fact, I don't deserve you."

No words can describe the pain that punctured my heart's core. I had wished that I had just turned around and gone home when I saw that Grace was not home. I betrayed the love of my life, Alonzo, and my best friend in the world, Grace.

Days had gone by; I could not shake my feeling of guilt. It was great that I had a few days of a break from my job. I was trying to spend more time with my children and Alonzo. One day, while me, Alonzo, and the kids were watching a movie, the doorbell rang. I thought that this was peculiar because I was not expecting anyone. I opened the door and there was Grace standing at my door in tears. I was in shock.

"Hey girl, are you okay?" I asked.

Grace walked by me and straight into the house and said, "We need to talk, right now!"

Alonzo greeted Grace and said, "We'll let you ladies have some time. The kids are ready for some ice cream anyway, right?"

The kids started screaming and celebrating as they rushed to put on their sneakers. I took Grace to my sitting room. "Girl, is everything okay?" I asked nervously. I knew Grace was confronting me about what happened between me and Tyrell at her house. I did not know how much she knew or how I would address it. I was trying to remain cool as I felt my heart doing endless somersaults in my chest.

"Girl, I am dealing with so much with Dane. Dane will make it, but I had to be at the hospital because we are still legally married. I had to make some serious decisions in Aspen. It was just so much, and then Tyrell broke up with me. Girl, why would he break up with me?" Grace said as she was sobbing.

"I guess it's hard for your man to see you worried about another man. Especially your estranged husband," I said as I rubbed Grace's back while she sat with her face in her hands.

"But how heartless is Tyrell for leaving me at this time."

I continued to sit there quietly just showing my support and trying not to say anything that would implicate me in the downfall of Tyrell and Grace's relationship.

"Karma, I really want to thank you for being such a good friend. Sometimes, I don't give you enough credit for how you try to look out for me. Getting me on The Real Perspective when you didn't have to do it did not go unnoticed. Although I am no longer with Tyrell, I am going to find my way."

"You are going to be just fine. I will do what I can to continue to look out for you," I responded.

After Grace and I sat and talked for a while, Grace left my house looking much better than she did when she first arrived. I felt like such a fraud. The guilt was eating away at me. I desired the day when all of this could be behind me and just be a wrinkle in my life's story.

Sometimes, you just need your mother. I was so distressed about my life and the mistakes that I had made. I needed to be with the one person who loved me no matter what, my mother. I went to her and Larry's house to visit. My mother always had a way of making me feel better. When I got to my mother's house, I was greeted by my sister Celine. After my mother had her stroke, Celine came to Los Angeles and never returned to Buffalo. Celine had been staying with my mother and Larry while my mother was recovering.

"Hey Celine, where's Mom?"

"She's asleep."

"Is everything all right with her?" I asked out of concern.

"Yeah, everything's good. We were out shopping, so she did a lot of walking today. She's just tired."

I was pretty much ready to go after that. I sure as hell didn't want to sit around and talk to Celine.

"Here, have a seat. I was just making a cup of coffee; do you want some?" Celine asked as she walked into the kitchen.

In an effort to make things less awkward, I said yes. As we sat at the kitchen table in near silence as Celine was getting the coffee cups, cream, and sugar out, Celine said, "So, how have you been?"

"I have been pretty good. Just busy with the kids and work. How about you?"

"Well, Todd and I are separated."

I gasped and grabbed for my chest pretending to be devastated, "I am so sorry to hear that."

"It's okay, one thing that haunted me is that when Todd and I were in town for your wedding, you told me to ask Todd the real reason why he no longer worked at his previous job. At first, I thought that you were full of shit and trying to throw me off. Then, I really put the pressure on him, and he confessed that he was let go for having an affair with your sister Jennifer. We stayed together, but right before Mom's stroke, I found out that he was still sleeping with your sister. Our daughter Rhea saw Todd texting, so she quietly stood over him and read some sexually explicit messages that he was sending to Jennifer. Todd's dumb ass didn't even notice Rhea there."

Celine kept her eyes on me as she was speaking. I figured that she was trying to see what my reaction would be as she was speaking with me. I remained calm, cool, and collected. I kept saying in my mind, "Don't let her see you sweat."

"Now, I have always wanted to know one thing. How did you know about Todd and Jennifer? Did Jennifer tell you?"

"Celine, I really think it's time for me to go."

"No, don't go. I am talking to you, woman to woman. I am grown. I won't get upset. In fact, I am glad that Todd and I aren't together. Things have not been good for years. I just have not been able to follow through with the divorce. Mom's stroke gave me a reason to leave the house. Plus, Rhea is away at college and there is nothing keeping me and Todd together."

"Celine, I am not sure you want to hear what I have to say."

"What? That my husband and your sister Jennifer are living together? They just moved in with each other," Celine said.

My mouth dropped. I was pissed at my sister Jennifer. I really had no idea that Jennifer and Todd were living together. Then, I began to think that this was not my problem at all. I had created enough of my own issues; I did not need to be bombarded with the issues of Celine, Todd, and Jennifer.

"Celine, I did not know about that at all. I promise you," I said.

"Listen, Karma, I feel like I am in the dark about a lot. Todd and Jennifer don't matter anymore. I just want to know the truth. I am tired of being in the dark. I feel like everyone is walking around knowing secrets about my marriage that I don't even know."

Finally, I just gave in and said, "I am going to tell you everything that I know." Celine sat her cup of coffee down on the table, sat up straight, and stared me in the face. I thought that Celine deserved to know the truth. "Okay, before my wedding, I had come home and heard some noises coming from one of my guest bedrooms. I opened the door, and Jennifer and Todd were having sex. I have spoken to both Jennifer and Todd about it. Todd said something about layoffs resulting in him losing his job and breaking things off with Jennifer. Jennifer told me that Todd was fired because she told someone at the job about her sleeping with Todd, and that person went straight to Human Resources."

"Why didn't you tell me?"

"Let's be honest Celine, you were not being very nice to me during that time. In fact, I don't think we ever had a relationship where we talked or when you looked out for me, and I looked out for you. You take any opportunity you can to demean me," I said.

"I guess you are right; I've been doing some soul-searching since being here with Mom. Life is short and when I really thought about our situation, I don't even really know why I have been so mad at you for all of these years. Then I started to really dig deeper since I have been in therapy, and I concluded that part of my resentment towards you is that I felt that your birth, your existence, broke up the family that I knew as a child. I blamed your birth for breaking up Mom and my father. So, I'll say this, I appreciate you for being honest with me. Moving forward, I will do my best to be a better big sister, and I hope that you can receive that. I am not asking anything from you other than to accept my efforts to show up better for you."

"Wow, Celine, that really means a lot to me."

Celine and I gave each other a genuine hug for the first time that I could remember.

"Wow, my babies getting along and hugging," I heard my mother saying.

"Momma, where did you come from?" I said. My mother had the biggest smile on her face.

"Yes Momma, Karma and I are going to work on our relationship," Celine said.

"Well, that is the best news I have heard in a long time," my mother said with such happiness in her voice.

I was dreading the day I would have to return to work while the crew was filming Tyrell. I knew that I could not avoid Tyrell forever. I had to put on my big girl panties and pretend like nothing happened. Oddly enough, this filming day included Tyrell conversing with Grace about why he broke up with her. The scene was taking place at a small but trendy coffee shop. I tried to avoid this day at all costs. I sat there behind the scenes, cringing, not knowing what was going to come out of Tyrell's mouth. Tyrell and Grace were sitting for coffee, and Tyrell proceeded to say that he was not as strong as he thought he was and that it would be hard to support Grace while she was so heavily involved in the healing journey of her estranged husband. Tyrell said that he thought that it was best for both of them to move on and Tyrell explained that he thought that Grace was still in love with her estranged husband. Then Tyrell went on further to say that he still had some unresolved feelings for someone that he needed to work through. When Tyrell said this, my heart sank. I started getting hot and sweaty. My anxiety was through the roof. I was praying that he would not mention me, look at me, or give any indication that he was talking about me. In fact, I didn't even know if he was talking about me. But Lord knows I was praying that he was not.

After the scene finished, I was trying to gather my things so that I could leave the coffee shop. I needed to go to the restroom before taking my long drive home. On my way to the restroom, Tyrell stopped me.

"Karma!" Tyrell said.

"Hey Tyrell."

"Wait, slow down Karma, we really need to talk."

"No, we don't; I need to get home to my family," I said in a blunt tone.

"Karma, I understand, but we need to talk. We need to talk about that day."

"Bye, Tyrell, I gotta go."

As I was about to open the bathroom door to walk in, Grace opened the door as she was walking out. Grace was looking at me and Tyrell. I proceeded to walk into the restroom. This moment made me really uneasy because I did not know what Grace heard, and I did not know how Grace was going to interpret what she heard.

When I exited the bathroom, Grace and Tyrell were in a heated discussion. I pretended not to witness the exchange and hastily walked out of the coffee shop. I was hoping that Tyrell and Grace's mics were off, and I was hoping that my name did not come up in their discussion.

Things between Alonzo and I had gotten so much better. I was spending more time with the kids, and I was spending quality time with Alonzo. Things were going so well that one day, Alonzo brought home a puppy. The kids had been begging for a puppy. Trinity started screaming and jumping up and down, "A puppy, a puppy, thank you Daddy." The twins Alonzo Jr. and Angel seemed a little afraid of the puppy, so Alonzo held the puppy so that all of the kids could rub her and get used to her.

"So, what is going to be her name?" Alonzo asked.

Trinity said without hesitation, "Her name will be Dream because she made my dreams come true today."

"Well, her name is Dream," Alonzo proclaimed.

The kids were having such a good time, and I was appreciating my life at that moment. Then, all of a sudden, I got a call from Tyrell. I ignored the call. Tyrell called me two more times even after I sent him a text asking if everything was okay. I decided to take the puppy outside for a little walk and return Tyrell's call. As soon as I got outside to return the call, Alonzo came outside.

"Baby, I'm about to move our cars into the garage so that I can shoot some hoops with Trinity," Alonzo said.

I just shook my head letting Alonzo know that I heard him.

"Karma, I won't keep you long, but I really need to talk to you," Tyrell said as soon as he answered the phone.

"Okay," I responded.

I was unable to say much because Alonzo was right there. Suddenly, I couldn't hear Tyrell. I was saying, "Hello! Hello!" Then I started to look down at my phone and saw that my phone had connected to my car. The same car that Alonzo was parking in the garage. I immediately started fumbling my phone to end the call. By the time I ended the call, I knew that it was too late. Alonzo closed my car door in the garage and walked towards me, infuriated.

"Karma, who were you talking to? And you better not lie to me."

"It was someone from work, why?" I replied.

"Karma, don't lie to me, who the fuck were you talking to."

"Someone from work, Alonzo."

"Okay, you wanna play games? Call him back, and don't you say anything about me being around. Let that man finish what he was saying."

"No Alonzo, I can't do that."

Alonzo snatched my phone and looked at it. "Who is Tyrell? You've been messing around with Tyrell, huh."

"What are you talking about, Alonzo?"

"I heard the man saying that making love to you brought back so many memories. Why would he say that, Karma? Is it true? Are you fuckin this dude?"

A flood of tears poured from my eyes, and all I could do was shake my head yes. Alonzo started walking in circles and holding his head. I had never seen Alonzo so upset.

"You haven't changed. You are the same selfish ass, immature little girl that did me dirty and left me in Buffalo after Aunt Betty died and after the miscarriage. You're fucking heartless! You out here doin hoe shit and I've been nothin but good to yo ass. You don't deserve me. Fuck, I'm a good man, and I know it. And yo trifflin ass is for the streets. I'm leaving, and I hope that one day you can realize how fucked up you really are. And if I find ol' boy, I'm fucking him up."

Alonzo began to storm off into the house. All I could do was put my hands over my face and cry. My deceit had finally emerged, and I feared that I had done irreparable damage to my family. By the time that I walked into the house, Alonzo was walking out with a bag that he had packed. The kids were asking, "Daddy, what's wrong? Mommy, what's wrong?

"Daddy has to leave for a while; I promise I will be back to get you," Alonzo said to the kids.

I just looked at Alonzo and said, "Please don't go, please don't go!"

The kids then began to cry saying, "Daddy, please don't leave! Please don't leave us!"

Alonzo couldn't even look at me as he left the house and slammed the door. The day that my family welcomed our new puppy, Dream, was the day that my life became a nightmare.

I have heard my elders say that what you do in the dark shall come to light. I felt that my one indiscretion with Tyrell not only came to light, but that light was painfully blinding. Alonzo was so hurt and blinded by pain that he could not see the woman that he fell in love with. I never wanted Alonzo to find out about me and Tyrell, and I especially didn't want Alonzo to find out the way in which he did.

I was convinced that Alonzo hated me. I hadn't seen him in weeks. Alonzo arranged for the nannies to pick up and drop off the kids so that he would not have to see me. I had come to the point where I knew that I had to tell Grace about Tyrell before Alonzo did. Alonzo did not really watch The Real Perspective but it would only be a matter of time before he figured out that Tyrell was the cast member that I had sex with. Alonzo was going to really be disappointed in me once he found out that Grace and Tyrell were dating. The truth was inevitably going to come out.

I called Grace one day and asked her if we could talk. Grace told me that she was in the process of moving and said that I could meet her at her new place. I agreed and told her that I would help her unpack. In my mind, Grace deserved to hear that I had sex with Tyrell directly from me. I knew that it would be a tough conversation, but I knew that it was something that I had to do.

When I arrived at Grace's new place, it seemed to be a downgrade. It was still really nice, but it was not like the beautiful place that she had before. It was a nice condo in a quaint neighborhood. When I walked into the condo, Grace seemed surprised to see me.

"Hey girl, I wasn't expecting you so soon," Grace said.

"Why not? I told you that I would be on my way. I walked into the condo and began to look around. There were boxes everywhere.

"Girl, what made you decide to move from your house?"

"Well, Dane was paying for it, and I wanted to start off fresh. Tyrell reminded me that I could never truly move forward if I kept relying on my past to finance my future."

"I completely understand that. Speaking of Tyrell," I said with hesitation in my voice. Then something peculiar caught my attention. I noticed Grace's couch. Grace's couch looked really familiar. That red and orange floral design. This looked just like the couch that Alonzo had bought for Aunt Betty. This was the couch that I damn near had to beg Alonzo to take out of our house. I knew that Alonzo had put the couch in storage, but what the hell was it doing here?

"Grace, where did you get that couch?"

"From me," I heard a male voice say. I looked to my right side, where there was a hallway. And there was Alonzo walking out of one of the back rooms in the hallway.

"Alonzo, what are you doing here?" I asked. Alonzo did not reply. "So, I guess you couldn't wait to get over here to tell Grace," I said.

Alonzo grabbed his keys and began to walk out of the door. I ran after him.

"Alonzo, I get it; you wanted to get back at me by sleeping with my best friend. But we still need to talk."

"Karma, you don't get it; I don't owe you anything, not a conversation, not my time, nothing. You made your bed, now lay in it." Alonzo continued to walk away.

"Wait, Alonzo, don't you love me? I know that we can still make it work. I made a really bad mistake."

"You're right, you fucked up Karma. I don't know if I will ever be able to trust you again. In fact, I have been questioning everything about myself. Throughout our marriage, I gave you my all. You did something to me that I had never done to you, although I could have. But the difference between me and you is that I respected you. You don't respect me. Fuck, you don't even respect yourself. So, move on because that's what I'm doing."

"But Alonzo, are you moving on with Grace?"

"It's none of your business who I move on with. But I will tell you this, Grace is a much better person than you. Grace has far more integrity. So, for the record, I'm not moving on with Grace. I am only helping a friend out, which is something that you know nothing about. You just fuck over your friends. And in the future, you need to be careful about how you treat people because karma's a bitch."

I followed Alonzo to his car. "Alonzo, let's put our egos aside and have a calm conversation. I know I was wrong, and I am sorry." As Alonzo opened the driver's door, I noticed a woman in the passenger seat. "Wait Alonzo, who the fuck is this?" I yelled.

The woman turned to Alonzo and said, "Let's go babe, you don't have to entertain her."

Alonzo jumped in the car, and he and the woman stared straight ahead, ignoring my existence.

When Alonzo drove off, I knew exactly who that woman was, she was Jasmine from the law office where Alonzo worked at. She was the woman who facilitated the signing of the NDA between me and Deshaun. I was crushed.

I keep replaying my last interaction with Alonzo in my head. I had never seen this type of hatred in Alonzo's eyes, and my soul hurt for both him and me. Alonzo's warm, soft eyes had turned cold, his soft embrace was nonexistent, and he was so callous because he was protecting his heart from further pain. The more I tried to reach Alonzo's heart, the more I was bruised emotionally by Alonzo's harsh words. In Alonzo's mind, I was an unwanted intruder. I no longer recognized Alonzo. It was like speaking to a cold stranger. Alonzo's loving emotions towards me had dissipated, and now I had to learn to live with my new reality. When Alonzo drove off with that woman Jasmine, I just stood there frozen like a mannequin. I never went back into Grace's condo; I was too distraught. Every fiber of my being was mourning the Alonzo that I once knew.

I have not received any closure from that day. Grace will not return my calls, and Alonzo will not speak to me. All I can do is speculate about what transpired with Alonzo, Grace, and Jasmine. This is overwhelming and confusing. This is all my fault.

Because of all of the chaos in my life, I needed to make some drastic changes. I resigned from The Real Perspective, but Roman Hart assured me that I would continue to get paid as an Executive Producer. I needed to do this for my mental health. It was not healthy for me to report to work and have to be exposed to Tyrell. Life for my children was a lot different because they no longer had the comforts of a two-parent household. And I needed to cleanse my mind, body, and soul. I had been moving far too fast for far too long. I needed to slow down.

After a few weeks of being at home, I have fallen into a deep depression. As I sit here with tears falling from my frail face after telling you about my story, I realize that every decision that I have ever made in life, whether good or bad, has landed me in this very moment. Further, I have learned that you can't escape karma. When you do bad, that bad will be reciprocated, and karma will chase you down like a famished leopard chasing its prey. And when you do good, karma will do the same. At the end of the day, karma is merciless. And when you mess up really bad, Alonzo was right; karma is a bitch.

Made in the USA
Columbia, SC
25 April 2025